END OF WAR IN
THERMOPYLAE

Belinda Harrison

Thermopylae Bound Series
(In reading order)

Princess Of Thermopylae
Chosen For Thermopylae
The Ker At Thermopylae
Dark Thermopylae
Far From Thermopylae
End of War in Thermopylae

DEDICATION

For all those bravely living their truth in whatever form that takes
for you.
And for those who love them for being who they are.

BELINDA HARRISON

PART I

Return to Trachis

1

"What you shall hear is not a tale I have shared with many, indeed parts of it I have never shared," Hephaestus stated as we made our way toward the Othrys Mountains and Trachis beyond. "But I hope you can accept what you hear and support the decisions made, and those still being made."

Lysistratos looked to me in confusion. "Just listen," I told him. I appreciated Hephaestus trying to pre-empt his story about Demetri ... about Demi with strangers and I could only hope that Moeris and Lysistratos would be as welcoming as I had been.

"Many winters ago I emerged from Hera's womb, a full-grown god, with the expectation of being just as strong and powerful as she, and my father, Zeus were. As they still are," Hephaestus continued. "As I slid from her body, she taunted Zeus that she had borne me alone, without help from him. He did not believe her, replying that he had planted his godly seed within her and from it, I was created. Their argument did not last long, neither suddenly eager to admit their part in my lineage when they saw the lameness in my legs preventing me from standing as tall as my other siblings.

"Before I could defend myself or prove I had talents that would outweigh my physical limitations, Hera threw me from Olympos. I fell for days through the clouds and the air, falling towards the mortal world far below until finally I landed on the island of Lemnos.

"The sea god Proteus found me and cared for me as my broken bones healed. Proteus was father to the Haliai nymphs who tended and guarded the sea, the sand and the rocky shores around Lemnos. Schools of fish and other sea creatures were loyal to them; obeying their commands and assisting them when ships crashed against the rocks and threw the mortals into the raging waters.

"Proteus taught me to walk again with the aid of metal frames around my legs and in return for his care I gifted Proteus and his family with fire to cook the fish they caught, and keep themselves and the injured sailors that washed up on their shores warm. When I had recovered enough, I helped Proteus build the first forge. I showed his people how to tend it and how to craft objects from the heat. Proteus told me the gifts I had given them was far more than he had given me with the metal frames, and insisted I accept something else – his youngest daughter, Cabeiro.

"Cabeiro was just a child, barely three winters old, but Proteus assured me that she was not as mortal as she appeared. She was not immortal but she would live for many, many winters and would bear me strong children should I request it of her. I thanked Proteus for his kindness, and his gifts, and assured him I would return one day, but first I had matters to settle on Olympos. I needed to assert my place amongst the other gods – lame legged or not.

"I returned to Olympos and proved my standing through a number of deeds, some honorable, most not so, until finally Zeus gave me the titles of God of the Fire and God of the Forge. I took my place among my family, my parents grudgingly accepting my existence and imperfections, along with my gifts.

"I remained in Olympos for a long time, and Zeus gave me a wife – Aphrodite, the Goddess of Love. At first I believed it was because I had proven myself worthy of such a gift, but I quickly learnt that he had given her to me so the other gods would not fight each other for her affections. I did not care much for Zeus' reasons and I loved her dearly, honored to have such a beautiful woman to call my wife.

"I wish I could tell you our marriage was a happy union, but it was not. Aphrodite did not love me or desire me the way I did her and she soon returned to her lover, my brother Ares. I did not know of their affair at first, but the all-seeing sun god Helios did, and he informed me of it. I arrived back at our palace to find my wife and my brother writhing together in our marital bed. Fury surged in my blood at the sight of them. They were oblivious to my presence and I silently retreated to my forge deep beneath the earth where I devised a plan to trap them. I would have killed Ares, killed them both for the betrayal, but I knew I could not. Zeus would have banished me again from Olympos, stripped me of my immortal powers and forced me to live as a mortal being for the rest of my days. Or perhaps he would have just killed me, even though he had told me he favored me more than Ares.

"For moons I worked on a net made of unbreakable chain-links and when it was finished, I strung it high above the bed in my palace, ready to catch the unsuspecting lovers. The links were so tiny that it was impossible to see the trap from afar and that was my intention. One morning I announced to Aphrodite that I intended a visit to my worshippers and would be gone many days. I knew she would not care which temple I named, her only thought would be how much time she and Ares would have together. I was not wrong as, with barely a glance, she wished me a pleasant journey and breezed out of the room, rushing to get a message to Ares. I knew then that my plan would work.

"I hid in the palace as Ares arrived, furious at how they flaunted their passion through every room in our home, but I took comfort that soon they would be discovered and made to cease their affair. When they took to our bedroom, I dropped the net onto them, ensnaring them in its power. They could not move or deny what they had been doing; caught in their lover's embrace. I appeared to them and told them it was not enough that *I* knew, I wanted every god and goddess on Olympos to know of their betrayal. I was certain my father would put an end to any future between them. I told myself that Aphrodite belonged to me, Ares could not have her; Zeus would not allow it.

"But when I took the lovers to Olympos, my plan unraveled – no one was outraged at the trapped pair, they only laughed that they had been caught by the lamest god of them all. They ridiculed me too, speculating that I had been unable to satisfy the Goddess of Love, and would never be able to as my body was not whole. I fled far below to my forge, leaving my wife and her lover trapped beneath the net.

"Eventually I returned to Olympos and spoke with my father. I told him that Aphrodite and I would part ways, but I would only release them if Ares paid me the bride-price I had paid when Aphrodite and I married. Zeus agreed, adding that Ares would also pay the adulterer's fine. I agreed to the terms and allowed them their freedom. I was not everything that Aphrodite desired, and she was not what I wished for. I wanted more than constant betrayal and lies from the woman I wed. I did not carry on as the other gods; marrying one and lying with another just because I could. I wanted a proper union of love and trust, and with Aphrodite that could never be.

"Over time I took other lovers, but none were satisfactory to me, none filled me with what I was looking for, no woman – goddess or mortal – wanted what I did. None that is until I returned to Lemnos and saw the beautiful sea-nymph who had been promised to me so long ago.

"I was hesitant to reveal myself to Cabeiro; such a beauty could not love me, just as Aphrodite had not. I told myself she would hide from me, scream at my damaged legs and refuse to lie with me should I ask it of her.

But I was mistaken, when Proteus finally convinced me to reveal myself to Cabeiro, she accepted me with open arms, listening to my struggles with Aphrodite and offering comfort in her arms and her bed.

"I had found my love, and our union produced three beautiful daughters, the Caberides, nymphs just as their mother was, and two blacksmith sons – Alcon and Eurymedon – who were known as the Cabeiri. The boys were strong and talented and it was clear from the moment they entered the world that they carried my godly blood inside them. They grew from infants, to boys, to men in one short winter and were soon running the forge I had begun with Proteus so long before.

"Cabeiro and I were immensely happy together and she did not shy away from the boys when it became clear that they had also inherited some of my lameness; for both did not grow taller than half the height of normal men. She loved them and cherished them with all that she had, just as she did me, and I did not want to leave when Zeus called me back to Olympos.

"I went of course, but promised Cabeiri I would be by her side again just as soon as I could. Whilst I was away, Cabeiro found she was with child again. She did not tell me the news, intending the baby's arrival to be a joyous surprise for me when I returned. But I was kept away for almost two mortal winters and I did not know of my child's existence until an old woman prayed to me and told me of the fate that awaited it.

"Cabeiro and our children had welcomed the impending birth with joy. There would be another in the royal line of the sea nymphs, fathered by Hephaestus, the great God of Fire. But when our sixth child arrived, healthy and strong, it was not celebrated. It was not a magnificent event. The baby was a Halfling. Part-girl, part-boy. Already developed. Immediately feared. Instantly hated. The child was not a demigod – not in the true sense of the word where strength or abilities were obvious at their birth. It was plain. It was … mortal. It held no power, it was as though none of my blood flowed in its veins. Being neither immortal nor nymph, this new arrival, this simple mortal, was a disappointment. He did not age as his brothers did, she did not display talents in the waters as her sisters did."

Lysistratos looked to me again, his eyes sliding across to Demetri as well and taking in the flat chest and short tunic, a slight frown creasing his forehead. "What does he mean part-girl, part-boy? You have … both male and female organs? Your chest is …" He waved his hand as if searching for the right word. "It's like mine. It's flat," he finally said.

Demetri took a deep breath and blew it all the way out before replying. "I had breasts. I don't have them anymore but that is another story, one that I will share with you if you want to hear it once Hephaestus has told us the rest of his tale." Lysistratos took an almost imperceptible step away from Demetri. I didn't miss it and I had to figure Demetri didn't either.

A flash of anger lit my blood but Demetri squeezed my hand and gave a small shake of his head. "Don't." I bit down on my response as requested but glared at Lysistratos.

Moeris stepped between Lysistratos and Demetri and addressed Hephaestus who stood on my other side. "Allow us to hear the rest of what you have to say."

Hephaestus nodded in return. "I think that best for now, things shall become clearer to you all as I explain."

I nodded in return, mouthing 'thank you' to Moeris. He inclined his head in acknowledgement.

2

Hephaestus continued with his story. "Within a few days of the child's birth, Cabeiro shunned it. She refused to see it, feed it, care for or love it. She gave the baby to Ophelia, the midwife who had helped her deliver, with instructions to throw it into the sea and never speak of its existence again. But Ophelia could not. She feared my wrath and kept the child hidden from Cabeiro and its siblings.

"When the child was a winter old, Alcon and Eurymedon somehow found out that their sister-brother was alive and took it, naked and screaming from Ophelia, intent on killing it themselves. Ophelia prayed to me, begging me to return. When I did, she told me of everything that had happened since I left, and of much I did not know from before.

"I thanked Ophelia for all she had done, resettling her far from Lemnos before setting out to find my sons. It did not take me long to locate them; they were behind their forge, a semi-circle of rocks hiding them from unsuspecting eyes. Eurymedon held the innocent child and Alcon the knife that would end its life.

"I intended to remain hidden, and I did – from Eurymedon and Alcon at least – but the baby's eyes captured mine, and I stared into the deep brown flecked with the same yellow as my own. I cannot say how she knew I was there, but our gazes locked and in that instant, a silent acknowledgement of our kinship passed between us. When Alcon drove the knife into my child's chest, I ensured the pointed tip did not touch her heart. In return, she appeared to understand what we must do, she did not cry out, nor make any sound, but his body went limp and her eyes closed. Somehow I knew that she – he – was destined for greatness and I was determined to do everything in my power to ensure he had the chance."

I drew a breath and held tighter to Demetri, noting with interest that Hephaestus referred to the child like I had when I first learned of Demetri's dual sex – a female from the waist up and a male from the waist down.

"The older boys worked quickly and I allowed them to believe they had succeeded with their murderous plan," Hephaestus said. I stayed out of sight as they wrapped the small body in a purple cloak, wreathing the head and burying it beneath the rocks, before fleeing the area. When they were gone, I took the body from the hole and placed it on a bronze shield, returning to my palace.

"I took the wreath and peeled the cloak away, finding the child alive beneath the layers with not even the hint of a scar from the knife on her chest. I held him to my breast as she stared up at me with wonder and innocence.

"I told no one of my child's existence and took her to a small town called Larissa. I knew the people there to be kindly and they worshipped the goddess Demeter, who favored them with an abundance of crops, so I knew she would never go hungry. I had considered Athens, where I was highly worshipped, but I did not believe a baby would be as well cared for there; there were more people, which meant more mouths to feed, and I believed that those who saw her would be more inclined to leave her where she was rather than take her and care for her.

"So, I left the child beneath a small statue of Demeter in a grove just outside the town of Larissa and waited with her until a group of women returning from the fields came across her. The women did not hesitate to take her back to their home or hide her from their master, even when they realized she was not just a she.

"They were not unkind to the child, but they were not fully nurturing either. They assigned no name, referring to it only as *child*, and no one took on a true mothering role. The child lived with them in secret until the age of four when it was discovered by the master of the house. He did not normally enter the small rooms that belonged to the slaves, but for some reason that day he did, and the child happened to be bathing in plain sight. He saw not only a betrayal by his slaves, who all truthfully claimed that the child was not theirs, but an opportunity for coin.

"He marched the boy-girl through the streets to the inns and taverns, attempting to convince the owners to allow him to use the child for all manner of ways in their private rooms, with the profits to be split between the two parties. I ensured none of them took him up on the offers. In the end the master saw the youngster as a burden rather than a use and took it to the slavers market to rid himself and make some coin anyway.

I sent a silent prayer of thanks to Hephaestus for what he had done for his child, knowing that Demetri's life had taken a turn for the better at that market.

"I could feel my blood pumping strongly through the child and I knew he would have exceptional skills in metalwork so I ensured that Spyros – the most talented metalworker in the area and a kind hearted man – was at the market that day and saw the master and young child. I knew Spyros' heart and that he would not leave the boy-girl to the clutches of the others milling about there.

"After learning the child had been left beneath a statue of Demeter, Spyros gifted him with the name of Demetri after the goddess. And with my assistance, Spyros decided to put Demetri to work in the Celator's hut rather than the fields, as well as outwardly raising Demetri as a boy, with the intent of one day allowing him – or her – to live as they wished.

"Satisfied that my daughter-son was safe, I returned to Olympos and turned my attention to Cabeiro and my other sons. I could not punish the boys for killing their sibling but I have not assisted them with their forge or answered their prayers and sacrifices since; they do not deserve such kindnesses after what they did.

"As for Cabeiro, Ophelia had told me many things, none of which made me want to ever return to *her* side as the husband and lover I had been before. It was not just the rejection of our child that I could not forgive, but the knowledge that she had used me only to father powerful sons and daughters, to keep her royal bloodline worthy. She had never truly loved me, and spoke of my blindness to the truth of her deception with glee to her friends.

"I still loved her dearly, but I could not forgive such a betrayal, and I could not pretend I did not know of it so I never returned to Lemnos. I did not want to see or speak to Cabeiro again. I did not want to hear her lies if she chose to hide behind them, but neither could I bear to hear her speak the truth.

"I had truly believed we wanted the same things; that we felt the same way about each other, but I was wrong and an innocent child had almost paid for my blindness. I cut all ties with Lemnos and the people there, never again aiding them in their quest for better metal products or blessing one of their own with the skills of the forge.

"I returned to Olympos but spent much time in Larissa as well, watching Demetri as he grew. When I left him beneath the statue winters before, I also left a small pouch with him. It was not an ordinary one made of animal skin and leather; I had laced it with crystallized carbon, which made what was inside invisible to those who would seek its contents. I added a drop of the child's blood to the pouch so that if, by some chance, Cabeiro or her sons ever found out he was alive, they would never be able to find him.

"My heart ached as I watched from afar. I wanted to love and care for my child as he deserved, to protect him from those who taunted and tortured him but I was afraid that my own enemies would use his existence against me and I did not want to add to his burden. I could see that even unconsciously he had questions about his mother, about who his parents were – he drew my face and the likeness of his mother, the nymph, with unnerving accuracy even though it had been winters since he had seen either of us, and he had never seen Cabeiro in her fish form."

"My mother," Demetri murmured, sudden clarity of who she was and why he had been compelled to draw her dawning.

Hephaestus nodded in reply, addressing Demetri directly with his next words. "Your skill with not only the designs you drew, but the silver you put them into, surprised even me. I had never seen a Celator carve such intricate designs for the obverse side of a coin into a block of iron, nor a design just as intricate for the reverse side. Your early coins did not quite have the accuracy, but as you grew, your pictures graced each side of the heated silver disks with unnerving perfectness.

"I was proud to call you my son, proud to call you my daughter. I was proud to know that you had come from my body, even if no one else ever knew of it. I hoped one day we would meet, but I did not know how or what would see it so until Ava came along and I found the opportunity I had been waiting for to meet you … and to hurt Ares and deny him what he wanted."

"And how did that come about? Where is Ares now?" Moeris asked.

"In a cage deep in the earth," Hephaestus replied. "He shall not see light again."

I explained what had happened since I left them at the Pass of Coela, Papou and Demetri adding their own perspectives when I had no answer for the questions Moeris or Lysistratos asked. "So that is how we find ourselves here," I finished.

Lysistratos drew me aside, his voice low when he spoke. "So you and Demetri are … you have started a relationship with him … her?"

"I have," I replied.

"How … I mean is he a boy or a girl? If he doesn't have breasts anymore then does that mean he has …?" He trailed off again.

"Demetri is the best one to answer those questions. If he or she wants to discuss it with you."

"But does it not bother you … that he had breasts?"

"I have fallen for someone for who they are, not the body they are in. Talk to Demetri, hear what he has to say, judge her on who she is, not what she looks like. I believe the two of you can become friends if you only get to know him."

Lysistratos was quiet a long moment before giving a single nod. "I can listen."

"Thank you." I returned to Demetri, to Demi.

"Everything alright?" she asked.

"Lysistratos has questions about you, about your past. He may not ask them tactfully, he may even offend you with them and I apologize on his behalf if he does but he wants to learn, to understand why I care for you and he will try and understand who you are as best he can."

Demetri nodded. "I can imagine it's difficult for him and Moeris to understand given that I introduced myself to them as a male, and then they learnt what they did through my father's story. It makes me wonder …" Demi paused but I remained quiet, letting her arrange her thoughts before she continued. "When we get back to Trachis, I don't want the same confusion to befall your grandparents. I want them to know who I am straight away. I want to introduce myself as Demetri. As Demi. As a Halfling in all senses – half-woman, half-man, half-god, half-mortal. I don't want there to be any question about who I really am."

I drew a breath, blowing it all the way out before I responded. "I can … appreciate that wish but … I do not know how it is going to be between Agrias, Melina and me when I see them again. When I return to Trachis with Papou and a thought of acknowledging who I am to the people there, of being the Princess of Trachis like I was always meant to be … it is complicated. Can it possibly wait just a little while?"

"I understand where you're coming from too but now that I've left Larissa I want to live my truth. I want to be who I really am. I've wanted it for so long and now finally I have the chance. Why should I have to introduce myself as one sex or the other?"

"Because you look like a man," Lysistratos murmured, re-joining us.

"Yes, but I am not just that," Demi countered.

"You are unless you tell people otherwise."

Papou neared, his hand on Demi's shoulder as he weighed into the conversation. "We do not have to make any decisions right now, allow us to see what happens when we arrive, and then a decision can be made."

"Agreed," Moeris nodded. "There is much to be discussed on our return."

TRACHIS

1

5th waning, Moon of Anthesterion 489BC

"Old pain must be set aside. We should not waste time blaming one another for something we cannot change. It is time we came together as a family, just as we were when Ava was a child," Agrias insisted.

"*My* child was not dead in those days," Melina yelled.

"Neither was mine," Papou added.

"That army was here because of you and your daughter," Melina countered. "*You* got Alexis killed."

"Do you truly think Alexis would have wanted to be anywhere but at Skylar's side, even in death?" Papou shouted, throwing his hands up. "Their love was strong. Through all they endured, it never wavered."

"Those thoughts may have comforted you all the winters you were far from here, but they are lies," Melina spat.

"This is not helping," Agrias sighed.

"Papou cannot be held responsible for what happened that night any more than the Persians can, not now we all know the truth that it was Ares who took them from us," I said, finally weighing into the conversation. "And we did not lose just my mothers, but my father – Thaddeus – too."

"You … you knew Thaddeus was your father?" Agrias asked, surprised.

"Not then, but Papou told me when we were reunited recently. You lost me soon after as well, though not to Hades."

"We did lose you, that is the truth, and I have regretted it every day since," Agrias agreed, taking my hand in both of his. "But we never stopped loving you, even if our actions did not show it. Not one of us," he added, his eyes finding his wife's then Papou's. The queen dropped her gaze to the floor, but Papou nodded to the king.

"You say Papou should have told you about Ares' involvement before he left, but what purpose would it have served? It would not have brought my mothers back," I addressed Melina directly, but she did not lift her eyes to mine.

"I wish Ares had taken my life that night. I would have gladly sacrificed it so Ava could grow with the love of her parents, and for you to still have Alexis," Papou murmured.

"Hush, Leandros," Agrias said, laying a hand on Papou's shoulder. "We should be thankful that Ares did not harm the rest of us. If you had been taken that night along with Skylar and Alexis, what would have happened when Ava reached her nineteenth winter and Ares gifted the amulet to her? The thought of *that* makes me shudder. Tell us of Ares, where is he now?"

"Hephaestus crafted a cage to hold him deep within the earth," I replied. "I am not foolish enough to believe it can hold him forever, but for now he cannot reach or threaten us. After I woke at Olympos, the nodes on my back where my wings had sat dormant were gone. Ares can no longer call me his Chosen One for with their disappearance, his potential hold over me is gone too. I feel it."

"And where have these past winters found you?" Agrias asked Papou.

"I returned to the north, not to Thrace, but to the friends I fled my tribe with before I lost Zita and received Skylar," Papou replied.

"They are well?"

"Yes. Though I do not know if they shall welcome me again."

"If that is so, then I urge you to harbor no sad feelings. I wish you to spend the remainder of your days here with us in Trachis, as I intend to spend mine." Agrias addressed me with his next words. "Both of you can have your old rooms here at the palace. I hope that you shall be happy here again, Granddaughter. That once again we *all* can be."

"Excuse me," Melina said, making her way across the balcony and through the closest walkway into the palace without a backwards glance.

"I appreciate the offer, my friend," Papou replied, all of us watching Melina leave. "But I do not know if your wife bears the same wishes."

"It shall not be an easy path," Agrias nodded.

I agreed, but did not say it out loud, wondering now that I was back in Trachis if I had made the right decision. So much time had passed and yet there was much hurt that remained. I had spoken words of putting the past behind us, but it was difficult not to still place blame with Melina and Agrias for banishing Papou and turning from me. The anger still burned inside me, as it obviously did Melina.

I was almost jealous of my grandfathers and the easy way they had been able to put aside their hurt and return to friendly terms. "I will take my leave as well," I told them. "I promised to show Demetri the hot springs."

"Come to the east banquet hall tonight, we shall all eat together and we can meet your new companion properly."

"If we are back, we will come, otherwise we will just get something from the kitchen."

"Oh. If that is your wish then I understand, but please, consider the offer."

I only nodded, leaving my grandfathers to speak alone, heading for the barracks where I had left Demetri – Demi – with Moeris a candlemark earlier.

2
Five moons later
Moon of Hekatombaion, 488BC

"And you have been feeling ill for how long?" the healer of Trachis, Podaleirius, asked as he checked me over.

"About a moon I suppose. It is not all the time, I notice it most in the mornings."

Podaleirius nodded, removing his hands from me again. "That is to be expected being that you are with child."

"What?" I gaped.

He grinned and nodded again. "Yes, I believe you are two or even three moons along. We can expect them in the winter, in Gamelion if I am not mistaken, or perhaps it shall be sooner."

"Why sooner?"

"You carry two children and I have seen it cause early birthing."

"What?" I said again. "*Two* children ... but ... how ... I ..." I did not go on, unable to comprehend what the healer was saying. Of all the things I had imagined I could be suffering from, *that* particular scenario had not crossed my mind. Demi and I had not discussed children or even the possibility that it could happen. I did not know how they – which is how we were now referring to Demi – would react to the news.

Since we arrived in Trachis and Demi's dual sex had been made known, Demi decided they would not be known as *he* or *she* but *they*, it seemed the best way to acknowledge both parts of who they were and for the most part, people accepted it. Lysistratos had taken a little longer to come to terms with it but to his credit he worked hard to understand what it meant for Demi and was now the first to explain it to someone who showed confusion or shut down any negative comments or reactions, which I was more than grateful for.

"Shall I allow Demi in now?" Podaleirius asked, interrupting my musings.

"Please," I nodded. The healer let Demi in and himself out.

"Everything alright?" they asked.

I drew in a breath and reached out for them to take my hand. "I ... er ... I am not sure."

Demi frowned. "What do you mean?"

"It ... appears that I am pregnant," I stammered.

Demi's eyebrows shot up. "You're what?"

"Pregnant," I replied.

They paced back and forth, eyes flicking between the floor and me. "Is Podaleirius sure?"

"Yes. Apparently ... we are expecting two babies."

Demi stopped pacing. "Two?" they repeated. I only nodded in reply. "I didn't even know I could father children ... I mean I suppose I should've considered it but ... well it never came up before ... and I suppose that makes me a father. A male role ..."

"Are you upset?" I asked, not sure I actually wanted the answer when I was so unsure of how I felt about the whole thing.

Demi stopped pacing and turned to me, a grin on their face. "No. I'm surprised ... shocked actually but not upset ... are you?"

"Not upset, but like you, I am surprised. I never saw myself becoming a mother. I never thought of *us* becoming parents, at least not in the way it seems we have ..."

"No, I can't say that ever crossed my mind either."

A knock sounded at the door and when Demi crossed the room and opened it, the three worried faces of my grandparents appeared around their shoulder. "We saw Podaleirius leaving the barracks and Moeris said you didn't train this morning," Papou explained. "Are you unwell?"

"Not exactly," Demi replied, stepping aside to let them in.

"I am pregnant," I told them.

"You are?" Melina asked.

"How?" Papou asked at the same time.

"The two of you have been attempting to start a family?" Agrias asked, confusion rather than anger tinting his words.

"Er ... not intentionally," I replied, a blush creeping up my neck.

"Did you know you could even ..." Melina fumbled.

"No, this is as much a surprise to me as it is to you," Demi replied.

"And you two are ... happy with this development?" she asked.

I nodded, catching Demi's eye. "Still trying to comprehend it, but yes, I think so."

"Then we are delighted too," Melina grinned, moving forward and taking me in an awkward hug. "Perhaps it can be a new start for us all. Heirs for all of our lines." She released me and met Papou's eyes, an understanding and perhaps the start of a slight thawing of their feud emerging. He nodded in return.

"Yes, a happy occasion indeed," Agrias agreed. "Perhaps you would now reconsider my offer of returning to live at the palace?"

"Maybe," I shrugged. I could see the merit in his words – babies would keep the soldiers awake at night and that would not be conducive to battle conditions if we were called upon for such – but I still wasn't ready to relinquish the position I held within the army.

Agrias let my answer be enough. "When are we to welcome this new addition?" he asked.

"These additions," I corrected, quickly adding. "Podaleirius believes I am expecting twins in the moon of Gamelion."

"Twins?" Papou echoed, a grin of his own breaking out. "That is the happiest of news. Do you know if either of the children are expected to be boys?"

"I have no idea," I replied. "Perhaps they will be like Demi ..."

"The test ..." Melina murmured.

"What test?" I asked, wondering if everyone would be as welcoming to our children if they were born with both sexual organs as they had been when Demi announced who they were.

"When your mothers found out you were growing inside Alexis, they carried out a test to determine if they were to have a daughter or son," Agrias explained.

I saw the question hanging on Demi's face and voiced it so they did not have to. "Does it matter? Can we not just love whatever and whoever our children are?"

"Of course, but ... no boys have ever been born to the line of the Chosen One. It would prove that you defeated Ares, that his power over you has been lost," Papou replied.

"Oh," I nodded. Ares and his line had not even entered my thoughts when I found out. I raised my eyes to Demi, who only shrugged, deferring the decision to me. "I suppose we could do it if you know how," I replied.

"I do," Papou nodded.

"Perhaps we could do it later today or perhaps even tomorrow," Demi suggested, taking my hand again. "But while we're all together perhaps we could discuss something else I've been thinking about." I watched Demi carefully, wondering what they were talking about.

"Of course, what is on your mind?" Papou asked.

"You have all accepted me as I am, agreed to refer to me as neither male nor female specifically as I asked. And I couldn't be more grateful for that but ... the last couple of months I've been feeling ... confused about who I am. I mean I don't feel different to how I always have, I embrace my female and male sides as much as I always have but ... I feel like maybe there is more female in me than male. I ... think I want there to be."

I frowned. "I do not understand. What do you mean?"

Demi tightened their hand against mine and drew me to sit on the bed of the room I occupied in the barracks. "You're a strong woman, a competent and respected soldier. The person who's lucky enough to be with you should be strong too."

"You are," I said, my frown deepening.

"I know," Demi nodded. "But for how I look on the outside, I should be a strong *man*. Someone who can stand at your side when you train and when you go into battle. Your partner should be a warrior, a protector, just like you are ... and that isn't who I am."

"You are not going to leave her, not now, not with the announcement of your children?" Melina asked, taking a step forward.

"No, no. Of course not," Demi assured her. "I am overjoyed at the prospect of becoming a parent, of being able to shower my children with love and family and a proper home where they will grow with kin around them." They faced me again. "What I mean is that I'm not comfortable being seen as an inferior male companion for you ... and I know that is how some people see me." I opened my mouth to refute their words but Demi squeezed my fingers and I stayed quiet.

"If I'm ever to sit on the throne of Trachis beside you, the townspeople can't be confused about their ruler – would I be their king or their queen? I will never be a soldier but they need to see me as someone strong, a leader, someone they can trust to lead them when needed and in this body ... I don't think I can do that."

My frown deepened and I drew my hand from theirs. Ruling Trachis was something I had barely discussed with Agrias, let alone Demi. "I think it is premature to presume that you ... or I ... will sit on the throne anytime soon. I am in no hurry to do so. There is a lot I need to learn before I even consider it and for now I am more than happy to continue my role with the soldiers."

"I know, but when ... if it doe–"

It was my turn to pace. "This is a discussion we should have had alone. Besides, you have brought the situation on yourself, *you* were the one who insisted everyone knew you were a Halfling. *You* were the one who wanted to dress as a man at certain times and as a woman at other times."

"Ava ..." Papou started.

"No, no, Ava's right, maybe I have brought this on myself," Demi agreed, a hard edge to their voice. "But having children ... this changes things. I know I could live as a man, be a father to our children but ... I'm ... that's not how I want to present myself anymore."

"So what are you saying? You want to live as a female?" I asked, stopping my pacing so I could look at them. "How would you do that? You can't exactly have your breasts returned to you and what abo–"

"Perhaps we should give you some privacy, allow you to discuss things together as a couple," Melina interrupted.

"I think that would be a good idea," Agrias agreed, Papou nodding his agreement as well, the three of them unable to get out of the door fast enough.

"Join us for dinner and we can discuss the test and ... other matters," Papou managed before closing the door behind them.

"Let me be your Alexis," Demi murmured when they were gone.

I frowned but raised my gaze to meet theirs. "What?"

"Let me be the one to stay here and be a mother. Let me look after our children while you join the soldiers whenever you're needed," they explained. "I'm not a fighter but as an able-bodied man it would be frowned upon if I didn't pick up weapons when required. I'm not a fighter – not like that. I'm not that person. I don't *want* to be that person. But you do. You are. And I won't ask you to give that up. When the times comes, let Trachis one day be ruled by two queens just as it was always meant to be with your mothers."

"Demi," I started, unable to figure out how to finish.

"I'm sorry to just spring this on you, I know it was wrong bu–"

"This is a lot ... the babies ... I need to process that, I think we both should before we make any other major changes. The timing is ..."

"You're disappointed with who I believe I am now I've had the chance to figure that out?"

"I did not know you were confused – I thought you knew who you were – Demetri, Demi, they, them, the Halfling."

"And I am still all of those things but I think I am Demi. I want to be Demi."

"And how would that even happen?" I repeated. "I doubt Podaleirius would be able to do anything."

Demi dropped their eyes. "I don't know exactly but I want to start asking the traders who come from Athens or Sparta if they've ever heard of healers being able to ... change someone." I shook my head, so many thoughts and words fighting their way to get out, all of which I knew I would regret if I let them escape.

I needed to get out of there. "I ... I need time ..."

"Ava, wait," Demi started. I shook my head and pushed past them out through the door. I headed into the palace, uncertain who I was looking for, or if I even wanted to talk to anyone about what Demi was asking.

Papou and Agrias were headed into the Throne Room but I stepped behind one of the bushes in the central garden and they did not see me before they entered.

"Who are we hiding from?" Eumelia's voice startled me as I spun to face her. She gave me a tight grin. "Melina saw me at the barracks when Phaidros and I were visiting Lysistratos, she said you might need someone to talk to."

I blew out a deep breath but nodded, pointing to the doorway to the eastern balcony. When we cleared the doorway and I saw we were alone on the balcony I told Eumelia what Podaleirius had found and what Demi had pronounced.

"I know you love Demi, all of her, all of him, and it is not like you haven't had both female and male lovers before but this is an extreme change, an actual, one would think *permanent,* change. If they were to find someone who could do what they are suggesting, would you want a female lover? Are you comfortable with that?"

"I just want Demi. I want them to be happy, I always have. It has never bothered me what body they came in, I fell in love with what was on the inside, not the outside. I mean I have got used to them having the … body parts they have but would I miss that? Honestly I do not know. It is a lot for Demi to give up and what about when I eventually leave the soldiers would they regret their decision, blame me for it?"

"There is that to consider," Eumelia nodded. "What we want can change over time, even if it is only slightly."

"The thing is, I do not think I can say no to what they want, it is not really my decision and if that is what makes them happy … if she is happiest being a woman, then how can I deny her?"

"It has to be partly your decision too, it cannot just be about what Demi wants. You have to be comfortable with the choice as well and if you do not want to be with a woman then you have to tell Demi."

"I know," I nodded. "I just need time to get my head around everything," I told Eumelia, echoing what I had told Demi.

3

Six moons later
Moon of Gamelion, 488BC

" Ava, wake up." Papou's voice pulled me from my slumber.
I struggled to lift my rounded belly and limbs from the bed,
noting that the sun was much lower in the sky than when I had reluctantly
lay down to rest.

"What is it?" I asked, my stomach clenching at the look on his face. I
amended my question. "Who?"

"Come," was Papou's only reply. I swung my legs over the side of the
bed, Papou taking my elbow and helping me to stand. "He is not dead, but
the healer does not expect him to last the night."

"Who?" I repeated, praying Moeris had got Demi to safety.

"Lysistratos." I quickened my steps but Papou held firm and I slowed
my pace again. "There's no need to hurry, there is nothing you can do for
him now."

I should have been by his side just like I had always – my aspis
protecting his right side as the man who stood beside me (Moeris usually)
protected mine. "What happened?" I asked instead.

"A number of soldiers surprised Demi and Moeris as they were leaving
the palace, Lysistratos and I saw it unfolding from afar. We rushed to help
but arrived late, Phaeops and Eton were there by then and they held Moeris
at bay with a sword to his throat, another at Demi's. Phaeops was crowing
at how they had finally caught up with 'the beast'. They had heard of a

person at Trachis who was referred to as neither a man nor woman and they knew it must be the slave they pursued from Larissa."

"You and Lysistratos would have been able to dispose of them easily, they would be no match for either of you. With their attention diverted, Moeris would have been able to jump in and help you as well," I countered.

Papou nodded. "I have no doubt of that but Phaeops and his friends did not come alone. The Dolopes joined them and they are far more competent fighters. We were outnumbered and while the real warriors occupied our swords, Phaeops took his revenge on Demi and their escape from those boys last winter."

I stopped where I was, gripping Papou's arm hard. "What do you mean? What happened? Where is Demi?" Papou drew a deep breath. "Papou," I urged, scared at his hesitation.

"Hephaestus has them."

"Why? What happened? Are they alright?"

"Phaeops … attempted to … to cut off …" Papou stammered, unable to say the words but indicating his groin area. "There was so much blood. I thought … I thought Demi would die and I called for Hephaestus but he already felt Demi's life draining away and appeared before I was even finished saying his name."

I closed my eyes, my legs threatening to give out. Papou held me up, wrapping his arm around my waist.

"Hephaestus shall ensure they return alive but … you should prepare yourself for when they do. Demi may not look as they did when you saw them this morning."

"What do you mean?"

"Demi was dying and was also going to lose the only … sexual organ they had left. They couldn't lose that as they had lost their breasts. Hephaestus agreed to find a way to change Demi into a woman, to return her breasts to her and … change what they had."

"How?" I frowned, tears prickling my eyes as I imagined not only the fear and loss, but the pain they must have been in. Demi and I had not spoken much on the subject of their becoming a woman since they brought it up the day we found out I was pregnant but we had made a number of enquiries with traders who came to Trachis and through healers Podaleirius knew. So far it had yielded no answers.

"I honestly do not know. It may not be possible at all but either way, Demi shall not be the same person they were when they left here."

I swallowed loudly. I did not care what they came back looking like, just as long as they came back to me. Alive. I could not birth our children or bring them up alone. I sent out a silent prayer to Hephaestus asking him to protect Demi and return them to Trachis as soon as he could. I sent a second one to Demi, telling them that I did not care what their body looked like, I just needed them here with me.

"I should have been there. I should have been able to protect the city from enemies," I murmured when my prayers were done.

"You know that is not possible, your children gro–"

"I should have been there," I repeated firmly. "What about Lysistratos? How is it he was injured so badly? Were you not at his side?"

Papou dropped his head before taking my elbow again and leading me toward the front of the palace. "No. I was distracted with the Dolopes and by the time I got through them, Phaeops had mutilated Demi and Lysistratos was perched above, badly injured himself but protecting Demi – ensuring Phaeops could not run his sword through their chest."

I blew out a deep breath. "That job should not have been Lysistratos'. I cannot lose Demi and I cannot lose Lysistratos. Not now."

As we neared the Throne Room, *Podaleirius, Moeris and another soldier* entered the front doors of the palace, Lysistratos' crumpled form on his shield between them.

"Ly, no," I murmured when they reached us. I swept the hair off Lysistratos' forehead, drawing a sharp breath. His remaining intact eye was closed. Blood covered him from head to toe. The red on his arms appeared to have been drawn from the enemy, but the rest belonged to him. A broken spear was lodged in his stomach, blood seeping slowly from the wound and dripping off the edges of his shield to stain the ground in the courtyard beneath.

"His hand," I murmured.

"Was lost to a sword. His eye from a second spear," Moeris replied, placing his free hand on my shoulder. "He fought valiantly to protect Demi, his friend, his best friend's beloved, a father, a mother, a son. He fought until his legs were severed below the knees and dropped him to the dirt, never to rise again and still he protected Demi."

My eyes trailed to the missing appendages, then back to my friend's face. His chest rose and fell. It was slow and wheezing, but regular enough.

"We must get him inside if I am to ease his pain on his way to the Underworld," Podaleirius said, adjusting his grip on Lysistratos's shield.

I wanted to tell him to save Lysistratos but the words stuck in my throat.

"Take him to the banquet hall," Papou directed, pointing to the room between the doors and kitchen.

The three men headed toward the room, Papou and I following.

As they settled him on top of a table, Moeris held out a length of leather to me. "He wanted you to have this. He said you would know what it meant." I closed my hand around the bloodied bronze at its end, squeezing it between my fingers, as tears rolled down my cheeks.

Lysistratos had had the necklace for as long as I could remember. It had belonged to his father, who died a moon before Lysistratos was born.

When Lysistratos' son Phaidros was born, Lysistratos made me give my word that upon his death, I would ensure it reached his boy. He spoke of it being a source of both pride and pain for Phaidros, as it had been for him, but he was determined to keep the tradition alive, even if Phaidros was a grown man by the time he received it. We did not speak of the agreement often, but before particular battles Lysistratos would remind me of my oath and what I had agreed to do if his life should end in the fight ahead. It seemed like today was to be that day and we had not even discussed it.

"I need to go get Eumelia," Papou said. "Will you be alright here?"

I nodded. "Do not let Phaidros come with her, he is too young to see his father this way," I replied, wiping my eyes.

"Of course." He placed a kiss on my forehead and one hand on Lysistratos' chest, his eyes closing briefly, no doubt sending up silent words of healing to the gods.

When he was out of hearing range, I turned to Moeris. "I should have been there, Moeris. We could have found a way to delay the enemy until I had birthed my children. None of you should have been facing them without me."

"That is not your role now, you are to be a mother. Your days as a soldier are at an end."

"No, I do not accept that. Mumma was still a soldier after I was born. She did not live in the barracks, so why can I not be the same?"

"You know of her fate only too well. Do not subject your children to the same." I opened my mouth to protest again but Moeris held his hand up to silence me. "I am certain you shall want to argue on the point further but now is not the time. I must return to the Plain. There are many pyres to make this day, for both sides," he said grimly. "The battle is done but were it not for Zeus' help, the one called Titormus may have crushed us all. He gives no mind to lifting rocks or uprooting trees and throwing them at his opponents, crushing them beneath before moving onto the next. He is the strongest man I have ever seen, and I heard several of the Dolopes refer to him as the second Heracles, which befits him."

It took me a moment to realize what Moeris had said. "Zeus?" I frowned.

He nodded. "Something else to discuss at another juncture – I am certain he shall visit you in time as well."

I kept further thoughts to myself, Moeris was right – now was not the time and our arguing and discussions would only prolong the grief of those who had lost a loved one. "Go," I nodded. "I will help *Podaleirius*." Moeris only nodded in reply.

*

I sat beside Lysistratos in the banqueting hall, a chair pulled up and awkwardly holding my newly-large frame. I had helped the healer apply bandages to the cuts and gaping holes across my dear friend's ravaged body, and washed the blood from his face and arms. The skin beneath his eyes was a deep purple and in stark contrast to the pale cheeks and chin. His empty eye socket was hidden by a wide bandage that wound around his forehead and hair. Where once his hand and legs had been, thick layers of material kept the ragged tears from view. I had packed cloth into the hole the spear had made in his stomach, Podaleirius ensuring a firmly tied length held it in place.

I kept Lysistratos' cold, unmoving hand between my warmer ones, hoping that Hephaestus was holding tight to Demi's, and that theirs was not so cold. I recalled the battles Lysistratos and I had fought together over the winters and of our reunion at the barracks when we were inducted as epheboi in the army in my twelfth winter and Lysistratos' eighteenth. I remembered too when we had learnt of the impending attack by Phaeops. I had immediately started to calculate what we would need to do before the enemies arrived before Lysistratos and Demi reminded me that I would not be able to join the soldiers, that I would not be taking any part in the defense of the town.

Had Phaeops and the Dolopes decided to come in the summer moons when almost all campaigns were fought, I would have been able to join them, our children already born. Instead they were already on their way and it became a moot point that I would be involved, I could not move with the same flexibility and speed I once had. I would have to remain at the palace when they came, unless I was prepared to lose my life and those of my children. Which I was not.

Still, I railed against the knowledge, clashing with Demi, my grandparents, Lysistratos and Moeris. I pleaded and demanded that someone be sent as an emissary, to discuss terms, anything to delay their arrival but in the end it was an argument I lost. Although I did not know of their arrival when I lay down earlier, I was angry with myself that I had slept while Demi and Lysistratos needed me.

"Though I love them with all my heart, the children inside me have made me weak. They have robbed me of promises made to you, my dear friend, and I am sorry," I whispered, raising Lysistratos' knuckles to my lips.

"His life draws to an end." *Podaleirius* said, his hand on my shoulder. "You must say your goodbyes now."

"You must fight, Lysistratos. Fight your wounds. Please. Recover for Eumelia and Phaidros and for me," I urged, squeezing his hand. "You must look upon your wife and child again. Do not leave us. Stay, I beg it of you."

I did not expect the words to have power, but Lysistratos' eyes cracked open. "Ava … You must remember … to gift Phaidros my necklace," he rasped.

I squeezed his hand tighter. "And I shall, when it is time. It cannot be so yet."

"It is ... Please, you gave me your word."

I closed my eyes and nodded. Deep down I had known when I saw him lying on his shield that he was not long for this world, but still I wished I did not have to say goodbye to him already.

"Ava, we have known each other ... so long ... and I have always been proud to ... call you my friend," he gasped. "I could always rely on you when we ... faced our enemies ... and when your time here is ended ... I shall look for you ... in the Underworld. Tell Eumelia I love her... and ensure Phaidros knows who I was ... and that I loved him."

Lysistratos closed his eyes again, taking one last gasp before his chest became motionless. Tears streamed down my cheeks and I pressed my fingers against his face.

"I am sorry," I whispered.

"You! This is your fault," Eumelia screamed, rushing into the room, her face as wet as mine.

"Eumelia, no," I cried, dropping Lysistratos' hand and knocking the chair over in my haste to get away from her as she advanced.

"You promised you would keep him safe, that you would always be by his side in battle, and yet you allowed him to go to this fight without you," she continued. "Where were you when he was being speared to death? When his limbs were being chopped without care from his body?"

"I could not ..." I began.

"You *chose* not to. Your belly is swollen with your children so you have forsaken all previous promises, but what about *my* child? You destined him to grow without his father for more than just the four winters it was supposed to be."

My breath refused to be caught, but I had no reply for her. She spoke true. I had made promises that would no longer come to pass. Except for the necklace, I would ensure Phaidros received it. I must.

"Eumel–"

"No! You promised he would return to me for good in his thirtieth winter."

"I ..."

"I shall never forgive you. You have taken a father from his son, how should I explain that to Phaidros when he is old enough to ask after him? You shall never be welcome at our table again and though we have only just learned of it, I shall call you sister no longer. Take your leave."

Eumelia righted the chair and dropped into it, grabbing up her dead husband's hand and pressing it hard against her mouth, screaming her despair around it.

I swallowed the lump in my throat. "As you wish," I whispered. "I am sorry."

4

"Demi," I cried, rushing forward as quickly as my rounded belly would allow. I took them – her – in my arms and held her tight.

"Ava," she murmured. "By the gods I am glad to see you again."

Hephaestus had visited me early that morning, telling me Demi was well enough to travel. He had been able to heal her, and the changes we had discussed were complete. Demi had sent him on ahead to ensure I was still comfortable with it, that I still wanted her back.

A week ago when Hephaestus had come to me after Demi was hurt and Lysistratos died, he told me he had been able to stop Demi from losing any more blood, and that he had someone who could help him change Demi to be a woman. I had not known what to say but I told Hephaestus that I just needed Demi back. Alive. Hephaestus nodded but insisted I decide if I would be comfortable to be in a relationship with a woman, if I would accept that that was who Demi was now. Demi wanted to know if there was still a future for us before it was done.

Hephaestus had let me think on it overnight and when he came back I gave him my answer: I did not care if Demi presented themselves to the world as a man or a woman. I loved them and I would love them in whatever form they took.

I released Demi, resting my forehead against hers instead. "How are you?" I asked.

"Thank you," Demi said at the same time. We pulled back and she gave me a tight smile.

"You first," I insisted.

"I am not in much pain anymore but … I feel different."

I swallowed. "Is that good or bad? I am afraid that you will regret this decision. What if … when I leave the soldiers one day you feel like you have made a mistake? What if you blame me for making you feel like you had to change yourself because you weren't seen as a 'strong enough man' to stand alongside me?" My fears poured out before she could answer my first question.

"Ava," Demi murmured, taking my hands in hers. "I promise that will never happen."

"But h–" She pulled me close, silencing me with a finger to my lips.

"I will never regret this. I feel more like myself than I ever have. I know now that this is who I am. Perhaps if Phaeops was alive I'd even thank him for what he did, for giving me the chance to become who I wanted. I thank *you* for still wanting me."

"It is not the way I wanted it to happen but, somehow, I know that I would never have stopped you doing it. I know why I love you and it is not for how you look on the outside," I told her, reaching up slowly to rest my hand on her chest – a chest that was no longer flat but softly swollen above her heart.

"And I am more thankful for that than you can ever know."

"Will you … show me … share with me who you are now?" I asked, suddenly shy.

Demi took a deep breath before nodding and closing the door to the room we would now share in the palace – the room my mothers had occupied when we all lived here.

I sat on the bed as Demi made her way back to stand in front of me, her fingers shaking slightly as she removed the fibula from her chiton, letting it fall to her waist just as she had at Mount Smolikos when she revealed what had happened to her in Larissa and what her body looked like because of it.

Her chest was no longer scarred. There was no sign of the trauma that had once lain there. Her right nipple was no longer missing, now positioned at the end of a rounded breast. The left side was shaped in a similar fashion, the middle of both curving together to form a valley between in perfect harmony.

Demi removed the belt at her waist and let the chiton fall all the way to the ground. My eyes followed its path over her stomach and down to where there was no longer a hanging appendage between her thighs. Dark hair hid what had replaced it but I did not linger for too long, my eyes instead travelling back up to meet Demi's.

She watched me, fear written across her face. I stood, eyes locked with hers as I asked, "May I touch you?" Demi only nodded in reply, her eyes closing. I drew my fingers across her chest. Her breasts were warm, soft, perfect. I trailed my fingers across her skin, letting both of us get used to the sensation, my palm sliding across the hardened nipple as I cupped her breast.

I circled Demi, my fingers following to the scars that remained on her back. "You did not want these removed too?" I asked, pressing my lips to the ones at her shoulder blade.

Demi shook her head. "No, they are part of who I am, a reminder of what I had to endure to become truly myself."

I only nodded in reply, not that she saw the gesture. I slid both my hands across the raised sections of her back before taking them lower over her bottom. Her breath caught as I moved them around to her hips and I paused, fingertips drawing small circles where they lay.

When she blew out the breath she held, I continued slowly to the front of her thighs, drawing closer to her new area but in no hurry – waiting for the cues from Demi to tell me when I should stop and when I could carry on with my exploration.

I kissed her shoulder again, tucking my front into her back as best I could with our children between us, my arms encircling her protectively as I journeyed. I could feel her heart thudding and my own matched it.

"I love you," I told her. "I have loved you for who you are on the inside, not the outside since we met." I kissed her neck. "Your body never defined if I found you attractive or not."

I slid my fingers to the apex of her thighs but went no further. "I will love you as you are, in this form, for *you*, from now until our days together are done." Without breaking contact of my fingers at her thigh, I returned to stand in front of her. She opened her eyes.

"Demi, you are beautiful and I love you," I smiled.

"Thank you," she whispered, a single tear sliding down her cheek. I swept it aside with my thumb, keeping one hand on her cheek as the fingers of my other ran through the short hairs at the base of her stomach and lower, exploring this new part of her, of us.

My female lover. My lover. My love. The mother of my children. My life.

5

7 winters later
Deep within the earth, 481BC

"Ares?" a voice cut through the darkness.

The god of war stood, wrapping his fingers around the cold, steel bars that had held him for so long.

"I am here," he replied, his voice cracking from disuse.

He watched the light bounce up and down the walls as his lover searched the tunnels. He ran a hand through his dark hair – he knew there would not be a strand out of place (just one advantage of being immortal) – but even so he wanted to look his best when she saw him. He adjusted the red, sleeveless leather vest so it exposed the hairs of his chest and inched his dark pants lower to hang across his hips in the suggestive way that had always pleased her.

Finally Aphrodite turned the corner and his breath was taken away, as it always had been, by her beauty. He put his hand up to shield his eyes from the bright light she held, but not before he noted the way her golden hair trailed over her shoulders to nestle between her ample breasts.

Aphrodite dimmed the glowing ball of flames she had conjured, allowing it to hang in the air as she rushed to the cage, her hands gripping his tightly.

"My darling, finally I have found you," she whispered.

Her breasts, barely concealed in her fitted chiton, rose and fell with each deep breath, her eyes taking in every inch of his body, as his did hers.

"I never doubted you would," Ares replied. "But I have done everything I could think of; I cannot be released from this cage."

Aphrodite smiled and held up a metallic object. "You can if you possess this."

"And just *how* did you come to be in possession of such an item?"

"Hephaestus and I may no longer be married, but when he partakes of Dionysius' sweet wine he is easily led on many a subject."

"When did you learn it was he who kept me imprisoned?"

"After the tale of what happened at Olympos was finally told, I was certain it was Hephaestus who kept us apart, and I made plans to free you."

"How long have I been here?"

"Too long," she replied, inserting the key into the large lock.

She smiled again at the satisfying 'click', the door of the cage swinging open with a metallic screech. Ares burst forth, taking Aphrodite in his arms, his lips finding hers and possessing them with a fierceness and passion he had only dreamt of since being held captive.

Aphrodite returned his affections just as ardently and they soon lay on the hard ground, clothes discarded, their love and devotion to one another reaffirmed. After a time, Ares pushed himself to his feet and gathered his clothing.

"I searched for you every day. I spoke to Hades, I spoke to the other gods loyal to you, I even searched for your Keres, but I could find no sign of you ... or them."

"The Keres?" Ares asked.

"Yes. I went north to the island of Aretias where you told me they lived, and to Lake Stymphalos, but they were not there. It does not appear anyone has been in either location for many winters; the lake oddly devoid of mortals or creatures."

Ares paused. He had not felt his winged chargers since the fight at Olympos. Not since Ava, with the aid of his own brother, had sent him to the cage Aphrodite had just freed him from. He had spent candlemarks pondering the knowledge, but convinced himself it was only because he was so far beneath the earth that their connection did not reach him. Now he was not so certain.

"I must go," Ares said, pulling his leather pants on.

"Where?" Aphrodite asked. "Do you not wish to enjoy one another some more?"

"There shall be time for more when I return."

"Zeus is not going to allow you back to Olympos, or me if he finds out I freed you."

"I shall go to Olympos when I am ready, but no one can know I have returned yet. Go back to Hephaestus' cage and lock it up. Take the key and ensure you put it back where you found it. My brother has not visited me for some time but if he realizes the key is gone, he may do so. I do not want him to learn I have gone."

"And where shall you go?"

"I cannot feel my Keres and I do not know where to search for them. I must find the Valkyrie, hopefully they can provide the answers I seek. When I am ready I shall send for you, in the meantime, stay at Hades' palace in the Underworld. You shall be safe there."

"Hades' palace? Bu–"

He pulled her to her feet. "Please, Aphrodite. If Zeus finds out I escaped from Hephaestus' cage, he shall look for you to draw me out. He must not find you."

Aphrodite hesitated before nodding. "I do not relish the thought of spending time in such a place, but I shall do so, for you."

"Thank you. Soon we shall call the thrones of Zeus and Hera in Olympos our own. We shall rule all other gods and put to death those who do not claim loyalty to us."

"You have spoken of such acts before, but it only saw you confined to a cage," Aphrodite grumbled.

"Do not doubt me, my love. I shall no longer rely on mortals to bring about my father's defeat. I shall find another way," he insisted, pulling her close once again. "Soon we shall have all that I promised."

"I hope so," Aphrodite murmured. "But you cannot allow your mother to know you are free either. You may have once been her favored son, but when she learnt of your intention to unseat her as well as Zeus, she vowed revenge on you."

"That is to be expected. Do not fear, I shall deal with her in time too."

Aphrodite pressed her naked body the length of his, his skin tightening at her touch as she ran her fingers through the hair on his chest. "You have been away for so long. I have found myself unsatisfied in many ways. I have taken no other to my bed, though scores wished it to be so. Is it not in your power to rectify such an oversight before you leave me again?" She slid her fingers from his chest to his stomach, but did not stop there, dragging them lower to squeeze him through his pants.

His breath quickened and he closed his eyes. He knew he could not resist what she was offering, he never had. From the earliest beginnings of their relationship, she had been undeniable, and even had he wished it, he could not have done anything but partake of the pleasures of her body. It mattered not when Zeus gifted her to Hephaestus, her heart had always belonged to Ares, and his to her. The celebration of Aphrodite and Hephaestus' union was barely complete before Ares was in their bed, taking and giving pleasure to the goddess he loved.

After so long alone in the dark, he could think of nothing more satisfying than finding himself wrapped in Aphrodite's embrace, skin against skin, his body inside hers as they moved as one. His hands found the softness of her back and he gripped her tightly, his body straining to be released from its confines. There would be time to find the Keres … later, when he had sated his lover. Perhaps he would be able to feel them again once he was above ground.

"Not here, my love," he whispered, his lips trailing down her neck and collarbone. "You deserve a soft, comfortable bed for what I have in mind."

"Do not take me to Olympos," Aphrodite whispered.

"Then where?" he asked, caressing the breasts before him.

Aphrodite moaned, pressing into his hands as she slipped her own into his pants. Ares gathered the soft mound between his lips and sucked gently. "Take me somewhere we shall not be discovered, somewhere we can spend candlemarks or moons in each other's arms."

"As you wish," Ares murmured. He kissed her again and they disappeared from the dark depths of the earth and the cage crafted so carefully by Hephaestus.

6
Valhalla, Asgard, North lands

"I want to speak with the Valkyrie," Ares announced.

The great hall of Valhalla was sparsely populated, the few warriors who found themselves in the home of their gods largely ignoring the man who spoke when they realized he was not familiar. They returned to their drink, their feast or their women with no further thought for him or his request.

Ares knew from the Valkyrie that the Norse gods brought their best warriors to Valhalla once they had died. They believed the men would help them change the outcome of the Ragnarök – a battle fated to see the end of the Norse gods.

A large, bearded man finally pushed himself from his throne at one end of the room and approached. "And what is your business with them?" he asked.

"I seek their counsel on matters from long ago," Ares replied, inclining his head as he realized that the speaker was Odin, ruler of the Norse gods.

Odin acknowledged him with his own sharp nod. "If the Valkyrie agree to speak with you, then I shall allow it, but do not keep them from their duty."

"Our conversation needs only to be brief," Ares replied.

Odin nodded again and returned to his throne, his wife asking a question Ares could not hear when her husband sat down beside her.

"We shall speak with you," came a voice.

Ares turned, finding himself face to face with a light-haired beauty he recognized. She wore the golden chest plate, which accentuated her high, full breasts, and appeared as though it had never seen battle. Her wheat-colored hair lay long over her shoulders and trailed her back, parting where brilliant, white wings extended from her shoulder blades.

"Eir," Ares nodded.

She led him into a second, smaller room where eight other women, all dressed in the same golden chest pieces and with the same golden hair, sat at a table. Eir indicated an empty chair.

"Why do you seek us after all this time, Ares?" the woman to his right asked as he took the offered seat.

"I seek information on my Keres. I cannot feel them as I once could. I want to know where to find them."

"The Keres are no longer," another of the women replied.

"You failed in your protection of them. You allowed their line to die out, and with it, their power has been lost," yet another said.

"What?" Ares asked.

"You have failed, God of War. We were led to believe you were undefeatable," Eir replied. "By providing you with a powerful gift, the Keres told us you would bring about a great new beginning in your realm. But it appears we were misled."

"You were given a powerful object and yet you were not able to bring about its full power. You could not make mere mortals do what you desired, what you needed them to."

"You allowed a mortal to better you, to separate the pieces of the amulet and reconnect them so she could use the power against you. You are pathetic. You are weak."

The women spoke quickly, their words overlapping one other, but Ares missed none of them and anger beat in his belly.

"You cannot speak to me in such a manner, I am..."

"You may be the *Greek* god of war, but you have no power over us north folk," Eir reminded him.

"We shall see about that."

The Valkyrie had no time to react as Ares rounded the table, slicing their throats. One by one they slumped against the table, dead. Their blood slid down the wooden legs and pooled on the marble floor by their feet. He paused in front of the last – Eir – his hand darting out to grip her by the throat, raising her from her chair until they stood eye to eye.

"I shall not allow you to call me weak. The mortal you speak of did not work alone, she had help from my brother, but I have no use for her any longer. All I require is the Keres and the pieces of that amulet and the future I seek shall be mine."

"What my sisters said about the Keres and the power of the amulet is true," Eir choked. "The Keres are dead, they cannot return. Their existence was linked to the amulet and when it worked against you, it also worked against them." Ares dropped Eir to her feet and she put a hand to her neck.

"But if the parts of the amulet were put back together, as they were before, could the power be restored?" he asked, pacing.

"Perhaps, but I cannot be certain. The mortal who betrayed you not only altered the amulet, but the power of the line."

"How is that possible?"

"She has borne two sons, mortal, healthy and unmarked. They have no power and as you know, bearing sons has never occurred in your chosen line. Other Ker were chosen to bear sons to father daughters with your line. But it is proof that the line does not continue. If you reconnect the pieces of the amulet as you wish, there is no way to tell if the power shall return in the manner you desire.

"When the amulet was made, it was very specific, it was made with your blood and that of the Keres. Its intent was to bring about the glorious victory the Keres had in mind for *you*. With the changes it has undergone, it is not possible to know what shall happen to you or for you if they are reconnected."

"So you are advising me to forget the amulet? Is there another way to obtain what I seek?"

"No, I cannot assist you in what you … seek." Eir's eyes suddenly rolled back into her head and she stood as still as the marble beneath her feet. Barely a moment later she blinked, shaking her head as if to clear it.

"What is it?" Ares asked with a frown.

"It may indeed be possible for you to harness the power of the amulet," she replied.

"Tell me," Ares demanded.

"You say you have no interest in the mortal who altered it, but she still has what you desire."

"Tell me," Ares repeated.

"They reside where they have since she defeated you – in her sword. You shall find the jet in the pommel at the end, hidden beneath a layer of silver. The hematite holds the guard to the tang of the blade. You must separate them from the rest of the sword, for it is protected by the blood of another."

"Hephaestus," Ares muttered.

"Yes. You must separate them and you must kill the mortal. Only then, after she has passed into your Underworld and the jet and hematite have been apart for a moon, shall the pieces obey your will once again."

"So we are to meet again after all, Ava," Ares mused.

"It is not only the sword that is protected by the other god. Your mortal is also still protected by him, you shall have to draw her out into a more …

intimate battle between the two of you if you want the sword," Eir warned.

Ares smiled. "Do not fear; I have a plan, one that I promised her would come a long time ago."

In an instant, Ares was at the Valkyrie's side, driving his knife deep into her neck. "It appears it is time I revisited the Persians," he murmured, pulling his knife out and wiping it against his pants.

Ares released Eir and she dropped to the floor in a pool of her own blood. He smiled before disappearing from the north lands of Asgard and the Norse gods who called it home.

PART II

Before

1

Anthela, Thermopylae, Greece
Moon of Hekatombaion, 480BC

The temple was hot and crowded with soldiers and delegates from many of the allied city-states of Sparta and Athens. Voices bounced off the marble walls as men shouted, trying to make themselves heard above each another.

In preparation for the Persians' latest invasion, ten thousand hoplites, including Papou and I, had marched to the Vale of Tempe a moon ago to set up a defense in the area. Almost the entire number joined us now at Anthela. Many stood inside the temple itself, the rest outside on the ground or on the seats where the council members gathered each spring to discuss their business.

Themistocles, an Athenian politician and general, held his hands up, shouting as loudly as he could until finally the voices around us quieted. "The Thessalians suggested the Vale of Tempe, tell me why you believe it is not suitable to stop the advance of the Persians," he said. A cacophony of voices erupted and he shook his head, yelling again for quiet.

"If I may," I said, stepping out of position near the front and addressing him, my head slightly bowed. The general nodded and waved me forward. "Aside from the fact that many regions of Thessaly are still considering submission to Persia ..." I started, quickly drowned out by protests from the Thessalian delegates.

"Quiet!" Themistocles bellowed over the din. "Ava shall be permitted to speak."

"There are too many paths south from the area," I continued. "We *could* position ourselves at the Vale, but there is no guarantee Xerxes and his men would take that road. If they chose to, they could take the Sarantaporo Pass instead."

"Then we shall position men there also," Themistocles frowned.

"No, we need all our men together. By all accounts, the Persian army far outnumbers ours and we need to provide a united front if we are to hold them back," I replied.

"You are certain of this?"

I nodded. "Yes. Not only did we see the various paths for ourselves, but it was confirmed by Alexander of Macedonia, who met us when we arrived."

"A Macedonian? Is this man to be trusted? Did Macedonia not submit to Xerxes' demands for earth and water when his ambassadors came last winter?"

"They did, but Alexander can be trusted. He does not want to be under Persian rule. He wishes for our success and provided the information willingly to us."

"He is also our late king's nephew," Papou added, stepping to my side.

Themistocles looked with interest between the two of us.

"He is right," I confirmed with a nod. "My grandfather, Agrias, former king of Trachis, was of the royal Macedonian Argead line, brother to Amyntas, Alexander's father. Until Agrias passed five winters ago, he and Alexander still spoke often and were united in their hatred of the Persians." Themistocles considered my words as I continued. "The Persian army has already crossed the Hellespont and, even though the Delphic Oracle predicted the storm that destroyed half their fleet, their cavalry and soldiers make their way through Thrace and will soon reach Macedonia. The remainder of their ships have been seen in the Malian Gulf approaching our shores. We do not have time for lengthy discussions; we need to mobilize our army as soon as possible if we are to have any chance of victory."

"Perhaps we should withdraw to the Isthmus of Corinth and block the path to the Peloponnese," Themistocles suggested.

"Why the Isthmus?" a man whose name I didn't know, but recognized as an Athenian, shouted. "Why not stop them before they reach Attica so they are not able to take Athens?"

"I agree, what do you believe would happen if Athens fell?" another of the Athenian soldiers asked.

"*We* would become the most powerful force in Greece, although it is a title we already claim," a Spartan warrior yelled. "Our boys are taught to be soldiers from their seventh winter, while you Athenians sit around, talking and pondering, only supplying armor to those rich enough to afford to be trained for battle. You are soft and it would not surprise me if Athens fell, but we shall not allow the Persians to rule the mighty Spartans, we shall drive them back across the waters where they shall perish beneath our sandals!"

His speech was met with more arguing and shouting until Themistocles took control once more. "Do you have another suggestion?" he asked me.

"Yes," I replied, holding up a map and unrolling it as I approached the altar in front of Themistocles. I spread it out and joined him behind the marble as the men crowded closer to see what I had in mind. "We won't let the Persians reach southern Greece at all, not Boeotia, not Attica and not the Peloponnese. The Pass of Thermopylae ... here," I said, pointing it out on the map, "is very narrow. When the Persians reach Thessaly they will have to take the road that leads through the Pass of Thermopylae between the mountains and the sea to continue south to Athens."

Themistocles studied the map. "How can you be certain of that?"

"Their horses would not be able to traverse the mountains to the west. They will come through the Thessalian Plain, and take this east path around the mountains, which puts them exactly where we want them. The wall once built by the Phocians, and recently rebuilt by my own soldiers, stands at twelve feet high and can provide us with protection as it runs parallel with the path. At one end of the wall is a very narrow section, or gate, where the wall meets the cliffs at the sea. The west gate is only as wide as one cart and it is *here* I believe we should mount our defense."

"It is a good plan," Themistocles conceded. "Even if they outnumber us, we would have the advantage of knowing the terrain of the area."

"Exactly," I replied. "We'll need more soldiers, but the ones we have here already can go to the wall and set up in the Pass. I believe you have command of the Athenian triremes also?" Themistocles nodded. "Good, they'll be just as important in the battle."

"How so?" he asked.

"As we've already seen, the Persian cavalry and soldiers march through lands they already rule. It's so their numbers aren't depleted by unnecessary fighting before they reach what they believe to be their final destination – Athens. But their ships follow them closely and that is of concern."

"In what way?"

"The middle gate at Thermopylae is accessible by sea, so we need to have two strategies in place, one for sea and one for land. We must make sure that their ships don't bypass Thermopylae and go directly south, which is why I suggest we engage them ..."

"In the Straits of Artemisium," Themistocles finished, his finger pointing to the Strait I had intended to mention.

"Yes. If we can repel them at both points then Athens and Sparta remain in Greece's hands and we have the opportunity to take back Thrace and Macedonia."

I watched as Themistocles studied the map again, weighing up everything I had suggested against what he knew already of the allied forces he was fortunate enough to have command of. Finally he gave a nod, addressing the men in the Temple.

"The majority of our soldiers shall defend our lands at the Pass of Thermopylae and at sea in the Straits of Artemisium, but we shall also have a smaller contingent waiting to defend the Isthmus at Corinth, should they be required. Athenian women and children are to be evacuated to Troezen, as are those from the region of Thermopylae, and they must remain there until we are victorious against the Persians." Themistocles turned and spoke to me personally. "Get the soldiers settled into position here. I shall send word to Athens and Sparta, mobilize the Athenian fleet and request more men to join you as soon as possible. It should not take more than a week or two for them to arrive."

"Thank you. Have no fear, Greece will be victorious at Thermopylae and your name praised for your defensive strategies," I told him.

Themistocles took my arm and we shook. "And yours as well Ava, Queen of Thermopylae."

The soldiers and delegates started to file out of the temple as I rolled the map back up and found Papou in the crowd. He shuffled towards me, his body far slower these days than his mind, much to his disgust. He was nearing his seventy-third winter and his time fighting as a soldier and travelling over the hills and mountains of Greece had started to wear on his body. He was stubborn though and refused to acknowledge that he needed to rest more often than he did, continuing to join the soldiers at training most mornings.

When I had found him in Konitsa nine winters ago, his grey hair and beard had been long and shaggy, reaching his shoulders in a tangled mess. Now though, he had only a smattering of grey wisps atop his head and above his ears that floated skyward when a particularly gusty breeze blew. His forearms and shoulders had lost much of their thickness and strength and his chest faced the ground more than the sky. Only his bright blue eyes were still clear and strong and they captured my own green ones as we met in the middle of the temple.

"I told you to sit during the meeting, Papou."

"I am not Damon or some hound you need to command. I am more than capable of standing upright for a candlemark or two."

"You are not as well behaved as Damon," I muttered.

"I have not lost my hearing yet, my darling," he replied. I shook my head and smiled discreetly but said no more, leading him to the doorway of the Temple without offering assistance; he would only be offended if I did. "You intend to stay and fight?" he asked.

"Of course."

"Demi shall not be pleased."

"No," I agreed.

"Perhaps she is right to want you at home."

"You cannot ask it of me, Papou. I would think *you* of all people would understand."

"I do my darling, but she and I spoke about a great many things while you were away. She adores you as much as she ever did and does not want to lose you."

"I do not want to lose her either but I cannot let the Persians take my home, my people. Not again. I won't leave Trachis and go to Troezen. Not when I can do something about it."

"You know it was not Persians who took your mothers. You know it was Ares."

"I do, but I am not foolish enough to believe that Hephaestus' cage will hold the god of war forever. The more time that passes, the more convinced I am that we're going to meet again soon. And with this latest advance by Xerxes and the Persian army I feel that *somehow* Ares drives it. Why else would they return after so many winters?"

"Hephaestus would have let us know if Ares had escaped."

"Maybe, but this is my home Papou. Our home; yours, Melina's, Demi's, Kadmus and Zenon's. I have to stay and fight."

"It is a home that you once abandoned because of the memories it held."

"So did you. But that was winters ago. I was merely a child and there was a lot I had to learn, to experience. People I had to find to finally know my place in this world. You most especially."

"I know, and of course I understand your wish to stay and fight for what you have here, but I gave Demi my word I would attempt to convince you otherwise."

"Male soldiers do not face this issue. No one asks them to lay down their swords and their shields and stay home with their families," I said, my voice rising.

Papou gripped my arm, stopping me. "Other soldiers are not my kin. I may not have many winters left in this world but I would rather spend it with you and my great-grandsons somewhere far from here. I do not wish to watch those boys lose their mother – to have to grow without you as *you* had to live without your mothers from almost the same age."

"You will probably outlive us all," I muttered, unwilling to acknowledge the rest of his words. "I won't change my mind. I won't let other soldiers fight without me in a place that is mine to protect. Not this time."

"The blame for what happened to Lysistratos does not lie with you. He died a hero, defending his homeland and his future queen from enemies; it is what he would have wanted."

I ripped my arm from Papou's grip, pain and guilt robbing me of my breath momentarily as my mind brought up Lysistratos' face the last time I had seen him. I swallowed loudly.

"What he *wanted* was to see his son grow up. He couldn't wait till his thirtieth winter when he could go and live with his wife and child. You did not know him like I did."

"And do you not wish for the same?"

"I already live with my family. I am queen, Demi is queen and I live in a palace and have slaves to run my errands or wash my hair. For the longest time this was not the life I imagined for myself. I did not want it to be."

"But it is now. When you returned you sought at least some of it. Why can that not be enough for you?"

"Because I am a soldier, Papou. After my mothers were taken from me, it was the soldiers who cared for me, who taught me and raised me to be who I am. I would not have survived without them. I will always be a soldier in my heart, just like you are," I replied, turning on my heel. I passed through the doorway of the Temple, stamping my way across to a large group of trees where the soldiers that I was to take to the Pass of Thermopylae waited.

2

West Gate, Pass of Thermopylae

Standing before the men shouting encouragements and commands felt good. It had been five winters since I'd been given charge of organizing the soldiers for battle – outside of training at the barracks at least. I used to revel in the faith Moeris put in me to lead our army, and it happened often back before I met Demi. Back before I knew who I truly was – Ares' Chosen One, descended from the line of the Keres. Before I lost Lysistratos, when life was simple – train, protect, win.

So much had changed, yet much remained the same. I trained with our soldiers as often as I could and I had not forgotten how to sharpen my weapons, how to wear my armor or how to set the men for phalanx formation. But I had not joined them in proper battle when our army was requested by Athens or its allies – my place now in Trachis as her Queen. A leader from the throne in the palace rather than from the barracks.

As I had told Themistocles, the Pass of Thermopylae was perfect for our set up; the wagon track through the west gate narrow enough for only one cart to roll through at a time, the east gate a little wider, with both having a sheer drop of cliff face down into the rocks and water of the Malian Gulf below. Between the two entrances sat a dusty plain and sandy beach known as the middle gate which stretched almost twenty itinerary along the edge of the Malian Gulf. Not only was it long enough for our phalanx to stand shoulder to shoulder in a large number, but it was about sixty-five feet wide from the water's edge to Mount Kallidromon. It was there the men now trained. The soldiers came from different tribes, but they all knew of the phalanx and what was expected of them. We were confident we could defeat the Persians there.

"Apologies for my late arrival, Queen Ava, but may I have a moment of your time?"

"Again! Keep the sides tight. I do not want to see sun between your shield and the man whose chest you're protecting," I called to the men before turning to the man who had spoken. "You may, and you are ..." I trailed off, taking in once-familiar features set inside the body of a fully grown man.

"Nikomachos," he nodded, though I didn't need him to say the words aloud to know it for myself.

He carried an aspis and sword, a spear tied to his chest in much the same way I had once worn mine. He seemed comfortable in his armor; the weight of his shield no bother to him. He was handsome, his face and arms tanned, cheekbones and chin strong. His hair was still dark and curled, his eyes a warm brown. He had always been tall for his age, but his thickly muscled arms and solid legs now created an imposing figure.

I smiled at my half-brother and took the outstretched arm he offered me. "You have grown since I last saw you," I told him.

"As have you, though I am not surprised to find you here in the role of Queen, or commanding an army. You rule them as Skylar once did."

I acknowledged the comment with a slight nod. "I didn't know if I would ever see you again but I have wished for it these past winters. We have a lot to discuss." I released Nikomachos and signaled to a soldier at the front of the phalanx. He trotted over obediently. "Continue to lead the men, I will be back soon," I instructed.

"Of course, my queen," the young man nodded. He returned to the men, another hoplite taking his place at the front of the formation as they ran through the drill again.

"Come," I said to Nikomachos.

We walked toward the sand, Nikomachos setting his aspis on the ground. "I have missed this place," he mused, looking out across the blue and green of the ocean. "Leaving Trachis after Father and Mother died felt right. Pamphilos was not so eager, but with Eumelia cared for in Lysistratos' home, it was easy to convince him to join me. To convince him that a life away from Trachis was best for us."

"I believed the same, though I did it through the soldiers," I replied. "Where did you and Pamphilos go? The day Lysistratos and I started with the other ephebes you were supposed to join us. Lysistratos searched but couldn't find you."

"No. I saw him in the agora early that morning when I was collecting food for our journey but I ensured he did not see me. I could not remain here any longer. I wanted to fight and kill, but I did not want the memories of the place. Pamphilos and I travelled to many towns, finally settling in Athens almost twelve winters ago," he replied, turning to face me.

"You fought for Athens at Marathon?"

"I did. I would deny the Persians their victory at any port or plain. That is why I have come here to Thermopylae," he nodded.

"As would I," I agreed.

"I joined the Athenian army as soon as we arrived in Athens, but Pamphilos hated the fighting. Still does. I have not actually seen him for two or three winters, he is a farmer and has a wife and two children – a boy and a girl. He would not come with me when I sent a messenger to ask him."

"Do you have a wife?" I asked.

"No. After … after what Mother did when Father died I have never wished for anyone to call me husband." He shook his head, as if to clear the old memories from it. "Tell me of Eumelia. Is she well?"

"I believe so but I haven't seen her for over eight winters myself. She and Lysistratos were betrothed when she reached her thirteenth winter, as had been arranged. They were very happy and she bore a son named Phaidros. Unfortunately when our soldiers fought against the Dolopes, Lysistratos was killed. Eumelia took Phaidros to live in Iolkos after that, and even though she has never known, I made sure they had a place of their own to call home as well as food on their table and enough work for Eumelia to keep those needs met while she brought up their son."

"You are a good friend, I am glad she had you. Do you hear from her often? Do you believe Phaidros shall take up sword and spear or is he peaceable as Pamphilos is?"

"I don't know. After she moved away, Eumelia cut off all communication with me. She blamed me for Lysistratos' death."

"If Lysistratos died fighting, then how are you to blame? As soldiers we understand that death can find us at any moment, and we accept that. Even the greatest of men must meet Hades when his time arrives."

"Agreed, but I could not fight alongside him as I had promised I always would," I replied. "I was due to birth my sons and could not raise weapons, even if my grandparents and wife had allowed me to."

"Wife?" Nikomachos asked, eyebrows raised. "You are more similar to Skylar than I imagined."

"It is a little more complicated than that but that is a discussion for when there is more time."

Nikomachos held my gaze for a long moment but eventually nodded. "Remaining to see your children grow should be a far greater promise to keep than standing beside men in battle."

"You sound like Papou Leandros," I smiled.

"He is still alive?" I nodded. "That is happy news at least. And you said you had sons?"

"I do. Two. Zenon and Kadmus – they're twins."

"Congratulations. Having siblings is, for the most part, a joy and when we were growing up I always thought of you as a sister, just as Eumelia was. I was almost seven winters old when the two of you were born and by the time you reached five *you* in particular trailed me everywhere, wanting to do as I did. I often complained about having to look after you when what I really wanted to do was watch the soldiers train or go to the hot springs with Lysistratos."

"I remember and we certainly all fought like siblings didn't we?" I grinned.

"We did, but when the time came and Eumelia needed me most, I could not be her big brother, nor yours. I could not be the one to look after her as I had before, that responsibility became yours ... and I am sorry for that."

"We can't change what happened back then, how we dealt with the losses we suffered or our own pain, but I have learnt many things since I last saw you."

"Oh?" he asked, eyebrows raised beneath his curled hair once more.

"Well just as you always treated me as your kin when we were younger, I looked up to you and Pamphilos as older brothers too, Tritonos as well when he was still alive and when I was nineteen winters old, I left the soldiers and journeyed to search for Papou. He told me a great many truths about my mothers and me, things I never knew. I learnt that you, me, Eumelia, Pamphilos and Tritonos were indeed family. Siblings. When I returned to Trachis and spoke with Eumelia about it, she was overjoyed and we became close again, until the Dolopes came."

"How is that possible?" Nikomachos asked with a frown, though he did not appear upset by the news, just confused. "My mother did not carry you; that was Alexis as I recall."

"That's right but Thaddeus was my father as well. He helped Mumma and Mother create me inside Alexis."

"Indeed?" he nodded. "When I grew and learnt of children and women, I did wonder at your creation. I suppose it makes sense; Father and Mother were always close with Skylar and Alexis."

"They were but it was Thaddeus' loyalty to them that saw him killed that night."

"He would not have wanted it to be any other way."

"No, but it was not fair on your mother, to lose him that way."

"For a long time I was angry with her. Angry at her cowardice. She lost her husband and her two best friends, but she still had the three of us. Eumelia was just a child, not yet ten winters. Pamphilos was fourteen and of a gentle nature, he needed her. I was sixteen and did not necessarily need her guidance, but still, she should have placed her pain aside and been there for us."

"Maybe sometimes losing the one you love is just too hard, no matter who is left behind."

"Perhaps," Nikomachos shrugged, though he did not appear convinced.

"After Eumelia left I wanted to find you and Pamphilos, to tell you of our connection. I didn't know if Eumelia would, as I didn't think she ever knew where you were either. But raising my boys and ruling Trachis have kept me busy and I was not sure where to start searching for you."

"But we are together again now."

"Yes. I'm only sorry we can't spend the time getting to know each other again properly until after we've faced the Persians."

"Perhaps when we have dispatched them, I can meet your wife and your children, we can invite Pamphilos and his family to join us and perhaps Eumelia would come too."

"I would like that," I replied.

Nikomachos reached out his arm to me again and I took it, surprised when he pulled me into a rough hug. He clapped me twice on the back and released me again quickly, a light blush creeping up his neck when he cleared his throat. "I shall join the other soldiers … sister," he mumbled, picking up his shield and shaking the sand from it.

"I will be there in a moment," I replied, a smile turning up the corner of my lips.

3
Thermopylae

Steam rose from the warm, clear water of the hot spring, the slow-moving mist hiding and revealing in turn my sons as they laughed and splashed one another. One fair-haired, the other dark, their natures were as different as the color of their hair.

I had returned from settling the soldiers at the west gate and in the Pass half a candlemark ago, making my way directly to the springs. I knew Melina and my sons would be there, despite the heat of the day, for none of them could resist the warm waters of the springs and the waterfall above.

Damon stood on the bank, barking and pacing, desperate to enter the water, but afraid of its heat when he dipped his paw in. Even after nine winters in Trachis, he hadn't got used to the temperature of the hot springs, preferring the cooler water of the sea or the Asopos or Melas rivers to swim in, but he always accompanied my boys and waited impatiently for them to finish.

Melina stood waist-deep in the water, shading her eyes from the early morning sun as she watched her great-grandsons. She held their sandals in one hand and had two thick cloths slung around her neck to dry the boys off when they had finished. The relationship between my grandmother and I had been repaired somewhat since my return, but she was far closer to my sons than she and I would ever be and I still preferred to call her Melina, rather than Yiayia. Had she still been queen, I probably would have referred to her as such, but that title became mine when Agrias passed five winters

58

ago.

The title and position were not something I had wanted early on in my life, and when I returned to Trachis I still wasn't convinced the title and position should be mine. Demi certainly had never entertained thoughts of being a king or queen when she fled Larissa. Then again, she never expected to learn her father was Hephaestus, God of the Forge, either. If our paths had never crossed, neither of us would be in Thermopylae now, of that I was certain. But where, or how the world would be, was not something I cared to dwell on often.

A light breeze lifted my dark hair from my neck and cooled the sweat which had formed there. I was delaying seeing Demi because after a moon apart I didn't really want the Persians and their impending attack to be the first thing we talked about. But if the weather was favorable, and they continued to travel at a steady rate, it might only be a week until they arrived.

Papou's words at the Temple of Demeter haunted me, making me question my decision to stay; knowing I had to send my family away was not what I wanted but it was the only way to keep them safe. The depth of love I felt for my boys, and how quickly and so completely they had captured my heart even before they arrived, still surprised me.

As they'd grown inside me, the tiny flutters of their movements became noticeable; one most active during the dark of the night, the other the light of the day. I began to embrace my new role with eagerness, as well as apprehension, speaking soft words to them and reciting stories of gods and heroes, just as my mothers did when I was a child. Demi had still been Demetri in those days, and loved them beyond imagining, laying hands on my belly and caressing the soft skin whenever I was in reach.

Our sons had arrived – within a moment of each other – two weeks after Lysistratos' death and a week after Demi became 'her' in all sense of the word. Zenon was first, his head covered with strands of dark, damp hair and the green of his eyes mirroring mine. Kadmus followed with wisps of blonde curled at the base of his neck and over his ears to frame his perfect Demi-like face.

Mere days after I had birthed the boys, I realized the double three-sided shape on my ribs had begun to fade and now the mark was gone altogether. I was grateful; I no longer had the constant reminder of Ares and the plan he once held for me.

My sons were no longer babies, but growing into fine young men, seven and a half winters old and full of dreams and thoughts that were their own. Zenon may have had the same dark hair and green eyes as me, but he had Demi's nature, preferring for the most part quiet pursuits rather than swordplay or chasing his brother or friends around the grounds of the palace or through the agora. He would spend candlemarks in the stables sketching the soldier's horses or sitting with Demi at the Temple of Demeter in Anthela, capturing the color of the waves as they lapped at the sandy beach the temple overlooked.

Kadmus on the other hand was – as Hephaestus often told us – the very image of Demetri as a young child, regardless of the curls that framed his face where Demetri's had hung straight to his shoulders. Kadmus followed me when I went to the barracks to speak with the soldiers, or pestered me to take him to the council meetings when I attended them. I had no doubt that, had I allowed it, he would have followed me into battle or on scouting missions as well. He wielded a sword as well as any Spartan boy his age and yet he relished the lessons and poetry Papou taught him, such as was the custom in Athens.

We taught the boys the philosophies and ways of both the Athenians and the Spartans, just as I had been taught and Mumma Skylar before me. We were not as strict with Zenon and Kadmus as the Spartans were about their soldier training and they did not live at the barracks with the hoplites. When it became apparent that Zenon had other talents and interests, we nurtured them instead.

And then there was the immense love Demi and I still felt for one another after so many winters together. It had been strong when we defeated Ares at Olympos but it had grown and changed as we did, and now we were even closer.

"So, you have sons, Queen Ava of Thermopylae," Ares said, a statement, not a question. I jumped, not having felt his presence before he appeared like I had so many winters ago. The knowledge was a surprise but I did not have time to consider the reasons behind it as Kadmus looked up, catching sight of me.

"Mother!" he cried with joy.

I raised my hand in response, a smile lighting my face automatically as he and Zenon came splashing towards me. Melina turned, smiling, and I returned it with a nod realizing that, though they all saw *me*, they didn't see Ares at my side.

Kadmus reached me first, wrapping his arms around my waist and hugging me tightly. I bent down, kissing the top of his head as Zenon joined us and Damon came bounding over to rub his head against my leg.

"You boys have grown since I last saw you," I said, cupping Zenon's chin and running my fingers through Kadmus' curly hair.

"Moeris has taught us a lot as well. Will you have time to come and watch us practice our lessons today?" Kadmus asked.

"Later perhaps, first I need to find your mother," I replied. "Hello Melina."

Melina placed her hand on my arm and squeezed. "I thank the gods for your return," she smiled.

"As do I," I replied.

"Come boys, we must return to the palace, Moeris shall be waiting for you," she said, draping the cloths around each of the boys and handing them their sandals.

"Can we stay just a few more minutes?" Kadmus asked, just like he always did.

"No, go with Proyiayia, you don't want to be late," I replied. Kadmus sighed but nodded his assent. I ran my fingers through the curls atop his head again and kissed his forehead. "I'll find you when I'm finished and you can tell me everything I've missed. You can both help me apply beeswax to my armor." That got a smile from Kadmus and he threw his arms around me again. "Would you tell Demi I have returned and that I need to talk to her? I'm going to visit my parents before I return to the palace," I asked Melina as I hugged my boys to me.

"Of course," she replied.

"Thank you," I nodded. "I would like to see any new drawings you have," I added, taking Zenon's sandals from him and helping him push his foot into the right one.

"I have a great many I wish to share with you," he replied with a shy smile that was so reminiscent of Demi's that my heart leapt at the sight.

I straightened and planted another kiss on his head. "Good. I will see you in a few candlemarks."

Melina put her own sandals back on and herded the boys and Damon back towards Trachis and the palace.

4

"They appear strong and healthy," Ares said when Melinda and my sons were out of earshot.

"How long have you been free?" I asked stiffly, turning and making my way towards the cluster of trees where I had laid my mothers' ashes to rest winters before.

"Long enough to learn many things," he replied. "I see *you* have changed much in my absence; you did not feel me nearby until I showed myself."

"So it would seem." I was not surprised he had made the connection as quickly as I had.

"Do you not find that interesting?" he asked, a smile lighting his face.

"No. I find I am relieved," I replied, though that was not entirely true. "Why are you here, Ares?"

"You always get straight to the point. Skylar was just the same. But come now, shall we not share what has happened these past winters for the two of us? My tale shall of course be much shorter than yours. I am certain you remember running me through with your sword on Olympos after you promised me so much and then went back on your word ... I found myself in a dark, lonely cage with no one to speak to ... oh there was the occasional visit from my *caring* brother – Hephaestus – but I have not seen him for quite some time. Perhaps he has forgotten me after all these winters."

"You seem to have retained your quick wit," I murmured.

"It is part of my charm," he replied with a grin. "But tell me, how was your homecoming? Were Agrias and Melina overjoyed to see you return? How did they feel when they saw Leandros with you?"

"They welcomed both of us."

"Is that so? But there was such animosity the last time your grandparents were gathered together."

"That's behind us now," I told him.

In truth, our return had not been easy at all. Agrias and Papou had welcomed the reunion quickly but it had taken many moons for myself and the king and queen to feel comfortable in each other's company again, longer for Papou and Melina. It was really only when the news that I was with child was announced that the barriers between us lifted. By the time Demi and I married when our boys were a few winters old, things were a lot better.

"Well, I am pleased to hear of it," Ares said. "And my father, Zeus, how is he? I understand he assisted against your wife's rivals … your wife who as I recall wore the clothes of men when I last saw him."

"How do you know about what Zeus did?"

"I have had time to find out a lot," Ares shrugged. "I know Zeus was grateful for your aid in stopping me from taking his throne and that that is why he helped you. But tell me, if he knew about my plot to take his throne, why did he not simply take me down himself? Why allow me to remain alive instead of killing me?"

"You can thank Hephaestus for that – he convinced Zeus that it was more of a punishment for you to be alive, with no way of escape, knowing you had failed. How did you get out anyway?"

"I have friends," Ares shrugged. He started to pace, a grin lighting his lips. "The boys from Larissa and the Dolopes were not as fierce as the Persians, but you shall face the yellow caps again before long. I believe you have joined with Athens and Sparta in defending Greece against them?"

"I will always defend Greece from Persian forces."

"You do recall what I told you just before you sent me to the cage, do you not?"

I shall come with armies, with assassins. I shall bring the full force of the Persian army down onto your head; the brothers, the sons, the fathers of all those you murdered, I shall fill them with the desire to conquer every city between Trachis and Athens and I shall not stop until you are dead or at my side.

"I remember," I nodded. "You're behind this latest attack then?"

"Oh yes, and the Persians come with fire in their bellies and weapons at the ready."

"I knew one day it would be so," I murmured.

We arrived at the cluster of trees and I sent up a silent prayer to my mothers and father as I leant against the cool bark of the nearest laurel. Ares' return made it even clearer that Demi and the boys would have to leave Thermopylae; I would not let him to use them against me.

"Do you actually believe you can defeat the Persians when they arrive?" Ares asked conversationally. "They have cavalry, archers, armored soldiers and the royal guard – whom they call the Immortals – not to mention six hundred warships. Their numbers reach two hundred and fifty thousand men. You do not have nearly as many."

"We have enough," I lied.

If his numbers were accurate then our own were far from sufficient – we had two hundred triremes, each manned with one hundred and seventy citizen rowers plus thirty sailors and water soldiers. Our navy was lucky to equal forty thousand men. But we had our hoplites and horsemen as well and when the rest of the allied city-states' men arrived that would push our numbers to sixty thousand. It would have to be enough. Besides, we had the advantage; this was our land, our mountains, we had superior knowledge of it and we were experienced at fighting on it.

"You hope you do," Ares grinned. "You have made a number of preparations for their arrival, not least of which are the soldiers gathered together through your newly formed city-state alliance. Tell me, how many tribes join Athens and Sparta?"

"Twenty-nine."

"Impressive indeed," Ares acknowledged with a dip of his chin. "You rebuilt the wall at Thermopylae also."

"Yes. The Phocians were crucial to its development. I renamed it the Phocian wall in their honor."

I watched him from the corner of my eye, wondering what his intentions were and why, if he was responsible for the Persians coming to our shores, he didn't bring them directly to Trachis to destroy me for what I had done to him. I pushed off the tree trunk, heading back towards Trachis.

"You don't seem angry with me for putting you in the cage and denying you your victory over Zeus," I mused.

"Oh I was for a long time, believe me, but I have … forgiven you. I do not seek your aid in the same manner as before."

"Then why are you here?" I asked, certain he hadn't forgiven me so easily. "If it's merely to tell me that you're the one who sent the Persians, consider your message received."

He laughed. "Tell me; is your beloved grandfather – Leandros – still alive?"

"Why?"

"You mortals are very good at keeping secrets, but eventually they come to light."

"Don't speak in riddles," I frowned.

"Very well. There is more from the past you do not know of and I know

I only have to sit back and wait. We shall meet again and all that is between us shall end." His hand shot out and took my sword from my sheath. He held it up, his brow furrowing as he examined it. "You have a new sword. Where is the one you used to confine me beneath the earth?" I grabbed for it, but he put a hand up. "Stay," he commanded, my arms and legs instantly immoveable.

"I don't have it anymore," I replied, willing my limbs to obey.

"Why do I not believe you?" Ares asked, smiling as he spun my sword around his wrist and taking a step closer. "You know exactly where it is, and you shall tell me."

"I doubt it," I replied.

He circled me, placing a hand at my waist. "I do not," he whispered, sending a shiver down my spine. He held the sheath against my thigh and slid my sword back into place. When it was secure, he rested both hands on my hips. "You and I have unfinished business, and *this* time you shall not come between what I want and what I am going to get."

"You're wrong," I replied.

He laughed again and removed his hands from my body, returning to stand in front of me. "We shall see," he grinned.

He disappeared, my limbs moving with ease again when he did. I ran the entire way back to Trachis, steeling myself for the conversation I knew Demi and I must now have.

5

I closed the door to the Throne Room so Demi and I could continue our argument in private. For all the winters of my childhood there had never been a door on the room but after I returned I had insisted on one being put on. At first I refused to even enter the space, meeting Agrias or Melina in one of the banqueting halls or on the northern balcony if we had important matters to discuss; the constant reminder of what I had witnessed so many winters before came too easily to mind each time I passed by.

It was not until Agrias had passed on and it was expected that I would hold meetings there that I finally faced what I had not before, making myself think of the room as nothing more than another I must use as queen. Most of the time I was able to convince myself that's all it was.

"Demi, I *have* to stay and defend our home."

Her deep brown eyes captured mine, the flecks of yellow shining as they caught the light coming in from the high windows. "No, leave that to the soldiers. Your place is with Zenon and Kadmus and me, not to mention Leandros and Melina. We should all leave together, tonight."

"You think a queen should abandon her people? To just run away when enemies approach? I have the training, I can do this."

"Thankfully you don't train as often as you say you once did," she fired back, quickly adding, "you think it's alright for me to leave, so why not you too? We're both queens to the people of Trachis."

"You wouldn't even *be* a queen if it wasn't for me. You aren't a warrior –

you can't understand how I feel."

"I … you … That's not fair."

I blew out a long breath to calm the heat that raced through my blood. It was not the first time Demi and I had fought about our different upbringings and my want to remain a warrior.

"I know. I'm sorry. Look, you know I am a soldier first, Demi. You have always known that about me. It was one of the arguments you made about becoming a woman – so you didn't have fight, that that would be my job in our family. I was incapable of it once, but I can't, I won't …"

"I would've thought that being alive to see our sons grow would have mattered more to you," she countered. "But obviously I see, just as it always has, it comes back to Lysistratos."

"What are you talking about?"

"You blame me for his death – for the fact he never got to watch Phaidros grow up. If Phaeops and Eton hadn't joined with the Dolopes and marched on us then …"

"Like you blame me for what *you* lost that day?" I growled.

"It wasn't a loss, not in the end. It was a choice, a decision I was happy to make for me. For you. For us. But you …"

"I never blamed you for what happened to Lysistratos but I should have been there, you know *that's* how I've always felt."

"How could you? You were about to give birth to our sons."

This was getting us nowhere. I blew out another breath. "Look, what happened back then is irrelevant."

"Is it? You still have the necklace for Phaidros. You hold onto the hope that one day Eumelia will forgive you and you can give it to their boy. But what about *our* boys? They shouldn't have to live without their mother like you did. Do you care more for a city than you do for your own flesh and blood?"

"How can you even ask me that?"

"I never stopped you when you marched with the soldiers to the Vale of Tempe last mo–"

"We weren't marching to battle at the Vale, we were scouting, preparing, there was no chance we would engage any enemies. But you knew that already."

"And yet you want to stay when they come here."

"I want to defend our home from an enemy so you and the boys have somewhere to return to. Can't you see that?"

"Then you *are* choosing the city over your family."

"I guess I am. But I'm doing it for you. For Zenon and Kadmus. I don't want to see you enslaved to the Persians, or worse, killed by them."

"I don't think the Greeks can win this battle," Demi murmured, dropping her eyes from mine.

"Why not?" I frowned.

She raised her gaze again. "I've heard the soldiers talking about the Persian army, their numbers are so much greater than ours. I fear they'll overwhelm our soldiers with ease. I don't want to lose you."

"Nor I you," I said, stepping closer and combing my fingers through the dark, wiry hair above her ears. "But I'm asking you to leave while I remain here not only because of the Persians but because Ares is here."

"What? How? How do you know that?" Demi asked, alarmed.

"He visited me today when I was at the hot springs," I replied, my hand cupping her cheek. "I'm fine, don't worry," I added before she could ask. "But I can't risk you being here. If you are, then Ares could use you against me or you could be killed by the Persians and I don't want either. If I go with you, you're still in danger of being used by Ares. He's waiting for something."

"What? Does he still believe the power of the amulet runs through you? Does it run through the boys?"

"I don't think so. I couldn't feel him before he appeared to me and neither of the boys saw him. But he wants my sword and until I know why, I beg of you; take the boys and leave." Demi placed her hand atop mine on her cheek. "I don't ask this lightly of you Demi, you must know that. I don't want to be separated from you or our sons, but I cannot have harm come to you. Our boys need you."

"They need both their mothers," she corrected, her hands sliding to my hips and pulling me close as she kissed me fiercely.

Her mouth was warm and tears prickled behind my closed eyes at the feel of her here with me, safe. Her tongue teased along my bottom lip, making my blood turn to fire. I had sorely missed her. Us, and it seemed she had too. As much as I had wanted to be with the soldiers, there was a large part of me that had also wished I was back in Trachis with my wife, reveling in the depth of our love, without the impending threat of Persians and war to distract us.

She slid her hands to my thighs and up beneath my chiton, fingers teasing and caressing me as my breath shortened.

Our argument paled into insignificance as we lost ourselves to each other and a love that had once denied the god of war his desire for domination over gods and mortals, and borne two healthy, beautiful sons. I may not have been seeking a new friend, or anything more, all those winters ago, but he … she had found me. I could not be more grateful for it.

*

Demi and I clung together as we regained our breaths, our tableau broken when someone cleared their throat.

"Apologies for the interruption, Queen Ava," a deep voice said, his words echoing around the Throne Room.

I turned and found the door ajar, a Spartan warrior kneeling, head bent towards the floor, just inside.

Demi and I released each other and I addressed the stranger. "Rise," I told him. "Who are you?"

"I am Leonidas. King of Sparta," he replied. "Themistocles sent word you needed more men, and I have brought them."

He got to his feet and when he raised his eyes to mine, I gasped. His dark hair was cropped close to his head, as was his beard, neatly following the straight line of his jaw from chin to ear. His face was lined but free of scars and he had probably seen fifty winters. His eyes were set squarely in place and captured mine in a manner that was so familiar I could not look away. Blue and clear, they complimented the face perfectly and for a moment I looked into a much-loved face from the past.

"Find Papou and bring him here," I murmured to Demi, my eyes never leaving Leonidas'.

6

"What is it my darling? What has happened?" Papou asked, shuffling his way across the Throne Room less than a quarter of a candlemark later.

King Leonidas and I had barely spoken since Demi had left to find Papou. So many emotions ran through me that it was both hard to look at Leonidas and impossible to keep my eyes from his. So much familiarity lay there and I was unable to take a full breath each time his gaze found mine.

I drew a shaky breath and held my hand out to indicate our guest. "Papou, I wish to introduce the King of Sparta."

Papou turned towards the man, raising his arm in greeting but pausing when their eyes met. Leonidas' mouth fell open.

"Leonidas," Papou whispered.

This had to be the secret Ares spoke of. Leonidas had Mumma Skylar's eyes, Papou's eyes; his face the exact image of Papou's when I found him in Konitsa. Papou had been older then of course, but there was no mistaking it; Leonidas was direct kin to Papou and to Mumma.

The two men regained themselves and shook each other's arms with a nod.

Papou stepped back and cleared his throat. "You are the son of Queen Anassa and King Anaxandridas?" he asked, his voice catching on the words.

"For many winters I believed Anaxandridas to be my father," Leonidas nodded.

"Oh, and who now do you believe to be your father?"

"There was once a young Thracian tribesman who came to Sparta. My mother named him as the one. If I am not very much mistaken, I would venture that you are he," Leonidas said slowly.

"I am Leandros of the Thracian tribe of the Bessoi," Papou nodded.

"My true father," Leonidas noted.

Papou nodded again. There could be no doubting the truth of the statement. Leonidas took Papou's arm and helped him to the nearby chairs, taking the one beside him as Demi came to my side.

"Do you think this is what Ares was waiting for?" he murmured.

"I do but I don't understand why it would be of concern to him," I replied.

"There is a lot about Ares we have never understood," Demi said.

"That is true enough," I agreed.

"Would you tell me how you came to know my mother?" Leonidas asked.

"Is it alright if we stay and listen too?" I added.

Papou nodded for a third time and I took the seat on his opposite side to Leonidas, Demi beside me. "I am not certain I know where to begin," Papou murmured, his hands fidgeting with each other.

"There is no need to rush, take your time," Leonidas said.

Papou took a deep breath and met Leonidas' gaze. "There is much about my Zita that I shall share with you, but for now allow me to just tell you of the night our daughter – Skylar – was born and how I found myself with Anassa and Anaxandridas."

"As you wish," Leonidas agreed, inclining his head.

"Zita's family killed her the night Skylar was born but I managed to evade them, travelling through the night and reaching the Temple of Artemis at Sparta the next morning. I offered the goddess prayers of thanks for our daughter's arrival, along with food, startled to learn I was not alone in the temple when your mother spoke.

"She and the king were both at the temple and invited me to their home. In return for providing Skylar with honey-sweetened wine, and a bed for me, they asked a favor of me. I initially hesitated, but soon found I had no real choice but to agree to it if I wanted to keep Skylar safe, and with me."

"What was the favor?" Demi asked.

"The king and queen had attempted to have children for many winters, the healers finally announcing that the queen was barren. The ephors of the king's council told him he must take another wife to bear sons for the line and he did so, though it was with reluctance for he loved Anassa dearly."

"Anaxandridas and his second wife had a son, my half-brother Cleomenes," Leonidas noted.

"They did, your mother also producing a son a winter later with another lover."

"My half-brother Dorieus," Leonidas nodded.

"Yes. I never met Dorieus but Skylar and I aided Cleomenes when he was king to expel Hippias from Athens."

"It was a great victory for Cleomenes, and aided the people to continue to support him despite their misgivings of his sanity," Leonidas said, turning to me. "My brother had ambitions and thoughts not often shared by the majority of Spartans, but he always believed he was doing the best for Sparta, a belief I shared for the most part."

I nodded in reply, having heard little of the rule of the former Spartan king, though the man himself and the friendship he shared with Mumma had been mentioned often when I was a small child, he having stood beside Mumma when she married Mother.

"So, with both Anaxandridas and Anassa having produced children with other lovers, they again attempted to have one of their own. Still they were unable and the queen yearned for a daughter," Papou said.

"I imagine seeing you at the temple with a daughter of your own, they considered taking her from you and raising Skylar as theirs," I said.

Papou nodded. "I am in no doubt it crossed the king's mind, but they saw how much I had endured with her already and offered another solution; that I lie with the queen and put a daughter in her belly." He drew a deep breath before continuing. "Just as the king had hesitated to take another wife, so too did I pause in the request. I had only just lost Zita and did not believe I could perform the act they asked of me.

"It was the queen who convinced me to join with her, speaking with passion of the child we would create. She told me our daughter would grow to be beautiful and strong. She would never want for food or coin and would be Princess of Sparta; revered, loved and educated. I went to Anassa's room the following evening."

"My mother did not allow you to mourn for Zita before she made you lie with her?" Leonidas frowned.

"No."

"But she believed mourning was so important, that everyone should be given the time to do so. It was how she taught me."

"Desperation makes people act in unaccustomed ways," Papou replied. "Do not think badly of your mother, she only wanted what her husband could not give her. She wanted to add a daughter to her family to love and cherish, just as I loved mine. She was kind and gentle and if I had not been willing to lie with her, I do not believe she would have allowed Anaxandridas to kill me and take Skylar, she did not want to be gifted a child in such a manner."

Leonidas shook his head. "No, I do not believe she would have either. It would have driven them apart, rather than closer together."

"Indeed. When we lay together, Anassa did her best to ease the pain I felt at betraying Zita's memory, of betraying my love for her. She asked me about Zita, what I had loved most about her, what had first drawn me to her. We spent many candlemarks talking and when the sun rose above the hills the following morning, still we had not been together in the most intimate sense. We stayed locked in her room all the following day, while Skylar was regularly fed and cleaned as if she was one of the queen's own children.

"When finally there was nothing more to say, she told me she would always be grateful to whichever god or goddess had seen fit to arrange our meeting and asked me if I would keep my word. I told her I would. She understood the words pained me to say them so she took a soft cloth and covered my eyes. She undressed me and placed my hands on her body, telling me to think only of Zita as we made our child."

"And so I was created inside her," Leonidas murmured.

"Yes. I did not remain in Sparta to find out if I had indeed placed a child inside the queen, but I learned of you of course, there was much discussion within the Peloponnese that the king and queen had finally had a child together. I never returned to the city, knowing you were better left with your parents. No doubt your heritage would have been questioned had I done so, we share many similarities, as you do with Skylar."

"My sister," Leonidas whispered. "Has she ever been to Sparta?" he added.

"Once. It would be almost twenty winters ago now."

Leonidas nodded. "I thought I saw a woman – a soldier – once in the agora. We had the same eyes. I went after her but did not find her."

"Yes. She knew you had seen her and she asked me of you when she returned, believing the two of you to be kin."

"She did not wish us to meet?" Leonidas asked.

"She did, very much so, but she was killed soon after she was in Sparta and the chance was lost."

"Oh, I am sorry."

Papou inclined his head.

"She was my mother," I offered, smiling tightly.

Leonidas stood, bowing low in my direction before holding his hands out to me, speaking again when I took them. "My dear niece, I am sorry for your loss. You must have been young when she was taken from you."

"Nine winters," I nodded.

"I regret that I never had the chance to meet my sister and I share your pain at her loss."

"Thank you … uncle," I managed, swallowing around the sudden lump in my throat.

Leonidas returned to his seat beside Papou. "Mother did not get her wish for a daughter, but she kept me and loved me just the same."

"And for that I am thankful," Papou said.

"She named me after you," Leonidas continued. "The king was not pleased, telling her that the Thracian tribesman was never to be spoken of again. But he did not ask her to change the name she had chosen; Leonidas, Son of the Lion."

Papou smiled. "I did not realize she knew my name meant lion man."

"She knew a great many things my mother, but her greatest desire was to learn the whereabouts of the young man who captured her heart in the Temple of Artemis. It pains me that she never did."

Papou nodded, his eyes finding the floor as he lost himself to his thoughts. I wondered what other secrets he held and if they too would ever be voiced.

"When did you learn that Anaxandridas was not your father?" Papou asked a long moment later.

"After I assumed the throne, nine winters ago," Leonidas replied. "Anaxandridas had been gone over thirty winters and my mother was not well. She did not wish to leave this world without telling me of the young man who was my father."

"She has since passed?" I asked.

"Yes, she joined Hades not long after she spoke of Leandros," he replied, his gaze falling to Papou again. "She cared for you a great deal and was saddened she never knew what became of you, or the daughter she said you travelled with."

"I am sorry for your loss, my son, but I am glad you had her for as many winters as you did."

"Gratitude."

"I offer my apologies as well," I said. "We both do," I added, nodding in Demi's direction.

"I thank you all for your words," Leonidas said, nodding in return before addressing Papou again. "My mother did not know if you knew of my birth, but I assure you, I did not come here seeking you, I am only here because of the Persian army that wishes to take our homes and our women from us. I did not ever expect to meet my true father, though it gives me great joy to do so."

"As it does me," Papou replied. "And here you sit, King of Sparta," he added, looking rather proud as he placed his hand on Leonidas' shoulder. "One of the most respected warriors to come out of Sparta and the only Spartan king to have ever trained at the agoge."

"You were sent from your home just as a common Spartan boy is?" I asked, surprised.

"Yes. I was not the first-born son so it was expected. I relished the challenge and discipline the agoge brought. My feats there are the reason I have been sent here now to aid you in the war against the Persians."

"How many men accompany you?" I asked.

"Three hundred Spartiates and thousands more from the allied states we gathered along our journey. The rest of my Spartans shall follow when the Carneia and Olympic Festivals end."

"What are Spartiates?" Demi asked.

"It means living with sons. I only brought men who had sons to carry on their line if they came back on their shield, rather than with it," Leonidas replied.

Demi looked at me with concern but I put a hand on her arm. "Don't worry. Leonidas and I will return with our shields."

Demi didn't look convinced, but didn't voice her thoughts.

"Ah, family reunions, such happy occasions," Ares' voice permeated the room a moment before he appeared, lounging across my throne.

Leonidas drew his sword from his sheath as I stood, my hand on the pommel of my own.

Ares continued to smile and looked each of us over. "It is true what they say; children take on their parents' features ... and so similar to Skylar," he mused. "Who would have believed you would find each other after all this time?"

"You don't expect us to believe you had no hand in this Ares. Why else would you have asked me about Papou when we spoke earlier?" I asked.

Ares pushed himself up from my throne and approached Leonidas, circling him as he spoke. "Actually, the Spartans made the choice to send Leonidas here all by themselves. But when I learned that the king of Sparta himself planned to lead an attack here in Thermopylae, I just had to come watch your reactions."

"You have known he and I were kin for many winters, just as I have. I am surprised you were able to keep the knowledge to yourself," Papou said, making his way forward to stand at Leonidas' side.

"It served no purpose to tell anyone," Ares replied with a shrug. "It is of little consequence even now, though it affords me some leverage," he added with a smirk.

"You told me you didn't return to seek those of your line, so why are you here, Ares?" I asked.

"I want the sword you used to put me in that cage."

"I already told you I don't have it."

"But you know where it is and you are going to tell me. Now."

"Why would I do that?"

"Because, if you do not, you shall find your family grows smaller."

Instantly Papou was against Ares' chest, Leonidas' sword at his throat. Leonidas stepped back in surprise, looking between Ares and his now-empty palm.

"What? How? Ares, god of ... war?" he spluttered

I grabbed hold of Leonidas' cloak and pulled him back to stand alongside Demi behind me. I took my sword out, holding it up as I approached Ares.

He watched me advance, a menacing grin on his face. "Do you intend to run me through with that?"

"No, because I know it wouldn't kill you, you would heal again in seconds."

"True, and in that time, your precious grandfather here would be dead."

"You will not kill him."

"Are you certain of that?" He pressed the iron against Papou's neck, drawing blood. "I allowed him to live once before, and that ended far from how I planned."

"Why do you threaten Papou – why not Demi? It was our combination that brought about your defeat and denied you what you had waited so long for at Olympos."

"Ava, what are yo–"

"You must know that I love her much more than my grandfather," I taunted.

"You speak true, but I have a far worse fate in mind for your wife," Ares smirked. "Not that I shall *physically* harm her." He released Papou and Leonidas went to him. Ares tipped his head to the side and paced the room, keeping his eyes on me. "Perhaps you *would* feel better if I held a sword to your lover's throat, hmm?"

"You know if you harm anyone I love that I will *never* give you what you want."

"Oh no, I believe you shall give me *exactly* what I want. You do not wish to lose any more family, do you?" I kept my eyes on Ares, but he didn't approach Demi. "Tell me where the sword is."

"No."

"As you wish," he said with a shrug before disappearing.

I turned, desperately scanning the room, wishing I could feel his presence like before. A moment later he reappeared beside Papou, grabbing his chiton and driving a hand against Leonidas' chest, sending the king flying across the room where he landed, dazed, at the foot of my throne.

I had barely taken two steps toward Ares before he drew Leonidas' sword across Papou's throat, spraying the floor with his blood.

"No!" I screamed. Papou slumped to the ground. My sword clattered to the marble below my feet as I caught him, sinking to my knees and cradling his head in my lap as tears wet my cheeks. Leonidas approached us, laying his hands on Papou's chest. "What do you want with the sword?" I screamed as my tears flowed.

"I know the pieces of the amulet are in it and I want what is mine," Ares replied.

"Hephaestus' blood runs through the sword, as does mine and Demi's. The jet and hematite will not obey you."

"Perhaps, but I still want the sword. I shall even allow you to join me. I shall forget how you betrayed me and lied to me and we shall have everything, just as we were meant to."

"Ava, I will help you. You obviously have history with the god of war, and whilst I do not know of it, he has taken my father before I got to know him. I shall fight alongside you with all I have to keep him from getting what he wants," Leonidas murmured.

"Such noble words, King Leonidas, but you know *so* little about your new family," Ares grinned.

"For the moment that is true, but it shall not always be so."

"So you think. You know, it is a shame you had only just met your father before his untimely death, but fear not, you shall soon join him in the Underworld. Meanwhile, my Persians shall pillage your city, rape your wife and enslave your child and there shall be nothing you can do about it."

Leonidas jumped to his feet.

"No! Don't let him goad you into fighting, it's what he wants," I yelled.

Leonidas paid me no heed, gathering his sword from the ground and slashing at Ares. The great god laughed and disappeared. Leonidas roared. "We shall defeat your Persians, Ares. No one shall lay a hand on my wife or child."

He fell to his knees beside Papou and when Ares reappeared beside me, I knew that Leonidas and Demi could not see him.

"Tell me where the sword is," he demanded.

"I will never tell you," I whispered, unable to reach my sword while I held Papou.

"Do not be hasty with your answer. Think carefully about those you care most for; you do not want their blood on your hands as well, do you? I shall return in a week. I expect you to have the sword."

He disappeared again and my tears fell freely onto Papou's chest as I held him and Demi held me.

7

My tears soaked Papou's chiton above his recently-stilled heart. Leonidas spoke quiet words beside me; whispered details of his life that he had obviously intended to share with his father now he had found him. I almost felt like I was intruding on their private conversation, but I had my own words and apologies to make to my grandfather.

"Papou I am so sorry I did not protect you. I didn't think Ares would hurt you. If I had, I would have removed you from Thermopylae with my own hands today," I told him, stroking the smooth skin of his head. "Of course you would have complained and fought me the entire way, but at least I would have known you were safe," I added with a smile. "You will find Mumma, Mother, Zita and Nasrin when you arrive in the Elysium Fields. None of you will understand where you know each other from, but you will all somehow know that you belong together, that you knew one another in a different time and place. Be happy with them Papou and I too will find you all when my time in this world is done," I told him, kissing his forehead.

A flicker of light announced another presence and Leonidas and I looked up. Hephaestus stood by my throne wearing a worried expression as he flexed his lame, twisted leg. His leather apron was tied as usual over his impressive barrel chest and orange chiton and his dark, curly hair peeked untidily from the sides and back of his oval cap.

Leonidas jumped to his feet, clutching his sword, and pointing it at Hephaestus. "Another god? Who are you?" he demanded.

"Leonidas, lower your weapon," I told him.

"I shall not," he replied stubbornly.

"He is not our enemy. This is Hephaestus, God of the Forge. Demi's father."

"Your … father?" Leonidas looked first to me, then Demi. Demi nodded in acknowledgement. "It appears I *do* have much to learn about this family," Leonidas murmured, lowering his weapon.

"And there will be time to explain all of it. Soon," I promised.

Leonidas remained standing and Hephaestus' gaze fell to Papou. He hobbled over, lowering himself onto his good knee and taking in the deep red line that ran across Papou's throat. "What happened?"

"Ares," Demi replied.

"I should have been here sooner. I came to tell you about Ares. I should have checked on my brother more often. I do not know how long he has been gone and I cannot understand how he escaped," Hephaestus' words tumbled out in a rush.

"The how doesn't matter, only why," I said, wiping the tears from my face. "He wants the sword, the one I used against him on Olympos. I wouldn't give it to him so he … he killed Papou."

"Why does he want it?" Hephaestus asked.

"He didn't say."

The door to the Throne Room crashed open. "Ava, the Persians have arrived, th–" Moeris started, before his eyes found Papou's body. He crossed the room and placed his hand on my grandfather's stomach. "What happened?"

"Ares," I replied. "Where are the boys?"

"I returned them to Melina."

"What news have you of the Persians?" I asked before he could question me further about the god of war.

Moeris tore his eyes from Papou's face. "They march this way and have almost reached the banks of the Melas River. They intend to take Trachis for themselves and set up camp between here and the sea. Their numbers are far greater than we could have imagined and stretch farther than the eye can see. You must send your family to safety; they are the only ones who still remain in Trachis."

"We can't leave now. We must give Leandros a proper burial, we must honor him," Demi said.

"There is no time," Moeris said, addressing me as he continued. "The Persians shall not rest for long, they may even march towards the Pass tonight."

"Moeris is right, Demi. The Persians have arrived much sooner than we anticipated … Hephaestus?"

"Yes?"

"Take Papou's body to safety, along with Demi, the boys and Melina."

"Where do you wish for me to take them?"

"Ava, no …" Demi objected.

I held a hand up to silence her, keeping my eyes on Hephaestus' face. "I don't know, but far from harm's way. Please. Build a pyre for Papou as we normally would; display his body, give him a procession to the pyre and have a relief made. Honor his memory and his life and send him with a coin on his lips for Charon in the Underworld so he is not stranded on the banks of the River of Lamentation for eternity."

"As you wish," Hephaestus nodded, leaning in close so his voice was not heard by either Demi or Moeris as he added, "what do you intend to do about Ares?"

"I don't know yet, but I am sure the answer lies with my sword. When you have my family settled, find me and we will make a plan."

Hephaestus nodded again and slid his hands beneath Papou's body. "I shall find a suitable place and organize the pyre. I shall return shortly, be ready to leave," he said, addressing Demi.

Moeris took his hand from Papou's stomach. Closing his eyes, he mouthed silent words to the man who had once been his trusted friend and a brave soldier beside him in battle.

I kissed Papou's forehead and removed my own arms, allowing Hephaestus to hug Papou against his chest and take him far from the place my mothers, my father and now my favored grandfather had been stolen so brutally from me.

Hephaestus disappeared silently and Demi stood, offering me her hand. I took it, attempting to order my thoughts. I knew Demi would be even more opposed to the idea of her departure, and my remaining, after what Moeris had told us, but I would not change my mind. I had to defend Thermopylae from the Persians and deny Ares whatever it was he sought. This time I couldn't do it with Demi by my side.

She opened her mouth, but I shook my head. "Wait," I told her. I indicated Leonidas as I locked eyes with Moeris, who had also returned to his feet. "This is Leonidas, King of Sparta. He brings three hundred Spartiates and several thousand more soldiers from the allied city-states, take them and march to the Pass. Block it immediately in case the Persians continue to press forward. Ensure our men are prepared for battle and I will join you as soon as I can."

"The men lather themselves with oil as we speak," Moeris confirmed.

"Good," I said.

Moeris bowed and offered his arm to Leonidas. My uncle gripped it with a nod before finding my eyes with his. "We shall see each other soon. We have much to speak of." I nodded in return as Moeris and Leonidas left Demi and me to speak alone.

Demi turned to me, fear and a plea etched on her face. I cupped her cheek in my hand.

She closed her eyes, her hands resting lightly on my waist. "You know my wish," she murmured.

"I do," I replied. "And you know that I would grant it if I could, but I cannot. I must stay here and defend our home. I have to ensure that Leonidas does not fall and that he returns with me to you. He is the only family I have left on Mumma Skylar's side now. I can't lose him too."

"But my father ... he could take us all far from here. He could protect us from Ares," Demi said, opening her eyes again.

"Ares would search for us. We would always wonder how close he was to finding us. We would constantly be moving from place to place, we would never feel safe. It is no life for our boys. It is no life for you."

"It was how your mother was brought up."

"And you know how that ended for her. I don't want to live that way, Demi. These past winters without Ares' presence in our lives have been a gift. I intend to enjoy many more with you; to see our boys grow and have families of their own. I want to be safe and never fear that Ares will come for me or my kin again. The only way to do that is to stay and fight."

"Do you think the sword will help you do that, just as it did on Olympos, even though it is what he now seeks?"

"Maybe," I replied.

"Then let me stay and help you, just like I did back then."

"No. Ares would cut you down as quickly as he did Papou if I refuse to give him the sword, and I ... I cannot feel him as I once could."

"Then that is even more reason," Demi argued.

I shook my head again. "I cannot lose you."

"Have you a plan then?"

I blew out a long breath. "Not yet, but I don't want you to worry. I will find a way to deny him and we will be back together soon."

I pressed my body the length of hers, kissing her fiercely. She wound her arms around me and pulled me even closer.

8

I held Demi for a long time, unable to bring myself to voice the thought I knew must be on her mind as well; this may well be the last time we saw each other in this world. Instead I concentrated on the feel of her body beneath my hands, each curve and dip, the smooth, strong muscles of her back, the way her arms felt wrapped around me. The sound of her heart beating strongly in her chest, the way her hair fell in that certain way across her forehead. I committed each to memory as we embraced.

"Give me your word that if the Persians are too strong, or you can't find a way to deny Ares, that you will get Leonidas and call my father to bring you back to me," Demi finally said, releasing me.

"I will," I replied, knowing that Leonidas would never leave Thermopylae until the battle was done – he was a Spartan and the Spartans never fled in the face of an enemy.

Demi closed her eyes, taking my hand and kissing my palm. "Return to me soon, my love, for this world is brighter when you stand beside me in it."

"I love you," I told her, wrapping my arms around her neck and pressing my lips to hers.

"I will gather our things and bring our sons and Melina here to say goodbye. Do you want me to tell them about Leandros?"

"No, I'll do it," I replied.

Demi nodded and kissed me again. As we parted, the door to the Throne Room swung open again and Melina, Zenon and Kadmus rushed in. Melina held two bags, as did each of my sons. Their travelling chlamydes were tied around their shoulders and Kadmus had his sword sheathed around his waist. Damon trailed them, tongue hanging from his mouth and nails clicking across the marble beneath his paws.

"Moeris says we must leave. He received word that the Persians were very near. We looked for Leandros, but could not find him, I thought perhaps he was with you," Melina said.

I swallowed loudly, motioning the three of them forward. "Papou … Papou is dead," I told them, my voice catching on the final word.

"No!" Zenon cried, turning and burying his face in Melina's chiton.

"How?" Kadmus asked. "Was it the Persians? I will cut them down where they stand," he insisted, gripping the handle of his sword.

"No, it was not the Persians," I said, pushing his sword back into its holder. "He was old but his life has held many happy memories, he will find peace in the Underworld."

Zenon raised his eyes to mine and I held my hand out to him. He took it and I drew my sons to me, kissing each on the top of their heads. "He was so proud of both of you, he loved you very much. Hephaestus will make sure you're able to say a final goodbye to him. Send him to the Underworld with honor and love and tell him you will see him again one day, when your own days in this world are done."

Kadmus pulled back from me, his brow creased. "You don't intend to be with us when we see him again?"

I shook my head. "No. Hephaestus will take all of you far from here, far from the fighting and the Persians. Somewhere you will be safe."

"If you're staying to fight the Persians then I am staying as well," Kadmus said. The set of his face reminded me of Demetri's long ago outside a cave in the Pindos Mountains when he stubbornly refused to let me climb Mount Smolikos by myself to find Papou. I lowered my face until it was level with his and put my hands on his shoulders.

"You must go with Hephaestus, Kadmus. I need you to keep Zenon and your mother and Proyiayia safe when Hephaestus returns to me. You have the training. Can I trust you with this?"

Kadmus' eyes bored into mine for a long moment before finally he nodded. "I will do as you ask."

"Thank you, my son," I said, taking him in my arms again.

"Where are we to go?" Melina asked.

"Only Hephaestus knows that," I replied. "It is best if I do not."

"You would never tell the Persians where to find us," Zenon insisted.

I smiled and put a hand on his cheek. "Of course not sweetheart, but some enemies have ways of getting answers, no matter how hard we try to hide them."

Demi met my eyes above the boys' heads, her mouth set in a grim line as Melina neared, holding her arms out. Demi took the boys as I allowed Melina to enfold me in a strong embrace.

"My dear child, the Immortals the Persians bring have never been defeated, but if anyone can, it shall be you and those you lead. You put much trust in the soldiers who fight with you, but you must remember that they are no more than flesh and blood as you are and you are far too important to lose. Come with us and we shall begin anew, far from this place and the haunting, hurtful memories it has held for so long."

I did not know what to say. Melina didn't speak of the painful memories of her past, only the happy ones and for her to do so now touched me deeply. I wished it was easy to abandon the soldiers, abandon the hills and the sea that I had called home for so long, but I was the daughter of Skylar, the granddaughter of Leandros; a soldier at heart, a protector. I could not turn from this place. I would stand and fight with everything I had to protect what was mine.

"I can't, but I will be with you as soon as I can," I finally said. Melina released me, taking Zenon and Kadmus by the hands as she hummed a quiet tune I recognized as one she had sung to me when I was very small.

"Perhaps you could convince Moeris to join us instead?"

"I will try," I nodded, though I doubted he would leave Trachis any more than I would, no matter how close he and Melina had grown since Agrias' death.

Demi approached, encircling my waist again. "Are you sure you won't change your mind?" she asked quietly.

"No," I replied. "Go and be safe. I will join you as soon as I can."

"I pray it is so," she said, caressing my cheek.

"All is ready," Hephaestus announced, reappearing beside Melina.

I inhaled deeply and nodded to him before meeting Demi's gaze again. I ran my finger along the line of her jaw, my thumb caressing her bottom lip. "I love you."

"And I you," she replied, taking my face in her hands and kissing me. "Be safe," she added when we parted.

I swallowed hard against the lump in my throat. "You too."

The boys approached, hugging me again. I kept my eyes on Demi's, vowing that I would never forget the way the brown and yellow flecks mixed together, and I prayed I would see them all again before long.

I released my sons, kissing both their foreheads. "Be safe and good. Look after Damon and do as you are asked without hesitation. We will all be together again before you know it," I told them.

"I will do as you ask, Mother," Kadmus replied.

"As will I," Zenon agreed.

I smiled at them both. "Good." I straightened and patted Damon on the head as he neared. "Take care of them, Boy," I instructed.

He looked up at me, drawing his tongue back into his mouth and pushing his head against my hand in reply.

Hephaestus approached as the rest of my family slung bags over their shoulders, Melina setting two aside that I presumed had been for me and Papou. "All is in order for Leandros' farewell. Where shall I find you when I return?" he asked.

"At the Pass with the soldiers, but before you return I need you to get my sword."

"Are you certain that is wise?"

"Ares is convinced it holds the key for him, but it doesn't obey his will, only mine. I defeated him with it once; I have to believe I can do it again. Your blood protects it but I can't find out what he intends to do with it until he sees I have it."

"You are certain he does not already know where the sword is?"

"No, it seems it's still cloaked from him, just as you suspected it would be."

"I do not believe it wise to bring him exactly what he desires …"

"It's the only way."

"And if he is somehow able to use the sword against you?"

"Is that possible?"

"When I aided you in crafting it I was certain it was not, but I do not know how he got free of the cage and I do not know who assists him since his return. We must be cautious."

"And we will be, but I need the sword."

Hephaestus nodded and turned to Demi. "Are you ready?"

Demi nodded, putting her hands on the boys' shoulders. Melina threaded her arm through Demi's and, as if sensing that they all needed to be touching, Damon nuzzled his nose into Kadmus' hand.

I swallowed and straightened my shoulders. Hephaestus gave a final nod and my family disappeared, leaving me alone in the Throne Room with only my thoughts for company.

9

I sat against the trunk of a laurel tree, my bronze aspis on the ground beside me. I had used it only a few times in battle, having purchased it on my return to Trachis after my old one was broken in the scuffle with Phaeops and his friends at Lake Xynias.

The bronze cuirass protecting my chest was also a new addition to my weaponry – I had previously favored only bonded leather and linen – but when word of the Persian Immortals reached me, I decided on an upgrade. After Demi arrived in Trachis with me, she took a position with Papou and Ophelos in their metal workshop in town and along with crafting coins and swords for our soldiers, she also made chest pieces – the one I now wore one of her latest and (in my opinion) best.

I ran a stone the length of my sword, sharpening the edges to deadly points. Leonidas and his Spartiates were gathered twenty or so paces from me, sending up prayers to the gods for the coming battle and offering the goat they had sacrificed.

Soldiers from Thessaly, Boeotia and Athens stood nearby. Some watched the Spartans, others practiced their battle formation and strikes, while more sat, as I did, sharpening their weapons. Whether it was a sword or the tip of a spear, each man took care and pride in his particular arsenal, not stilling his hand until he was satisfied it was ready to do the job he would ask of it.

Shields lay scattered on the ground, against the few trees of the area, or looped over men's arms and I marveled at the different pictures on the bronze and wooden faces. The Spartan shields displayed an array of pictures; most had the Greek letter – Lambda – on them which stood for Sparta's ancient name of Lacedaemon. It was one of the most recognizable symbols of any army in Greece and similar to the three-sided shape Mumma had had on her arm, although it didn't have the third side across the bottom.

Other Spartan shields featured the symbol of the Dioscuri called the Krotalon; a musical instrument I had only seen a handful of times and one that I'd never cared much for the sound of when the wooden pieces were brought together. The Dioscuri were the brothers of Clytemnestra and Helen of Troy. Along with their sisters, the twins were born to Leda, but there was much debate about the boys' fathers. It was said that Castor was the son of the great Spartan king – and Leda's husband – Tyndareus whilst Polydeuces was said to be the son of Zeus. Despite much debate and investigation, no healer had ever been able to tell which children were Tyndareus' and which belonged to the god. Two snakes and a spider also graced the shield; the snakes again representing the Dioscuri, whilst the spider honored the goddess Athena, the protector of the Spartan army.

I was surprised that the nearby Athenians did not display images of Athena – for whom their city was named – on their shields as well, but they were still easily recognizable for any who knew of the great city and its coinage. Their shields held the same owls that graced their coins, the owl a symbol of Athena and her wisdom.

Leonidas' shield design was the only of its kind and I wondered if it was because he was king. Lining the very edge were hundreds of small white dots on a black background and from the middle, curving lines in black and white streamed towards the edges. It was the Spartan symbol for the moon, a symbol associated with Artemis, the patron goddess of Sparta.

A number of black shields displayed a half-moon, which was a sign of respect to the power of Aphrodite and Eros, whom the Boeotians from Thespiae worshipped avidly. Other Boeotians held shields with the snake-dragon painted on them that represented Drakon – an early ancestor of the Spartans.

The shape of Heracles' famed wooden club graced the faces of many Theban shields, others bearing the Sphinx, a monster with the head of a woman and the body of a lion, which was said to have once been sent by Hera to guard the pass to the city of Thebes.

The Phocian and Thessalian shields were simple; a black rounded shape with a line that ran through it for the Phocians, and a bull's foot in the center of the Thessalians'. I was not certain what either symbol stood for, though the Phocians' shape could have symbolized the oracle at Delphi.

After Phaeops and Eton were killed, their families fled Larissa and the region of Thessaly entirely in fear of retribution. The Thessalians became loyal to us and there was talk of them adopting the shield design of our soldiers, Agrias and I spoke at length on the matter, but I told him they should keep their own, for though they called themselves our allies, we never asked them for submission to our rule.

When Agrias left Macedonia, he didn't bring a shield with the sixteen-pointed sun of his homeland with him, and as the Malians he joined with at Trachis didn't carry shields either, he didn't insist on pictures on his soldiers' shields. It remained that way until Mumma and Papou came, and Agrias learned what her shield's picture stood for. By the time my mothers were killed, every soldier carried an aspis with her symbol prominently displayed. The one I now carried, along with those of the other soldiers from Trachis, still did. It was a solid black picture of a dark figure – neither male nor female, adult nor child – kneeling, its face upturned. When I was given my first shield, Moeris had told me it meant we fought for those who could not fight for themselves. That we would protect those who could not protect themselves.

As I looked over all the different pictures, I couldn't help thinking of the gods, goddesses, heroes and stories behind them and when my eyes found the picture of a deer on a Spartan shield, I was reminded of a story Mumma told me about Artemis and her five golden-horned deer. It was one that the old healer of Trachis – Gnosidicus – had shared with her when she was recovering from the injury she received on her way to the town. I hadn't thought of it in winters.

"The Spartans pray to Artemis for good fortune in this battle," Moeris said, interrupting my musings as he came to stand beside me.

I looked up, noting that his eyes roamed the area around us, barely settling in one place before continuing to the next, his head barely moving. First the Spartans to his right, then the deep blue sea in front, then the west gate of the Pass to his left. Back and forth, constant movement, constant attention. I had made Melina's request for Moeris to leave Trachis with her when I saw him at the Pass but, as I had expected, he would not leave his home, no matter how much the answer pained him.

"Why don't they ask for assistance from Athena?" I asked. "I was led to believe it was she who was the protector of Sparta."

"She is one of the protectors, but the Spartans believe that Artemis protects their soldiers as a mother protects her young. Athena provides them with the strength they require to defeat their enemies, whilst Artemis protects them from injury."

I only nodded in reply as Leonidas and his men started to dance, stamping their feet and sending dust high into the air while clashing their swords and shields together.

"The Athenians offered prayers and a sacrifice to the great goddess Athena before the Spartans arrived, so perhaps we shall have more than just one goddess' favor when we meet the Persians," Moeris added, raising his voice over the clanging of the metal.

"We will need all the help we can," I agreed.

"The number of goddesses you manage to call on for favor shall not change the outcome of this battle," Ares drawled, appearing beside Moeris. Moeris reached for his sword as I jumped to my feet and pointed my own at Ares. "The Persian numbers are great. The Greeks do not stand a chance," he continued.

"Do not be so confident of that," Moeris said, raising his sword.

"I must admit, I admire the arrogance of Greek soldiers, always believing you shall win, no matter the odds. It makes for entertaining viewing, and much bloodshed," Ares smiled. "But with the festivals being held in Sparta, you do not have the required number to hold the Persians back for long."

"What do you want, Ares?" I asked. "You gave me a week. It's been less than a day."

"Perhaps our conversation would be best held in private," he suggested.

"I shall not allow it," Moeris rumbled.

"It's alright, Moeris, Ares won't harm me; I have something he wants. Take my aspis and aid the men in their preparations for battle. Talk with Leonidas, ask if he's had word about when the rest of the Spartans are due to arrive, and how many they bring."

Moeris looked between me and the god of war, but finally re-sheathed his sword and picked up my shield. He turned on his heel, heading straight for Leonidas, who had finished dancing with his Spartiates.

"The sword is being retrieved as we speak," I told Ares as I lowered my weapon.

"I presume it is my brother who aids you once again?"

"He does."

"I knew you would agree to my terms."

"I agree to nothing. I said it's being retrieved, I didn't say I'd gift it to you. What do you want with the pieces of the amulet you believe it holds?"

"Why would I tell you that? You would only attempt to find a way to deny me what I wish for."

"You assume I do not already have a way," I countered.

"There is that arrogance I spoke of," Ares laughed. He was suddenly behind me, his hands on my waist as he spoke low into my ear. "You shall not defeat me this time, Mortal. The amulet's power is as lost to you now as it was to me when you placed the pieces into the sword so many winters ago."

"Oh? How have you come to that conclusion?"

"You said yourself you no longer feel any connection between us," Ares replied, dropping his hands from my body. "I am able to come and go beside you and you have no knowledge of it. You are as ordinary as any other man here; you do not know of my presence unless I wish it to be so," he added, circling me until he stood in front of me again.

"So you think the amulet's power has reverted to you?"

"Not yet. But when it does, you may take comfort in knowing it was *you* who aided me in my defeat of Zeus and the other gods that stand with him."

"I will not allow that."

"You shall not have a choice, believe me," he said, a triumphant grin spreading across his face. In a flash of blinding light, Ares was suddenly thrown sideways, landing several feet away with a thud. From his place in the dust, he laughed. "Nice to see you again, Brother," he smirked as Hephaestus appeared. "I believe you have something for Ava?"

"Leave this place. Now," Hephaestus warned, producing a ball of light in his palm.

"I shall go," Ares said, holding his hands up in front of his chest. "But this is far from over between all of us. I shall return and when I do, Ava shall give me what I want."

"She shall give you nothing," Hephaestus growled.

"That is something you can only wish for," Ares said, turning his attention to me again. "I *know* how this battle ends and it shall not be as the Greeks wish. The Persians are going to be victorious and neither you, or the Spartan king, can stop that, no matter what he believes awaits him."

"Destiny is what we make of it, it constantly changes and only the Moirai have the power to weave the loom, not you. The future is not yet written," I said.

"So you hope," Ares smirked, disappearing.

Putting my sword away, I turned to Hephaestus. "Is Demi safe?"

"Yes. She i–"

"No," I cut him off. "I don't want to know where you took her or my family, it's safer for all of them that way. Ares believes the power of the sword and the amulet are lost to me, but not to him. He intends to use it to once again challenge Zeus for the throne. Is it possible he could control my actions and my thoughts like he did when I first used the amulet?"

Hephaestus shook his head and lifted a shoulder. "I do not know. My blood protects the sword and you. I cannot see how he could break that and I do not feel it has diminished in any way. Are you certain that if he is able to use the sword, as you could the amulet, he would not just simply kill you?"

"No. He would take far too much pleasure in seeing me suffer. More likely, he'd make me kill Zenon and Kadmus as punishment for denying him what he sought last time."

"How can you be so certain?"

"Before Ares killed Papou, he said he wouldn't *physically* harm Demi, that he had something far worse in mind for her. You know how it was after I used the amulet against the army in Konitsa; Demetri hated and feared me," I told him, almost unconsciously reverting to how I'd known Demi back then. "He fled so I couldn't harm him or use him for my own personal gain. If Ares makes me kill our children, the act would effectively sever all ties I have with those I love in this world. I would be free to join Ares; I would *want* to join him because Demi would no longer love me. She would despise me and I would have no wish to continue living as I was."

"I suppose it is possible," Hephaestus conceded with a nod. "It would indeed be difficult for Demi to live with the knowledge of what you had done, especially if you showed no regret for the act ... and you would not if you were under Ares' influence again."

"I know."

"Perhaps I should return the sword to its hiding place," Hephaestus said after a moment.

"No, I have a plan but ... you're able to feel Ares' presence, aren't you?"

"I am."

"Good, because I can't, and if what I suggest is possible, Ares cannot know of it."

"Tell me," Hephaestus said.

10

When I had begun to put the plan together in my mind, I realized that what I'd said to Demi and Papou was no longer true; I couldn't be a soldier for Greece in the battle against the Persians. I couldn't stay and fight for the place I had been born in, the place where they called me Queen. I could not be that person – that soldier. I could not risk being killed by the Persians; my obligation was far greater than that. It was true that if the Persians defeated us here, the rest of Greece would no doubt fall into their hands, but if I could not deny Ares the pieces of amulet in the sword, then every mortal and every god would suffer a far worse fate.

With his Chosen One, Ares' intention had been to take the title of King of the Gods from his father, Zeus. If he was successful, the world would be thrown into chaos, no mortal would ever live in peace again, there would be no beauty left anywhere in our world – only perpetual war, death and destruction. The gods themselves would be killed if they didn't embrace Ares and carry out his wishes. When I learnt of his plan winters ago, I had fought with everything I had to deny him.

For my plan to be successful now, I had to embrace a much more important role than simply a soldier. I had to choose family. I had to become a mother who would protect not only *my* sons, but those of all the mothers in the mortal realm. There was only one way to keep us all safe from Ares for as long as we walked in this world; I had to find out if what I heard so long ago was true.

I gathered a deep breath, releasing it all the way before I spoke. "I once heard a story about Artemis and the five golden-horned deer she used to pull her chariot. The deer were sacred to the goddess and many men fell by her hand when they attempted to capture or kill them. The great hero Heracles was even set the task to capture one as the third of the twelve labors he had to carry out after he killed his wife and children. Most mortals believe that the worth of the deer is in the golden horns or bronze hooves, but they were far more precious than that."

Hephaestus considered me a long moment. "How so?" he asked.

"Artemis guarded the deer so fiercely because their blood is the only thing known to kill a god."

Hephaestus inhaled sharply, his forehead creasing at my words. "Hind's blood," he said slowly. I nodded. "If your plan is what I think it is, then our conversation cannot continue here in the mortal realm. We must go to Olympos and speak with Zeus."

"The story is true then?" I asked, my own breath catching and eyebrows high on my forehead.

"We must go to Olympos," was Hephaestus' only answer as he lay his hand on my arm.

"I seek the one who believes himself in charge here," a voice announced, startling us.

I looked around, finding a dark-skinned man standing at the west gate of the Pass. He wore a white chest piece over a yellow tunic that matched the yellow cloth on his head. He kept his only weapon – a long spear – strapped to his back, but his voice did not waver as he faced our army.

"Wait," I said to Hephaestus.

Moeris approached the man, Leonidas by his side. They kept their weapons sheathed, although their hands rested on the hilts of their swords, just as mine did. "What is it you seek?" Moeris asked.

"I come with an offer from Xerxes, the noblest and fairest of Persian kings. He wishes you to lay your weapons aside and suffer no bloodshed at this place. He offers you your freedom and the honored title of friends of the Persian people. He shall see you resettled on lands far better than the ones you hail from and he shall bear no ill-will for the defense you have mounted here," the man said.

Several of our soldiers laughed derisively while others shouted insults and rejections to the proposal as they picked up their shields and spears and created a phalanx formation behind Moeris and Leonidas.

"As you can hear, we do not accept such terms. We wish for nothing from your king and we are certainly not *friends* to the Persians," Moeris replied, spitting on the ground beside his sandal.

"If this is the entire number you have to rebuff our advance then you would be well advised to consider the offer my king makes to lay down your weapons, lest you die in vain."

"Come and take them," Leonidas said.

"Our arrows shall block out the sun," the Persian warned, glaring at Leonidas, fingers inching towards the spear at his back.

"Then we shall have our battle in the shade," Moeris replied.

The Persian looked from Leonidas to Moeris to the soldiers behind them, no doubt trying to find a man who didn't support what his leaders were saying.

"As you wish," the Persian conceded, obviously finding no weakness among the Greek army. "But we shall show no mercy when we descend upon you and by day's end there shall be many widows and children who mourn for husbands and fathers who should have accepted the Persian king's kindness when it was offered."

"So it shall be," Moeris said.

The Persian soldier retreated along the narrow path, his eyes never leaving Moeris'. When he had disappeared from sight, Moeris turned to his men, pulling his sword from its sheath and sliding his arm into the holds in his shield as he addressed them.

"It appears our enemies do not believe we can match the strength and might of their soldiers. They believe their idle threats can make us flee our position here, too afraid to stand and face them. But we shall not be driven away. We shall not fear their advance, we welcome it!"

The men shouted their agreement, hitting their swords against their shields, much as Leonidas and his warriors had done as they sacrificed to Artemis.

"We shall stand proud and fight bravely for our homes and our lands." More excited words greeted his speech. "We shall fight to protect our women and children and we shall not allow Xerxes to call our lands his own!" A cheer went up from the gathered men. "The Spartans fight with us and we call them brothers. They have a saying – come home with your shield or on it and I say to you that we shall *all* return to our wives and our families with our shields. Many songs shall be sung about our deeds here, your names shall be lauded in your hometowns and across all of Greece as the victors at the Battle of Thermopylae. We shall fight with honor and be victorious!" A deafening roar filled the Pass as the men beat their swords and shields together in approval.

"We'll leave as soon as I've spoken to Moeris and Leonidas," I shouted to Hephaestus over the din. He nodded in reply and I headed towards my old friend and the newest member of my family.

They saw me approaching and stepped forward to meet me, the soldiers ceasing to bang their swords and shields, returning instead to their preparations for the coming battle.

"I need to leave for a short while."

"Why? I thought you wanted to be with us when the Persians arrived,"

Moeris frowned, re-sheathing his sword.

"I do, but there's something I have to do first. There's no time for explanations, but it concerns Ares. I need to keep my family, and a great number of others, safe from the god of war."

"Then I shall accompany you," Leonidas offered, putting his own sword away. "They are my family also."

"That's not necessary, I will be with Hephaestus, he's the only protection I need and you are needed here at the Pass," I replied, placing my hand on his arm.

"I wish we did not have to be separated," Moeris said. "I pray for your swift and safe return, my friend. Thank you for sharing your intentions with me this time."

I nodded in reply. "I hope to return before night greets us, so don't dispatch the entire Persian army before we see each other again," I grinned, holding out my arm to him. "You know my hatred runs deep for their blood."

Moeris ignored my outstretched arm and pulled me into a hug instead. He gripped me tightly and I heard the grin in his voice when he spoke again. "I cannot make such promises."

We released each other and I gave both men a final nod, returning to the laurel tree where Hephaestus waited for me.

"I'm ready," I told him, taking the hand he offered.

My arms and legs grew heavy, just as they had when I travelled first with Ares, then Hephaestus, many winters ago. The Pass disappeared and I was plunged into complete darkness, the feel of Hephaestus' hand in mine the only assurance I had he was still with me. I closed my eyes against the swirling sensation in my stomach, finding Hypnos when the pressure of our journey became too much for my mortal body.

11

When my feet touched solid ground again, I found myself in the pure white palace where I'd defeated Ares so long ago.

"Ares' palace? Why is Zeus here?" I asked, raising my eyebrows.

"The section that once belonged to my brother is gone – the rooms that were not destroyed by your battle removed by Zeus himself. This is now part of my father's home," Hephaestus replied.

I took in the room, surprised to find it had been restored similarly to its former occupant's tastes. When I drove my sword into Ares' stomach, I'd caused a deep crevice to split one room from the next. My wings had erupted from my shoulders and agony engulfed me from head to foot, hot flames threatening to burn me from the inside until Papou struck me and I passed out.

Before I woke again, Papou and Demetri believed I'd used the final earth element of the amulet and would belong to Ares for all time. Thankfully I had not – the presence of Hephaestus and Demi's blood flowing through the individual parts of the amulet in my sword, altering the effect of Ares' power and the amulet's original intentions.

Light streamed in from the rounded windows, reaching the roof of the cavernous, high-ceilinged room. Doric columns stood between the windows and along the perimeter of the room within the walls. Another set of columns formed a square and the floor between them was tiled in a brilliant blue and archways led off into other rooms.

"It has been many winters since you visited me here on Olympos, my son. What sees it so now?" Zeus' voice filled the room.

"We seek your approval in a dire matter, Father," Hephaestus replied, turning me to face the greatest of all the gods as he appeared sitting comfortably in his throne before us.

"I see you bring a mortal with you. It has been many winters since we saw one another, Ava."

"Indeed," I replied.

"I hope you shall bring less destruction than on your last visit," he grinned.

"That is my intent," I replied, inclining my head in a gesture of respect.

"Approach. What is it you seek?"

I stepped forward, meeting Zeus' bright green eyes. His hand stroked his white beard, face open and inviting as he waited for my question.

I cleared my throat, slightly nervous about my plan now. "As you are aware, Ares has spent the past nine winters locked in the steel cage Hephaestus crafted to prevent him from challenging you for your throne and title," I started. Zeus nodded. "He managed to free himself, or someone helped him to escape. He visited me in Trachis, his intent still the same as ever. The parts of the original amulet remain in the sword that sent him to the cage, and he has learned of this truth. He believes the power I once possessed is gone and that he'll be able to harness the power himself and bring about what he has desired for so long."

"You wish to know if this is true?" Zeus asked.

"No. I want to ask a far greater favor than that." Zeus waited for me to go on and beside me, Hephaestus sucked in a deep breath. "Regardless of whether Ares can use the amulet or not, now that he's free, he will continue to search for ways to bring about what he wants. I fear he'll once again try to use me to help him. I don't want to find myself sided against you and if Ares can indeed harness the power of the amulet then I would be powerless to stop him. We all would be. I want to deny him of not only his current attempt to take over … I also want to strip him of his immortality forever. *That* is what I seek your approval of."

Zeus looked at me for a long moment, his body leaning forward ever so slightly. "I do not hear words asking me to carry out the task for you. So how do you intend to do what you speak of?"

The light that had been streaming in through the windows darkened and a large, full moon provided the only light until torches lined the walls and burst to life.

"I want to use hind's blood," I replied.

Zeus froze as he stared me down. He did not speak for many moments, his jaw clenching beneath his beard, brow furrowed. When he did, it was Hephaestus he addressed. "You spoke of hind's blood to a mortal?" he asked coldly.

"No, Father. She knew of it already. I told her nothing," Hephaestus replied hastily.

Zeus' eyes found mine again. I squared my shoulders and held his gaze. "You understand that using hind's blood against a god would not just strip him of his immortality; it would end his existence."

"I do, but I see no other choice. You can't simply send him to Tartarus as you did your father and the other Titans when you overthrew them; Hades has always sided with Ares and would release and aid him in whatever way he could, regardless of the wrath you would rain down upon them," I replied.

Zeus opened his mouth, but did not speak. He continued to look between me and Hephaestus as he considered his next words. "There are other places I could banish Ares to," he finally said.

"And it would always be possible he would return. You wouldn't know who he'd spoken to or what weapon he would bring with him to achieve his desire to lead the gods," I said carefully. "You know what would happen if he was able to defeat you; he would kill you and anyone who stood with you. He would cause endless suffering and destruction in my world, brothers killing brothers, mothers killing daughters, for no other reason than because Ares wished it. He would target the mortal women who have borne you children and he would inflict the Erinyes on them and cause them an eternity of pain and suffering, until finally they flung themselves into the Underworld to escape the terrors. And you can only imagine how the Underworld itself would be; there would be no Elysium Fields, only endless pits of Tartarus where he and Hades and the Erinyes would rule with cruelty and despair over all who found themselves there.

"I know you care for us mortals more than any other god or goddess here on Olympos, and it is not just because you are king, it is because you see us as important to the gods. You believe your power would be lost if we did not exist. I know what I ask and I know you are reluctant to agree because he is your son, but Ares is dangerous and he seeks to rob you of not only *your* life, but the lives of those you hold dear." I drew a breath and waited.

"It is indeed a dark day when a father would consider allowing his son to be killed without intervention," Zeus murmured, his voice somber as light started to fill the large room again. "There are many gods and goddesses who have not seen eye to eye with me in the many winters I have ruled, but never have I considered having them killed. Punished, yes, but never something so final, it does not sit well beneath my breast.

"When Ares was a child he spoke of taking my place when he was older, and I was proud of his words, believing them to be a son's respect and honor towards his father's duties. But I know now that his quest for power, and my defeat especially, would not be favorable for many of the immortals here on Olympos. What Ares does not realize is that each god and goddess plays an important role within the mortal world below. If he was to bring about the destruction you speak of, he would have no one to worship him, no mortals to fight for him; they would kill each other at his will and yet a new generation would not grow to take their place."

"Unless he brought them back from the Underworld somehow," Hephaestus noted. "It would not be the first time it has happened, and that did not end well."

Zeus shook his head slowly. "You speak the truth my son; once a soul has left the mortal realm, they are forced to drink from the River of Lethe. They lose all memories of their former life. If Ares was able to return mortals to the world they once walked, they would bear no resemblance to themselves or function in that uniquely mortal way."

"He would have the power to change many things, Father," Hephaestus said. "Making recently departed mortals drink from the river may only be the first."

"Perhaps," Zeus conceded. "Ares is the only one who has ever admitted freely that he would do as you say and kill me if I did not relinquish my title. It pains me that my own flesh would discard me so easily, but I see that perhaps I was always fated for such an act. As you mentioned, I overthrew my own father – Kronos – when I grew from childhood, just as he overthrew his father, Ouranos when his time came."

"But you defeated Kronos to free your brothers and sisters from his stomach; you wanted your siblings to be free and with you, not because you wanted to be the most powerful ruler on Olympos."

"There are some who do not see it that way," Zeus replied, his face taking on a thoughtful look.

I allowed the quiet to drag out between us before I spoke again. "Will you let me use the hind's blood against Ares to keep all of us safe from his desires?"

Zeus' eyes returned to mine, their green sparkling like jewels in the sunlight. "I shall allow you to attempt it," he finally said. "Although it is Artemis who possesses the blood and I do not know if she shall agree to aid you. Ares is, after all, her brother as well."

"She harbors no fondness towards Ares," Hephaestus corrected.

"Perhaps, but it is she who now holds your plan in her hands. If she agrees to assist you, you have my approval; if she does not then you shall have to find another way to deal with Ares."

"Do you have a plan of your own to deny Ares if I'm not successful in my task?" I asked.

"I believe you shall find a way. You are strong for a mortal and you have outwitted Ares before, just as your mother before you, and her mother before that. I have faith that all shall end as it is supposed to," Zeus replied.

I frowned, but was unable to press him further as he disappeared in a flash of light so bright that I threw my hands up to shield my eyes from it. When I uncovered my face again the torches were glowing around the walls and the windows beside me were dark.

I frowned, but turned to Hephaestus. "Is Artemis here on Olympos?"

"No, but I know where we shall find her," he replied. "Come." He held his hand out again and I took it.

12

I woke, finding myself this time in a thick, green forest with Hephaestus still holding my hand. The trees around us were close together and from somewhere high above me a bird called. I couldn't identify either its position, or its type, but its song continued to accompany us as we made our way through the dense firs, cypresses and pines.

"Where are we?" I asked, taking my hand from Hephaestus'.

"Artemis' sacred grove in the mountains of Taygetos," he replied.

"I should've brought something for her. I've heard that only those who bring wildflowers or sacrifices are allowed to look upon the great goddess or hear her voice."

"It is not necessary, you travel with me, she shall speak to us when we find her," Hephaestus assured me.

"Indeed I shall." I searched the woody copse until my eyes found the speaker. I gazed upon her for only a moment, before bowing my head and dropping to one knee. "Rise, my dear," she said in a voice soft and inviting.

I did as asked, noting that Artemis' face was chiseled with the same beauty and preciseness I had once observed in Ares'. Her enchanting dark green eyes were set above a neat nose and full, pink lips. She was more than beautiful and it was no wonder that many mortals had fallen in love with her and attempted to make her their own – with dire consequences. Her hair, with its gentle wave, was a deep brown, mirroring the color of the trunks of the fir trees around us and she kept it back from her face with a light green hairband.

She wore a simple white chiton that reached to her knees, held together at each shoulder by brass clips in the shape of leaves. She clasped a long silver bow at her left thigh, her quiver of arrows sitting between her shoulder blades and held in place by a fine length of leather that crossed her chest between her breasts. Her arms were strong and muscular and, though I knew she was much older, she appeared no more than twenty winters.

A large stag stood beside her, its presence causing my heartbeat to increase. Its golden horns and bronze hooves caught the slanted light that filtered through the trees and shone brightly. A movement just behind the beast caught my eye. I reached for my sword, but Hephaestus stilled my hand, and as my eyes focused, I realized it was just a nymph. Everyone who knew of Artemis knew she was attended by twenty nymphs, a gift from Zeus, when she was a child. The nymph approached Artemis and took her bow, resettling herself on a patch of bright green grass beside several others. More nymphs hid behind trees, only their faces peeking around the trunks to watch us. There were no other deer in sight.

"Hello, Brother," Artemis said, holding her arms out to Hephaestus.

Hephaestus limped over and grasped her warmly, his lamed body putting him barely a head shorter than her. "My dear baby sister, how does this day find you?"

"Very well, and you?"

"Troubled I am afraid. We seek your aid in a very … delicate matter."

"I see, and have you plans to introduce me to your young companion?"

"Of course. I bring with me Ava, Queen of Trachis in the region of Thermopylae. Ava, this is my sister, Artemis, Goddess of the Hunt and Childbirth."

"I am most honored to meet you," I said, lowering my eyes once more.

"Gratitude, my child," the goddess replied. "And what is it you seek me for this day?"

"Ares has found a way out of the cage we sent him to and, just as he always has, he seeks to take father's throne," Hephaestus replied without hesitation. "Ava has a plan to deny him this wish, but it requires extreme measures, and we come, together, in the hope that you shall assist us and allow us to carry out such a feat."

"How?" Artemis asked.

"We need some of your hind's blood," I answered.

She tilted her head to the side and regarded me silently. "Hind's blood?" she finally repeated. I nodded. "What do you know of hind's blood?"

"I believe it has the power to kill a god or goddess," I replied.

"And you wish to use it against my brother?"

"I do. I believe it's the only way to stop him from ever taking Zeus' place as head of the gods and slaughtering those who don't agree to join him and aid him in his quest. I want to protect not only the gods and goddesses, but mortals as well; if Ares is successful then life for us all would be dire indeed."

The forest around us darkened and the nymphs lit torches and made small fires where they sat, the light reaching Artemis, Hephaestus and me even though we were standing quite a way from them.

"It is a bold request. The killing of a god by another is something that Father has strictly forbidden. I shall not go against him."

"We have Zeus' blessing if you are willing to gift us what we seek. You would not be expected to carry out the deed yourself; I will be the one to do it," I assured her, silently noting that she wasn't denying what the blood could do.

"Ares is a god, how do you expect to get close enough to get it into his blood? Do you seek to lift a glass with him in his honor, having added the blood to his skyphos? Or perhaps you intend to become amorous with the god of war and somehow trick him into ingesting it while you linger in his embrace?"

"Neither of those choices interest me," I replied. "But I can get close enough to do what is needed."

"I shall need time to consider it," Artemis said.

"I have never known you to defend Ares, Sister."

"Your words are true, Brother. But it pains me to know that my agreement would be responsible for robbing Ares of life. He has never done harm to me, indeed he barely acknowledges my existence, and never as kin as you and I do."

"But do you not see that this is how it must be?"

"I know you have had your issues with him for many winters, especially since he took Aphrodite from you, b–"

"Please, Goddess Artemis," I interrupted. "I beg you to agree to my request. We wouldn't be here if there was any other choice."

Artemis' large eyes returned to mine and her face hardened. "And why should I, Mortal? Whilst it is true that you prayed to me for protection when you bore your sons and your mother called for me when someone birthed you *and* your grandfather thanked me outside Sparta after your mother's birth, I do not see that you or your family have honored me in any other way. You built no temples or shrines to me, you did not worship me or send prayers and sacrifices for protection in battle. When you married, you were not chaste; you had partaken of a man's body before the blessed day."

"What happened in Konitsa between Ava and Demetri was not her fault, neither of them wished for their relationship to begin in such a manner," Hephaestus assured her. "It was Ares and his amulet that caused them to be together."

"I do not speak of the one who managed to capture her heart, Brother.

But of the men and women she was with before."

"When I served as a soldier?" I asked. Artemis nodded. "I didn't have a choice; such deeds were expected of me. To refuse would have offended my host and I would never have committed such an act."

"Were there not other ways you could have honored such hosts?" Artemis asked.

Hephaestus again intervened on my behalf. "She did not grow as other young women do, Artemis. She did not have her mother to teach her your ways of chastity and the protection of the same. She was not sent to your temple to serve you and learn of your ways when she reached the age."

The nymphs began to extinguish their fires and torches as the forest lightened around us once again and Artemis stared silently at me for many moments, her head tilted to one side as if she was listening to the wind in the trees around us. She finally gave a small nod of her head.

"Dear sister, when you were just a child in our father's lap, you asked him for a silver bow to aid you in your love of the hunt. Father asked me to oversee its production and I agreed, having Brontes, Arges and Steropes forge the weapon you now use with unnerving skill and precision. You said that one day you would repay me the debt of its creation and if you agree to aid us now, I would consider your debt clear."

"Before I make my final decision, I would consult with our father."

"I shall accompany you," Hephaestus offered.

"I shan't be long, I do not need you to escort me."

"I am afraid I do. Whilst it troubles me to consider, there is a chance you may go to our brother and tell him of our plans, and I cannot allow that."

"You hurt me with such words, Brother ..." she paused and tilted her head again. "Come, we shall go."

Hephaestus took Artemis' outstretched hand and before I could say anything they were gone.

As I waited for them to return, I took in the forest around me. The nymphs stayed where they were, peeking shyly from beneath long lashes or between strands of brown hair. I smiled and raised my hand in a wave but the movement sent them scuttling into the trees.

I lowered my hand again and leant against the nearest tree trunk, trying to remember who Brontes, Arges and Steropes were. It was a few moments before it came to me – they weren't men Hephaestus spoke of but the immortal Cyclopes. It was said that Zeus, Poseidon and Hades had freed them from the pit of Tartarus where the Titans had put them many winters before. In return, the Cyclopes made a weapon for each god; thunderbolts for Zeus, a trident for Poseidon and the helmet of invisibility for Hades.

The Cyclopes were twice as tall as Zeus or any of the Olympian gods, and had only one eye in the middle of their foreheads. They lived on the

Isle of Lipara, to the west of Greece's shores. Toiling there day after day in Hephaestus' forge, they were known not only as strong and mightily skilled craftsmen, but stubborn beasts quick to anger. The mortals of the area did not dare venture too close to their home where sparks and hot liquid often sprayed from the top of the mountains.

I hoped that Hephaestus' suggestion of the debt and Zeus' assurances, would be enough to convince Artemis to help us. I couldn't let Ares have the parts of the amulet, but without the hind's blood I had no idea how to defeat him. The Lernaean Hydra that had once guarded the entrance to the Underworld was said to have deadly blood but I'd never heard that its blood was fatal to gods, only mortals. Besides, Heracles had killed it and its hundred heads many winters before my birth.

Before I had the chance to consider it further, Hephaestus and Artemis returned, with light rather than sound, marking their arrival beside me. I immediately looked to Hephaestus, who only lifted his shoulder in response.

"It appears my father agrees that there is little else to be done about Ares," Artemis said, her voice grave. She took a deep breath before she continued. "If you are successful in taking my brother's life, I ask you never call on me for favor again. On the other hand if *he* defeats *you*, then I suspect neither you nor I shall see another winter in this world."

"I do not doubt it," I nodded.

The forest's light receded once more, and again the nymphs lit torches and fires. Artemis joined them, settling herself on the bright green grass in their midst and indicating I join her. I stepped between the young women and sat across from her.

"The blood of my hinds is not something I part with willingly," she said. "It is with a troubled heart that I even consider it." The goddess did indeed look troubled; a faint line marred her flawless forehead between her eyebrows and her mouth dipped ever so slightly at each corner.

Knowing she would be directly responsible for killing another god, her brother no less, would obviously weigh heavily on her long after I had carried out the deed. I could not tell her that I understood the sacrifice she would be making or how the decision would feel. Doing so was to risk her wrath as well as her denial of what I needed to stop Ares once and for all. If I was to get what I came for, I would have to convince the great goddess of the hunt to bestow it in a way that she could live with hereafter.

"What can I do to persuade you I am worthy enough of such a gift?" I asked.

Artemis was silent a long moment. "Before I name any such wish, I want to know *how* you learned of the hind's blood and the power it holds. I was quite unaware mortals knew of it."

I had to think for a moment. "I would've been … six winters old. My

105

friends and I were in the open grassed area between the barracks and Melas River at home in Trachis. Our horses disturbed a brown horned viper, the snake biting my mother's horse and killing her and the young boy – Tritonos – who was riding her. I raced over on my colt, Philo, but the viper rose up as we approached and I was thrown to the ground, knocked unconscious by the fall.

"When I woke, I learned my left arm and leg were broken and, if I wanted them to heal properly, I couldn't move them for over a moon. Being an active child, I couldn't stand the thought of staying still for so long, so Mumma told me stories. Her own father had told her about ancient heroes, so she started with those, adding in tales the healer of Trachis – Gnosidicus – had shared with her when she was recovering from wounds of her own. He spoke of the gods and the Titans that ruled before them and how Zeus defeated his father, sending him to Tartarus for all eternity.

"Gnosidicus spoke of his own heritage as well; that he was a descendant of Asclepius, God of Medicine and Healing and that he knew of a way to kill a god. Mumma was never convinced of the truth of the story and I too had my doubts. Until today, I have never spoken of the supposed power of the hind's blood, not even as just a fanciful story to keep my own children entertained. When I heard stories about Asclepius from others, I did wonder about the truth of the tale, but I never repeated it."

"What stories?" Artemis asked, as the sky around us brightened.

"Well, the story of Asclepius' birth is well-known," I replied. I paused but Artemis nodded for me to continue. "Apollo was in love with a mortal woman named Coronis and they spent many nights together until Apollo was called back to Olympos. While Apollo was away, Coronis fell in love with a mortal man named Ischys. A crow informed Apollo that Coronis had been unfaithful to him and Apollo flew into a rage, cursing the crow for not having pecked out Ischys' eyes before he saw Coronis. So fierce was Apollo's curse on the crow that it turned all the bird's white feathers black, and caused all crows from that time on to be black in color. Apollo's sister … er … you … felt Coronis' betrayal just as fiercely as your twin. You killed Coronis in revenge and threw her body onto a pyre. Apollo was devastated at Coronis' infidelity, but also distraught that he'd never look upon her face again, so he returned to see her one last time.

"When he saw Coronis' body through the flames of the pyre, he realized that she carried his child inside her and, working quickly and desperately, he freed his unborn son, giving him to the Centaur, Chiron, to care for and teach him about medicine. Chiron taught Asclepius everything he knew and helped him to become the talented healer he was."

"What about the story of Asclepius' death? Was that often spoken of as well?" Artemis asked.

"There are many versions of it," I nodded. "Some say it was Zeus himself who struck Asclepius down."

A small sigh escaped Artemis as she plucked at a piece of grass. "That is true. Asclepius' death was my fault and I wish, even to this day, that I had not asked him for the favor which caused my father to unleash the power of his thunderbolt." I held my breath, hoping the goddess would go on. "There were few men, mortal or immortal, that I trusted or called friend, but Hippolytus was one of them. When he was just a boy, he came to my temple. He wanted to serve me in the same manner young girls did. He vowed to protect his chastity and live only for the hunt. He promised to hold sacred all that I do and I accepted him with open arms. There were others who were not pleased with his choices, his stepmother Phaedra for one, and when he rejected her advances, she accused him of raping her. Hippolytus' father – Theseus – had him killed.

"I sought out Asclepius, who I learned had been given two vials of Gorgon blood by Athena; one was a deadly poison, the other was able to perform miraculous healing. He told me he had already brought two people back from the Underworld with it, so I asked him to bring Hippolytus back for me. Asclepius did as I asked and I sent Hippolytus across the sea to live with the Romans. For Asclepius' aid, I rewarded him with gold, which he planned to use to build a house with many rooms to treat up to a hundred patients at once.

"Unfortunately, Hades and my father discovered what Asclepius and I had done and neither was pleased. Hades was concerned that with this new power in the mortal realm, he would be denied the souls he had always received to place in the Elysium Fields or the pits of Tartarus, and that his power over the dead would be greatly diminished. Father on the other hand raged and said we had disrupted the natural order, that when someone found themselves in the Underworld, no matter the circumstances, they must stay there, and that those who did not would find themselves severely punished.

It was then he unleashed his thunderbolt on Asclepius and sent him to the Underworld, along with Hippolytus and the other two souls Asclepius had brought back. Father then found Athena and made her destroy all the remaining vials of Gorgon blood she had. He went to the Gorgons, telling them that if they ever gave their blood to a mortal or immortal, he would end their lives.

"When Apollo found out, he too was incensed, not at Asclepius and me, but at my father for killing his son without consultation. He did not dare kill the king of the gods, they feuded for a long time before Apollo finally told Father he understood why he had done what he had. Father conceded that Asclepius' talents as a healer were wasted in the Underworld and removed him again. He made Asclepius a god on the promise that he never spoke of hind's blood to the other immortals, and especially not to mortals."

"But how did Asclepius even know about the hind's blood?" I asked. "Obviously he broke his word to Zeus otherwise *I* wouldn't know the story. Why does Zeus still let him live on Olympos?"

"He never broke his word." It was Hephaestus who replied and I jumped at his voice; I had completely forgotten he was there.

13

Hephaestus sat beside Artemis and me, resting his back against a large boulder as he explained.

"Before Asclepius was made a god, he already knew the story of the hind's blood and spoke of it to his son. He did not break his word to Zeus; just failed to inform him that he had already told someone about it. As for how he learned of it, that was Apollo's doing. Apollo spoke of Artemis' deer and their blood to Asclepius so Zeus would make him an immortal upon his death. Zeus did not want such information to be known by just anyone, so Apollo used it to save his son from mortal death long before Asclepius learned to raise souls from the Underworld and incur Zeus' wrath."

Artemis took up the story. "When Asclepius was still just a boy, Apollo visited him at Chiron's. He told him of his heritage and how it was me who killed his mother for her betrayal of his father. Naturally, Asclepius was angry and promised to avenge his mother by killing me. Apollo told him he was to carry out no such act, that he was destined for far greater standing as a healer. He told Asclepius that he would save the lives of scores of mortals, finding new ways to heal both mind and body and that his sons, grandsons and many generations of his descendants would be known as the greatest healers ever to have lived. The lure of such promise tempered the child's wish for revenge and he promised his father that he would learn all he could from Chiron and make him proud.

"Winters later, Apollo returned to Asclepius and spoke of my golden hinds. Apollo told Asclepius that he did not speak of the power of the hind's blood so he could take his revenge on me, but so that when his mortal life came to an end, he could bargain with Zeus to make him immortal."

"Wasn't Apollo concerned that Asclepius would try to use the blood anyway?" I asked.

"No, by that time all Asclepius was concerned with was his medicines and helping his fellow mortals recover from the ailments which troubled them. He had indeed become a great healer, a respected healer, and he had no desire to stray from that path," Hephaestus replied.

"How many other gods know what hind's blood can do and when did you learn it was fatal to your kind?" I asked. The nymphs began their now-familiar ritual of lighting their torches and fires, and for the second time since I had left Thermopylae, a large, full moon graced the sky above.

Artemis was quiet a long moment before she spoke again. "I shall share those answers with you but when I have done so, you shall tell me *why* I should put my trust in a mortal. If I am satisfied with your answer, you can have what you came for, if not, you shall not leave my grove with your knowledge."

I swallowed loudly. "I ... I understand." She nodded in reply and drew a deep breath.

"The hinds were created long ago by Kronos. Kronos learned from his mother, Gaia, that he would be overthrown as king one day, just as he had taken the title from his father. He carried out many deeds hoping to prevent it."

"Like swallowing his children after his wife Rhea gave birth to them?" I interrupted.

"Yes, and by creating five deer whose blood was so toxic, it had the power to kill his immortal children," Artemis replied. "My father learned of their existence from Rhea after she gave Kronos a stone to swallow, instead of her youngest son. She told Zeus that if he helped her free his brothers and sisters and dispatch of his father for eternity, that she would allow him to have the deer for himself, to keep them safe."

"Why didn't Zeus destroy the deer so they could never be used against him or his brothers and sisters?"

"I do not know the answer to that. He was young so perhaps he believed he may need them one day to preserve his own status as king of the gods."

"Which it appears is exactly what has happened," Hephaestus mused.

"Indeed," Artemis agreed. "Rhea and Father decided they would not tell the other siblings of the power the deer held. They feared it would cause unnecessary fighting between them all and that the blood would be used unjustly. Most mortals believe that I captured the deer myself after I received my bow and arrow from the Cyclopes, but the truth is that my father entrusted me with them, and the secret of their blood, when I left Olympos and came here. He chose me because I had vowed to remain chaste, and so he believed that no man or woman – mortal or otherwise – would ever find their way to my bed where I may be prone to whispering secrets as we lay together. He also knew that I would never use the hind's blood against another god or goddess, no matter how they wronged me. He could not say that about the rest of his family."

"So how did Apollo find out and how did you?" I asked, addressing Hephaestus.

"Apollo heard Father and me speaking the day he gave them to me," Artemis replied. "But I swore him to secrecy and he promised to tell no other immortal."

"And Father had told me of them a winter earlier, when he had me make an impenetrable enclosure for them. It made him uneasy that such a powerful weapon was so near and he did not want harm to come to any of his children or kin," Hephaestus added.

"Oh," I murmured.

"So, now you know what we know – what few immortals and even fewer mortals do. Tell me, why are you, a mere mortal, worthy of the blood of my deer, of something so powerful it can end the life of a god? Why should I trust you with it and how can I be certain you shall not use it against me the first opportunity you get?"

I drew a breath and chose my words carefully. I would only have one chance to convince her I was worthy enough.

"My life, as that of many mortals and immortals, has not been easy. My mothers were taken from me when I had not yet reached my tenth winter and I became a soldier to escape the pain and loss of their deaths. My Mumma Skylar lost her own mother the night she was born and grew without her love and guidance. My grandmother Zita was a Ker, the last full Ker in the line of Ares' Chosen One and it was she who began the task of denying Ares what he most desired. For over fifty of our mortal winters, the women of my family have worked against the god of war to keep those in our world, and yours, safe.

"The night I was born, Ares and his Keres were in Trachis. They believed I was the Chosen One they had waited for, but I did not bear their three-sided mark as they expected, so they left. Nine winters later, Ares returned and killed my mothers because they refused to teach me his ways and to tell me of my ancestors.

"When Ares came for me in my nineteenth winter, my mark was fully formed; two three-sided shapes with the bottom line removed between and on my ribs rather than my left shoulder like my kin. I was strong enough to use all four elements of the amulet and I could've brought about what Ares wanted. I could've given him what he'd waited for. But I had the love of a grandfather who wouldn't let me give up what my mother and grandmother before me had started. And I fell in love with a runaway slave who brought their own special gifts to help me deny Ares of me, the power I held and his wish to be King of the Gods.

"This time will be no different, but I beg of you to let me have the hind's blood so I can keep all of us safe from Ares' evil plans, and to ensure it's the *last* time Ares tries to take Zeus' throne. I do this for Zeus, Hephaestus, you and the other immortals who would seek to stop him and I do it for my world where animals and beauty and kindness exist. I do this for me, for Demi and our children, but I also do it for every man, woman and child in the mortal world.

"Ares has taken almost everyone I hold dear from me, and he would do the same to you. If he's able to use the amulet and defeats Zeus, then your forests and your animals would all be killed, and how long do you think it would be before Asclepius or Apollo told him of your deer, or sought them out themselves? If Ares knew of them he would get what he wanted even quicker and I will not let that happen. I will not shy away from what must be done and I cannot fail.

"I have nothing more sacred than my word to give you and I beg you to believe that I have only the highest esteem for you and that I'd never harm you." I held my hand out and Artemis took it, holding my forearm with her cool, strong fingers. "Hear me now when I say that I, Ava, Queen of Thermopylae, promise never to threaten you, oh great goddess Artemis with the blood of your hinds. I will never use it to take your life. I will never destroy a god or goddess with the blood, other than Ares and I will never ask you for favor again. I give you my word and if I break this solemn vow, may I be sent to the deepest, darkest pit of Tartarus to spend the remainder of my days in eternal torment."

Artemis' green eyes searched my face as her fingers tightened ever so slightly on my arm. "You speak of Skylar's line as though you share blood with her. With them. But was it not Alexis' body you grew inside?" she asked.

"I cannot explain it any simpler than that part of Mumma Skylar and part of my father, Thaddeus, were taken and put into Mother Alexis' belly. I was created from that and the blood of all three flows through me. It was Hera who saw it done."

"I see," she murmured, releasing my arm. Artemis held my gaze for only a moment longer before turning to Hephaestus and speaking so quickly that I couldn't catch even one word she said. Hephaestus replied just as swiftly and looked to me as Artemis pushed herself to her feet, the first ray of dawn lighting the forest around us.

"It appears you have managed to convince my sister of your worthiness, despite her misgivings," Hephaestus announced.

I lowered my head to Artemis, getting to my feet and releasing the breath I hadn't realized I'd been holding. "Thank you, my goddess," I murmured.

"I shall allow you to gather the blood you seek from my deer, but you must take only the amount I allow you to have and no more."

"Of course," I replied. "I have no use for more than what's required for the task I have to carry out."

"I am pleased to hear that. You shall gather the blood from my deer, just one drop from each. But, as I am certain you can appreciate, you shall receive no assistance in the retrieval from Hephaestus or me."

"I understand," I replied, not wanting either to be harmed. "How do I catch them? I understand your deer are fleet of foot and took Heracles a winter to catch just one of them. I don't have such time to spend on it."

"I shall assist you in their capture," Artemis replied.

She disappeared, returning almost immediately with four of her five deer. She gave a gentle tug on the ropes that held them and they joined the one that had remained at Artemis' side while we spoke. She produced another piece of cord and tied it around the fifth deer's neck, handing the ropes to me.

Each animal was a slightly different color across the head, back and stomach, although the brightly shimmering golden horns and bronze hooves were identical. The original deer was a reddish-brown and had spots of pure white along its flank and down to its tail. The tail itself, and the underside of its body, were white, its large brown eyes watching me carefully. The second and third deer were the same color as the first, although they had no spots on their flanks. The last two were slightly smaller than the others, and had brown rather than red running the length of their backs. Their tails and stomachs were not as bright as their companions; they were instead the color of a white chiton after a day of traipsing through the dry dust of the agora or along the narrow paths of Thermopylae.

I tethered each of the magnificent animals to a nearby tree, my heart beating fast beneath my chest, knowing how close I was to an animal so rare, and that would be misused by so many, if they knew about it.

Artemis and Hephaestus stood on the other side of the glade and Artemis' nymphs had joined them there, their faces a cross between apprehension and curiosity.

"How do I take just the one drop from each?" I asked.

"Make a hole above the back of the hoof with the tip of your sword. There is only a little blood there and it shall drip slowly enough for you to catch it in this," Artemis replied, throwing me a small amphora.

I caught the clay container in one hand; it was a sturdy piece, similar in design to the amphorae used to transport olive oil or wine on ships or from the agora, only much smaller. It fit into the palm of my hand and had a lid made of wood and twine to keep the contents safely inside.

I tucked it into the leather belt at my waist before unsheathing my sword. The deer shifted uncomfortably around me but I spoke quietly to them, much as I had done when I first tried to convince Philo that my intention was not to harm him, but to befriend him. Of course in this case, that would not be entirely true, but I hoped the pain I caused the hinds would be fleeting.

I approached the smaller, light brown specimen its eyes large within the white patches around them. I reached out and rested my palm against its short, course coat. The deer calmed almost immediately and I drew my hand from head to tail in long strokes, watching as the hairs smoothed then returned to position.

As I had with Philo when he had stones caught in his hooves, I ran my hand down the hind leg of the deer, drawing my sword higher as I brought its hoof off the ground.

I continued to reassure it, but paused, turning my head to address Artemis. "I won't be harmed if I touch the blood, will I?"

"No, the blood appears only fatal to gods," she replied.

"I hope that's true," I muttered.

I closed my eyes and took a deep breath. Opening them, I brought my sword down, piercing the skin of the deer with the very tip. The animal screeched, splitting the calm of the forest around us and sending the others into a panic. I dropped my sword to the ground and gripped the hoof tight, freeing the amphora from my belt. I held the container beneath the hole as the deer bucked wildly in my grip, its antlers narrowly missing me as it reared its head in an attempt to break free.

A single drop emerged from the skin and I scooped it into the mouth of the amphora, pushing the wood into the top and sealing it tight. I released the deer's foot and, careful to avoid its antlers, picked up my sword, splitting the rope and freeing it from the tree. It took off into the dense woodland, still screeching and snorting as it ran far from me and my weapon. Artemis raised her hand, shooting something into the forest. It must have hit the deer, for all at once its cries quieted. My eyes snapped to the goddess and I was surprised when she smiled.

"I healed his leg. You must hurry if you want to extract blood from each of them; they now sense the fear of their brother and shall not make it easy for you."

I nodded and held my sword up again, choosing the next deer. It moved away as I approached, but I followed, barely attempting to calm it as I picked up its hoof. It was reluctant to comply, but I soon had it firmly in my grasp and drove the tip of my sword in, gathering the blood as I had the first.

I continued with the last three, slicing through their bindings and setting them free when I had the blood so Artemis could heal them. I replaced the wooden lid of the amphora and secured it with its twine, before taking one of the frayed ends of rope from the tree and separating it into individual strands. I checked the strength of one strand and, satisfied that it would do the job, pulled it from the rest, tying one end around the mouth of the amphora and the other to my leather belt.

"I see you are a queen of your word, Ava," Artemis said, as she and Hephaestus approached me again.

I only nodded. "I thank you most sincerely for the hind's blood and I hope you won't be offended when I say that Hephaestus and I must return now to Thermopylae."

"I understand, and I believe your presence there would be much appreciated by your soldiers."

I dipped my head to her once again as Hephaestus stepped to his sister and grasped her tightly. "Stay safe, and know that you have done a great service to all of us. Ares shall not defeat our father and he shall not be permitted to destroy the world and all the beauty it holds."

"I wish you luck my brother, and wish the same safety for you. When Ares learns of our betrayal, he shall not show us mercy, as we have not shown him any thus far." Hephaestus nodded silently as he released Artemis. "Good luck to you, Mortal. I wish you and your family well both now and in the future," Artemis added.

"Thank you again, great Artemis," I replied, bowing to her. I held my hand out to Hephaestus. "Let's go get the sword, then we have a defense to mount and a battle to win."

He nodded in reply and took my hand, my eyes closing automatically when my feet lifted off the ground.

14

When my feet touched down again I opened my eyes, instantly drawing my sword as I took in the sight around me. Thousands of bodies lay strewn across the Pass of Thermopylae. Rich red stained the dirt from the west gate, along the beach and into the sea of the middle gate, the last rays of sunlight peeking over the mountains bathing the Pass in a red hue which only enhanced the bloody scene. The battle had clearly been fierce but I was heartened to see more fallen men and weapons from the Persian army than the Greek.

"The battle has begun," Hephaestus murmured.

"So it would seem," I replied.

"Ares is here," Hephaestus whispered.

"No doubt he can feel the sword." I held my newer sword out to him. "Let's swap them now and then you should go."

"Do you truly believe this is the best course of action?" Hephaestus asked, reluctantly taking the weapon from his orange chiton.

"I do," I replied, wrapping my hand around the once-familiar hilt.

It felt good to hold my old sword again. The leaf-shaped blade was still sharp and deadly, weighted perfectly by the pommel at the opposite end where long ago the jet from the amulet had been encased. The hematite had been mixed with iron and held the guard and blade together but it was impossible to tell there were two separate materials. The length of leather which had once held the amulet around my neck was wrapped around the hilt to help with the grip of the weapon.

"Go far from here, if Ares somehow gets what I have, I don't want him to use it against you," I said, sheathing the sword.

"I shall not be far, you need only call for me and I shall return."

"I appreciate everything you've ever done for me, for Demetri, for Demi. We wouldn't be here if it wasn't for you," I said. "But if I fall by Ares' hand before I carry out my plan, you have to get the sword before he does. Put it back where it's been hidden all this time and ensure he never finds it. Protect our family. Don't let Ares find them or harm them."

"It shall be done, you can be assured of that," Hephaestus replied. We embraced one another as someone called my name.

I released Hephaestus and turned, finding Moeris and Leonidas rushing towards me, their eyes scanning the area as they approached. Both still carried their shields and weapons and were covered in blood which didn't seem to be theirs.

"Thank the gods you have returned," Moeris said, nodding briefly in Hephaestus' direction. "We were worried you had been captured by Ares or killed."

"My journey took longer than I had hoped. I saw the beginning of the new moon but we couldn't return until we had what we needed."

"The new moon?" Moeris asked. "You have only been gone six days, but I assure you, we could have used your expertise and skills many a time."

"Six days?" I asked.

"Time with the gods moves at a different pace than in the mortal realm," Hephaestus reminded me.

I should've remembered; many winters ago Ares told me that waiting nineteen mortal winters for my mother, and then me, to be strong enough to use the amulet was a great deal longer than he was used to. Now I understood; a moon to the gods was only a week to us.

"The Persians did not attack right away; they waited four days, perhaps believing we would reconsider Xerxes' offer and surrender ourselves to him. But after dawn yesterday, they came. Their numbers were great, but we were mightier and when they sent in their Immortals, we did not flee in terror, we felled them just as we had the others," Moeris reported.

"How have our men fared? I see a lot of Persian soldiers lying on the ground here, where are the rest of our soldiers?"

"They wait by the water and in the hills around us, more stand at intervals along the wall. We lost many, but less than the Persians."

"I shall take my leave," Hephaestus said. "Here, put the amphora in this and tie it around your neck, you do not wish for harm to come to it if you have to battle. Remember, you only need call my name and I shall return."

Hephaestus put the small pouch I had once used to carry my mother's amulet in my hand and gave me a tight smile. I nodded in response and did as he said, tucking the pouch and its precious contents beneath my cuirass.

He disappeared and almost immediately Ares arrived, materializing behind Moeris. I took Moeris' arm, drawing him towards me, before doing the same with Leonidas.

"What is it?" Moeris asked, turning.

When his eyes settled on the god of war, he held his sword higher. "Ares," he muttered.

"I see you have the sword," Ares grinned, his eyes finding my sheathed weapon. "I am glad you changed your mind."

I drew it from its holder and held the iron blade up, catching a ray of sunlight and covering his chest with the wide slant. "I wanted to prove to you how wrong you are about it."

"Give it to me and I shall prove how wrong *you* are for I believe our time together is at an end."

"Not yet. You've sent Persians to my home and I will not gift you the sword before I've had a chance to use it against them. You ensured I hated them, that that hate burned within me for winters, even after I learned they weren't actually responsible for my mothers' deaths. Now you present me with another opportunity to send them to Hades and I will not be denied of that."

"You continue to surprise me," Ares laughed. "And I do so enjoy watching you fight, so I shall grant you your request. For a short time at least."

"General!"

We all turned as a young Athenian soldier ran toward us, jumping over fallen warriors as he neared He was covered with blood and dirt and a gash above his left eye leaked red down his cheek. Moeris stepped out to meet him.

"General, the Persians are retreating, we can claim victory here at the Pass, just as Queen Ava said we could," he panted, a smile stretching across his white teeth.

Ares laughed again. "You foolish boy. The Persians do not run away after only two days of fighting, though the Greeks have lasted longer than Xerxes expected."

"What is Xerxes' plan?" I asked, raising my sword in Ares' direction.

He held his hands up, keeping well away from the pointed end as he replied. "You have a deserter amongst you. A young man named Ephialtes told Xerxes of the mountain path and he leads the remaining Immortals and scores of soldiers up there as we speak. They shall soon outflank you and crush your defenses."

"We need to send all the men to the east gate at once," Leonidas urged.

"No, that could be Xerxes' plan," I replied, halting him with a hand on his arm. "We can't trust Ares' word. Xerxes might have it seem like they're retreating to outflank us but when we send all our resources to the east gate,

Xerxes' men could flood in from their original position, spearing us in our backs as we await their arrival from the opposite direction."

"I agree," Moeris added. "I shall send some men to the entrance of the west gate, just as before. Leonidas bring your Spartans, and I shall gather the remaining Thespians, Thebans and my men. We shall take to the wall and guard the east gate. No Persian shall get past us, unless we wish it to be so."

"Good. Kolonos Hill will provide you with the best vantage point behind the wall and Mount Kallidromon is also close by. Send the Phocians along the path through the mountains to delay the Persian arrival."

Ares laughed again. "You shall have plenty of time to form your defense, however inadequate it is. The Persians march quickly and strongly, but they do not intend to attack until the sun touches the water in ten candlemarks."

"We will be more than ready for them," I growled.

"Perhaps. But when they burst through your lines – and they shall burst through your lines – you have a candlemark to send as many of them as you can to the Underworld before you and I finish what we began so long ago."

I turned to Moeris and Leonidas. "Go, I'll meet you at Kolonos Hill and together we'll repel the enemy." They both nodded and took off, taking the young soldier with them. "You told Ephialtes about the path," I stated.

"*Reminded* him," Ares replied with a grin. "It is surprising how easy mortals are persuaded to turn on their own people when gold is involved."

"Yo–" I began, but he disappeared. I yelled in frustration and ran towards Kolonos Hill, gathering as many able-bodied soldiers from the battlefield as I could.

15

Leonidas and I leant against the solid stone wall that threaded its way over Kolonos Hill. Torches lit the area around us and almost a thousand men stood, barely speaking, scanning the darkness outside the wall for any sign of the traitor and his new Persian friends.

Behind us, the hill descended into a wide, open field before meeting the shoreline. If the Persians tried to come over the wall instead of continuing to the east gate, there would be more than enough room for us to form our phalanx and crush them against the stonework.

"You were able to gather all you needed whilst you were gone?" Leonidas asked, his eyes finding mine.

I preferred speaking to him in this half-light, his eyes were not such a vivid blue to remind me of those that I had loved so dearly and lost so cruelly. "Yes but let's not speak of it; it's of no importance to this battle with the Persians," I replied.

"As you wish," he nodded, taking no offence at my answer.

"Tell me, why did you agree to come here if you are now king of the great Sparta?"

"For many of the same reasons I suspect I find you still here. I love Greece with all my heart and it angers me when those from across the sea attempt to take her from our rule. Gods know, we quarrel enough between ourselves without having to defend our shores from those further away."

"That is true," I agreed.

"At least our hatred of the Persians has seen us come together; Spartan,

Athenian, Thessalian, Boeotian, it matters not where we call home, for we stand as one against the yellow caps and their desire for our lands."

I nodded my response, understanding how the Spartan people would've been persuaded to choose Leonidas as leader, regardless of his lineage. His way with words was similar to Moeris' and he could've easily rallied his people or his soldiers to stand beside him in whatever cause he asked of them.

A young soldier from Thespiae joined us at the wall, laying his black shield with the picture of the half-moon against the stonework. He nodded to Leonidas and me and began to repair his spear, which showed many notches and dents along the length of its handle. I looked down at the shield, thinking of Aphrodite. I could not help wondering if, when the young Boeotian prayed to the goddess of love for assistance and protection in this battle, would he by extension be praying to Ares with *his* belief of a Persian victory?

I shook my head to dislodge the thought, but it occurred to me that Aphrodite could have been the one who freed Ares from the cage. The strength of her love for Ares was well known – the story went that she and Hephaestus had hardly been paired together by Zeus before she returned to Ares' arms, often inviting her lover to her bed while Hephaestus was away at one of his forges. If Aphrodite had somehow found out Hephaestus was holding her lover captive then it was also possible she'd found a way to release him. When I spoke to Hephaestus again I'd let him know my suspicion.

I cleared my throat and indicated the shield against the wall. "Have you prayed much to your goddess for protection in this battle?" I asked the Thespian soldier.

The young warrior cast his eyes to his shield briefly before meeting mine again. "I do not pray for such aid. I do not fear for what happens in this battle, nor others I may find myself in. I, as all my tribe do, walk towards my fate without thoughts of returning alive. Aphrodite loves me dearly and I know that when my time in this world is done, she will gather me in her arms to love and care for me forever more."

Before I could do more than raise my eyebrows at his words, the young man took his shield and moved off to join his fellow countrymen further down the wall.

A thoughtful look crossed my uncle's face as he watched him go before he addressed me again. "My decision to be here is not just because I am king. It is also based on word I received from the Delphic Oracle. The Oracle said I must choose; either I could allow Sparta to fall beneath Persian sandals or I could throw myself headlong into battle, with the knowledge that I would never return home to my wife and young son. The Oracle said nothing would stop the Persians marching through our lands until one of those two outcomes were achieved. So here I am, determined to stand and fight for as long as I am able before I surrender to Hades in the Underworld. I do this willingly, here in Thermopylae, rather than sitting at home and waiting for the Persians to tarnish Spartan soil. I do this so no Greek ever has to bow down to Xerxes or his men, so that future generations of Persians know the might of Greece and do not seek to take our lands from us again. I will not celebrate my victory with my soldiers or my family. It is not my fate to do so."

I didn't know how to respond, but I recognized the set of his jaw and knew he wouldn't change his mind; he would not save his own life just so he could watch his beloved Sparta fall. Perhaps that was why he'd only asked for Spartiates to join him; perhaps he didn't think it was fair to ask young men to fight alongside him when they had no one to carry on their name. I couldn't fault him for those decisions but I hoped he and the oracle were wrong – that Greece *could* be victorious here in Thermopylae and Leonidas would return to Sparta with his shield. I wanted the chance to get to know him properly.

Neither of us spoke for a long while but it was me who finally broke the silence. "If I'm unsuccessful in what I have planned, then I don't think I'll be returning to my family either," I told him.

He only nodded in reply, neither of us willing to voice any other regrets we may have.

I caught his eye and gave him a tight grin. "We should get some rest, we have a long day tomorrow and need to be at our best if we're to bring about Greece's glorious victory."

"Until the morning," he agreed with a single nod.

I leant my aspis against a nearby tree trunk and settled myself against the rough bark, placing my sword beside me as I closed my eyes. Images of Demi, Zenon and Kadmus floated through my mind and I sent out a silent prayer to them, hoping they were safe and comfortable wherever Hephaestus had taken them. I didn't expect to sleep much during the night but I knew I needed to get at least a few candlemarks if I was to hold my own against the Persians.

Hypnos was kind and found me quickly.

16

"What is it?" I asked, instantly awake, my hands reaching for my weapons.

It was still dark, but the torches illuminated soldiers running to the wall and the east gate in a great flurry of movement.

"The Phocians met the Persians on the mountain path, but fled as cowards," Moeris replied, taking his hand from my shoulder and gripping my outstretched arm, pulling me to my feet. "We find our enemies have almost reached the east gate and I fear we do not have enough men to repel them now."

I hadn't slept well; my dreams full of old memories and voices and it took me a moment to remember what Moeris was talking about. I'd dreamt of a time when I was not a soldier, when I was not a lover, a mother or wife. Back when I didn't know I was Ares' Chosen One and my mothers were both still alive.

I shook my head to clear the images and belted my sheath around my waist. I picked up my aspis and slipped my arm through the handholds, drawing my sword and flexing my hand around the hilt.

I spoke as I followed Moeris towards the east gate. "We just need to hold them back, I still believe Xerxes will send the bulk of his men in the west gate, his cavalry wouldn't have joined the march through the mountains, so maybe there aren't many with their Immortals. Yesterday you told me you cut the Immortals down just like you did the other soldiers and today I fight with you, we will defeat them."

Before I could add anything further, a cry went up from the gate. Twenty or thirty enormous Persian soldiers broke through the defense. They crashed through our startled soldiers, using their shoulders, metal armor and wicker shields to drop them to the ground. They pulled axes from their belts and cut down the nearest man while the next wave, dressed in leather armor over their colored chitons, spread out rapidly and drew arrows across their bows, firing them into the nearest of our soldiers and felling them with deadly accuracy.

I tightened my grip on my weapons and charged towards the nearest Persian; a giant of a man with an axe in one hand and a short spear in the other. He saw me coming and fended off my attack with the handle of his spear, swinging wildly towards my stomach with the axe in his other hand. I jumped back as the head narrowly missed my bronze cuirass and jabbed my sword at him again, finding the meaty flesh of his thigh. He dropped to the ground, still swinging his axe, as blood spurted from his wound. It stained the ground thoroughly and I drew my sword across his neck, preventing him from returning to the battle or to Xerxes and his homeland.

With blood thumping loudly in my ears I turned my attention to the next soldier, taking his legs from beneath him and driving my sword into his chest when he fell. The next I relieved of his hand, along with the bow that was drawn tight in it. Driving my sword into him again when he met the ground before moving onto the next enemy.

Chest heaving, I cut my way through countless more Persian soldiers, taking a steadying breath when an even larger man approached. He spat loudly on the ground beside us, blood tinging his spittle from a blow he'd received to his lip. He was a much worthier opponent than the others I'd already faced. He blocked and parried with deft skill, thrusting both his shield and spear towards me with precision and outwardly little effort expended. Our weapons met with metallic rings, mixing with sounds of the same from the soldiers around us.

This soldier was just like we'd heard – a true Persian Immortal, favored by Xerxes for his skill and strength. I knew I would have to concentrate hard and rely on skills I hadn't been challenged to use in a long time to deny him his victory over me.

We traded blows, metal hitting metal, ducking, weaving and raising dirt, sweat dripping from us as we fought. Twice his spear found my skin, drawing thin lines of blood across my arm until I relieved him of it. I'd believed the advantage to be mine, but he found a discarded axe on the ground and continued to attack with it. The axe sliced through the air and had it connected with any part of my body, I doubted I would've been able to continue.

My arms started to shake, my shield heavy on my arm as I defended the constant attacks. Each time his axe hit my sword it reverberated through my entire body and I realized that I didn't possess the stamina of battle I once had. I frowned, drawing on my wits and inner strength and set to work, attacking rather than defending. Unfortunately my movements were not fluid and I stumbled as a wild swing meant for the soldier's neck unbalanced me. I had barely regained my footing when he charged for me, I waited until the last moment before spinning out of his way, but his shield glanced mine and I reeled unsteadily. He took advantage, approaching me again as I brought my sword up. He was on me in moments, and far too close for me to stab at him with any power. For the first time in battle, fear invaded my thoughts and I found myself frozen in place.

Suddenly the soldier gave a startled yell and his eyes rolled up into his head. He fell forward and the movement drew me out of my inertia. I jumped out of the way, finding Ares standing where the Persian had, sword bloodied and a grin on his face.

"You appear to be out of practice, my queen," he said, stepping forward and touching the tip of his sword to mine.

"Perhaps it is just a ruse to fool my enemy," I replied.

"Perhaps," Ares acknowledged. "But I do not think so."

He took one hand from his sword and, with beams of light as long as pieces of string, he picked up the Persian and flung him away as though he was a child's plaything. The soldier crashed into a pack of men – some of his own, some of ours.

"It's time we finished this," I said, pressing my sword against Ares'.

He gripped his sword in both hands again, head tilted as he spoke. "With a sword fight, just as we did on Olympos? You place much trust in that old sword."

"Why not? You think the power that runs through it has been lost to me. I, on the other hand, am not convinced. But go on, if the power I had has truly gone then you need only wave your hand and you would possess it rather than me … perhaps you know you can't control the sword. Perhaps you're *afraid* if you hold it, the power will turn on you and you'll end up back in a cage, or somewhere even worse?"

His smile disappeared. "I am not afraid to hold your sword." To prove his point, he took one hand from his own weapon and tried to call mine to him. It stayed where it was.

"It seems like the power isn't lost to me after all," I grinned.

"Or perhaps it is only Hephaestus' blood running through it that keeps it in your grasp."

"Maybe," I acknowledged. "And if that's the case then I request your permission to anoint my sword for … luck before we face one another in our final battle."

Ares laughed and dropped his sword to his side, leaning on its pommel as he pushed it into the dirt. "You mortals are strange creatures at times."

I took the pouch from beneath my armor, drawing the amphora of hind's blood from it.

"What is that?"

"Blood," I replied with a shrug.

He laughed again. "Does my brother's blood require replenishing after all these winters? Does his influence become impotent when it is not used?"

I smiled but said nothing. I crouched down and carefully tipped the five drops I had collected onto the blade of my sword. Soldiers continued to fight around Ares and I and I hoped we weren't in danger of taking a stray spear or axe.

I drew my finger through the blood and along the blade, surprised at the way it immediately spread itself across the width. I turned my sword over, finding it had made its way through to the other side, beading on the surface as though I had already placed drops there.

I stood, dropping the amphora in the dirt and crushing it beneath my sandal. I faced Ares, holding my sword in his direction once more.

"It's not Hephaestus' blood I honor my sword with, but hind's blood. Are you familiar with what it can do?"

"What it is *rumored* to do," Ares corrected, his smile faltering ever so slightly. "I have heard stories, but I gave no truth to them. If I had, I would have disposed of the animals long ago, along with my *sister* if she had attempted to stop me."

"Your disbelief is to your detriment now," I grinned.

Ares returned my smile and flicked his hand to disarm me just as he had before. I opened my mouth to mock his attempt, but the sword broke free of my grip and landed in his palm.

"No! How did you do that?" I screamed, flailing uselessly after my weapon.

Ares laughed, throwing his own sword away and halting my approach with a sudden burst of purple light. It engulfed me, lifting me from the ground and trapping me inside. It wasn't the first time I'd seen Ares use it and I knew my attempts to break free would be useless.

"It appears the blood of Artemis' hinds does indeed have power, but not the kind you were led to believe. Did you not feel the moment the sword lost Hephaestus' protection?" I shook my head. "Well I did and I am certain my brother did too, but he shall not interfere."

Ares raised his palm again, revealing the foot thick shield that surrounded us. Soldiers slammed against it, driven by the thrusts of their enemies. Leonidas approached at a run. He raised his sword, intending to break through, but was thrown backwards, landing heavily in the dirt with a puff of dust.

"Leonidas, no!" I cried as he got up and rushed forward again. He smashed his weapons against it time and again until finally he was beset by six Persians. He slashed at them with his shield and sword, felling several in his attempt to get to me. "Don't try to free me. Save yourself. Save Greece," I screamed. My pleas went unheard and Leonidas was overcome by the Persian soldiers.

Nikomachos came to Leonidas' aid, driving his spear and bloodied sword through enemy sides and stomachs. "No, Leonidas, no," I wept, pounding my fists against the bubble that held me as I sank to my knees.

Nikomachos felled the soldiers above Leonidas, but the more he killed, the greater the number that swarmed towards them. The Persians disarmed my uncle, taking limbs and weapons indiscriminately as they attacked the brave Spartan king. Leonidas' body stilled, the axes and spears sticking out of his body and I lost sight of him and Nikomachos in the melee.

"Such a shame," Ares murmured, bringing my thoughts back to him and the awful knowledge that he now held the only weapon I had to defeat him with.

I got to my feet, placing my hands on the inside of the bubble and glaring at the god of war.

He drew his hand down the blade, turning his palm to me to show how much hind's blood he had removed. "This blood holds no power for you. You, your mother and her mother have all denied me what I wanted for too long, but finally, you shall stop me no more. Finally I shall have what I want."

"You can't have what you wish for Ares, don't you see that? I won't let you become ruler of the gods."

"And how do you plan to stop me? You speak brave words, yet you are trapped, and there is no way for you to get free unless I wish for it to be so."

"Release me so we can do battle in a fair fight so the victor can say he or she won fairly."

Ares grinned again and shook his head. "No. I do not see that happening. I intend to take what is mine and if I have to keep you there so you cannot stop me, then I shall," he shrugged.

Ares drove my sword into the ground and knocked the pommel from the end. Gripping it between his thumbs and forefingers, he broke it in two and freed the jet hidden there. He then turned his attention to the guard, snapping the hilt from it like it was a twig. He ripped the guard from the blade and looked at me, triumphant.

I held my aspis tight against my left side as my breath faltered. I stepped backwards until my shoulders touched the other side of the sphere before rushing forward, slamming my shield against the colored cage that held me. I bounced off, the reverberation far greater than anything the giant Persian had inflicted, but I kept my footing.

Ares laughed when I ran forward again, crashing against the side and trying to weaken its hold. Hephaestus appeared in a flash of light, banging his fists on Ares' shimmering shield, but that too was to no avail. Ares turned to his brother, indicating my dismantled sword and holding the pieces of amulet up, a victorious grin crossing his face. Hephaestus yelled loudly, threatening Ares with every punishment he could think to name as finally Ares released me from the bubble that held me aloft.

17

"I have waited so long for this day," Ares said. "Once I believed I needed someone to aid me in my desire to become King of the Gods, but now I realize that all I ever needed was myself."

"You haven't won, Ares," I panted, getting to my feet.

"No? And how do you intend to stop me? You no longer have the pieces of the amulet."

He was right and I had no idea how to deny him of anything anymore but ... perhaps if I could distract him, Hephaestus would find a way through the larger shield around us.

"How did you get free from the cage?" I asked, bringing my aspis back across my left side.

Ares smiled, slipping the jet and hematite into his leather vest and picking up his sword from the dirt. He spun it around his hand and held it up to face me. "I wondered when you were going to ask me that," he smiled. "You are not the only one who is looked fondly upon by a god, or in my case, a goddess."

"Aphrodite," I breathed.

"Naturally. When she learned that my brother had aided you on Olympos, she knew he must be behind my disappearance. She searched and searched, until finally she found me."

"But how did she get you out? Hephaestus assured me there was no way you, or any immortal, could break those bars."

"He spoke true, believe me, I wasted much time and energy attempting to. No, my clever lover had Hephaestus plied with enough of Dionysius' strongest wine that he would tell her anything she wanted to know; and that knowledge led her to the key that fit the lock on my cage."

"Hephaestus would've never invited Aphrodite into his home, he's never forgiven either of you for the betrayal and shame you brought him with your affair," I argued.

"He would if she appeared to him in the guise of another – say a follower of Dionysius who brought the great god of the forge some of the finest wine as a token of their continued friendship?"

I opened and closed my mouth. It was indeed possible that Aphrodite was able to trick Hephaestus in such a way; after all, Dionysius *had* helped Hephaestus long ago and Hephaestus had often spoken of his respect for the wine god.

"So the two of you are reunited. Is she with you now – to see you become what you've always wanted?"

"No, a battlefield is no place for one of such beauty and when I eventually rise as king, it shall not be here in the mortal realm, but on Olympos where all the gods shall bow before me or die by my hand."

Hephaestus threw fireball after fireball against the shield, but still it didn't break.

"*When* you rise as king? Now that you have the amulet pieces aren't you going to seek your new position immediately? Or are you afraid that too many of your kin will still see you as an unworthy leader and laugh at your attempt?" I taunted.

Ares was instantly at my side, his muscular arm holding me motionless against his chest as the blade of his sword pressed against my throat. "We are done now, you and I," he whispered. "You shall defy me no more. You shall not stand in my way and play havoc with my plans. Once you were my Chosen One and I would have given you anything you desired. Now you are nothing to me ... Brother," he called. Hephaestus held back his next attack, eyes widening when he saw how Ares held me. "You bettered me once by aiding this mortal, but now you shall watch her die and when I become king I shall come for you and destroy you, along with our sister, and her hinds. You shall suffer my wrath and I give you my word, it shall be worse than anything you have ever suffered before."

"Ares, do not do this," Hephaestus begged. "You have what you want, release Ava and I promise that when the time comes we shall both submit to whatever you ask of us."

"I will not," I insisted. My heart hammered beneath my chest, but my voice was still strong.

I had once believed Ares wouldn't kill me – that I was too important to him – but now ... I knew he truly believed he didn't need me. I was nothing to him. He hadn't hesitated to kill Papou to get what he wanted from me and now he held me behind a shield that no god or mortal could break to get to us. He was done.

"Always so ready to defy me," Ares mused, amusement rather than malice in his voice. "But this ends now." He released his grip at my throat and pushed me forward. One pace from him was all I managed before he drove the cold, hard steel of his sword into my back and out through my stomach, slicing through the bronze cuirass as if I wasn't wearing it at all.

For a moment it felt like a light breeze had found its way beneath my tunic on a summer's day, caressing my stomach with its coolness. Then the searing, hot pain infused my blood and I screamed.

"No!" Hephaestus roared, helpless to do anything from his place.

Ares ripped the sword from me and I looked down as my hands found the gaping mess of my wound beneath the bronze. A myriad of sensations engulfed me; pain, anger, despair, loss. I stumbled towards Hephaestus, coughing. Blood flew from my lips, staining my chin and the ground as I willed my legs to carry me just a little further. I could not die. I couldn't let Ares win. I had to reach Hephaestus; somehow he would help me.

I could hear Ares' slow footfalls behind me as I stumbled and collapsed to my knees. Rich red covered my hands, spilling out onto the dirt in front of me and I pressed painfully against the hole, wishing I could stop it from leaking out so fast.

Ares knelt beside me, lifting my chin until our eyes met. "With your death, the amulet's power shall be restored to me and I shall rule both my realm and yours, as I always intended. Once it would have been you by my side, immortal and magnificent. Instead you are here; mortal, weak, dying. You are nothing."

"Then why prolong it? What are you waiting for?" I gasped.

Ares smiled, lifting his sword and running it through me again, twisting it as he snarled.

I opened my mouth but whatever words I had intended for the god of war caught on the blood filling my throat. I coughed, bringing up more of it and spitting it out. I tried to take a deep breath through my nose, but my chest constricted against the effort.

Ares pulled out his weapon and got to his feet, dropping a coin beside me. "I shall tell Hades to expect you soon," he said. "You were always a worthy adversary, but your reliance on immortal aid has only seen you defeated this time."

"I … will … find a … way," I choked.

"It is over," Ares replied and with those words, he disappeared, as did the shield around us.

Hephaestus was immediately by my side and I slumped against him. "We must … not let him … have…" I started as a shimmer caught the corner of my eye.

"Hush, save your strength, I shall take you to Zeus, he shall heal you," Hephaestus said.

"The shield …" I whispered. Hephaestus looked up, seeing what I had; Ares had trapped us inside again.

He closed his eyes, his brow furrowing slightly. "I cannot break through Ares' defenses, but my father shall come to us." The words were barely spoken when a flash of blinding light lit the area.

I craned my neck to see Zeus join us on Kolonos Hill, a deep scowl creasing his perfect forehead. He held a thunderbolt in his hand. He met my eyes briefly before raising the long spear and striking the shimmering field around us, breaking through it with only two hits and arriving at my side before I blinked again.

I tried to speak, but my voice died in my throat and Zeus put his hand on my shoulder to quiet me.

"Please, you must heal her, Father," Hephaestus said.

Zeus turned to him and spoke in the same rapid manner that Hephaestus and Artemis had spoken in her forest. I tried to make out what they were saying but a wave of nausea swept over me. I closed my eyes, memories, voices and faces from the past filling my vision.

The first time I saw Philo, his skin slick and dark with the wetness of his birth, his wide brown eyes watching me with curiosity as his mother licked him clean.

My first day at the barracks; Lysistratos and I paired together as we showed the gathered crowd why we had been chosen to join our army. I got the first win, he the last, and by the time the sun went down, we had rekindled the friendship that would endure many winters.

Moeris telling me I had been accepted to train with the ephebes. I had been unprepared for the hard work and strength of character that awaited me as I fought to progress past the training stage and become an elite hoplite in Thermopylae's army. I was unaccustomed to sleeping on the hard ground or training with sword and shield or spear and shield for candlemarks each and every day. I had not anticipated the freezing temperatures I would have to endure while on watch, or the cavernous noises of snoring men around me, but through it all, Moeris stood by me. He encouraged me and challenged me at every turn, pushing me harder than anyone else and celebrating with me as I rose through the ranks as I had always wanted.

Agrias teaching me the histories of each of the tribes under his rule as king of Trachis, taking me to meet each of the leaders, ready for the day when they became my people and my responsibility. Thanatos took Agrias from us one night while he slept and I was always thankful that he had not suffered as so many of my family had when their time in our world was done. Melina and I took his body back to his homeland of Macedonia, burying him with his ancestors, just as he had always wanted.

Melina holding my hand and humming her tunes as we walked through the agora buying food or special items when I was no more than four or five winters.

Mother sitting me in front of her large mirror, brushing out my hair before bed while Mumma tended her armor. They would tell me stories of heroes and of their love. Mother was always so proud of Mumma's actions against a man who tried to take her from Trachis, and in turn Mumma was humbled and embarrassed Mother still spoke of it so often with me.

Papou Leandros sitting outside the barracks, preparing his leather armor with beeswax, the smell drifting over to meet me as I sat beside him. He drew the wax across the leather in long strokes, always careful to ensure the entire surface was evenly covered.

The way Zenon looked at me with those bright green eyes that matched mine, the way they sparkled and his face lit up when he described a particularly beautiful sunset or the color of the water in the Malian Gulf.

Kadmus' fierce determination when he trained, the way he thrust and parried, mirroring my movements as I showed them to him, the small line of frustration that separated his brows when his actions were not perfect.

My beloved Demi; our first meeting at Lake Xynias when I pulled a boy through the rocks and onto the bank; the way the yellow flecks glittered in his brown eyes and his chest heaved as attempted to regain his breath. How he had fled from me the first time I had used the amulet, only to return to tell me of Philo's sad fate.

Our trip to Mount Smolikos when Demetri emerged as Demi – the boy-girl who stole my heart and shared with me a hidden, frightening truth about who they truly were. I thought I had lost him ... her for good when the mountain collapsed beneath our feet.

Konitsa – when we were together for the first time, our attraction for one another reaching a fever pitch thanks to the amulet and my use of it for the third time.

The first time we were intimate in Trachis. Love as well as lust drove our joining, the amulet gone, along with Ares. A new beginning for both of us in a place once familiar to me, but strange to have returned to after such an absence. Demi had not left me when our passion was sated; we lay together. We whispered our desires for one another and for the future and it was the most perfect moment I had ever known with them.

The first time we were together after Demi was changed and our sons were born. The slow exploration of her new body, the way she allowed me to learn and caress and worship her just like I had before. How much she trusted me, us, our love.

"Demi ..."

I willed my eyes open again, shields on the ground before me, their owners' dead or dying beside them. Persian, Spartan, Athenian, Boeotian, Theban, there were so many. My eyes found a Spartan shield, the symbol of the Dioscuri streaked with blood. Zeus and Artemis mustn't have known the hind's blood would break the hold of another god. If they had, I was sure they would've told me. I had to tell them, or Hephaestus. I tried to speak, but blood bubbled in my throat, making me cough.

"Hush child, do not tire yourself with words," Hephaestus whispered, tears flowing down his cheeks. "Everything shall be as it was meant."

I had to tell him, to stand again and fight. To take the pieces of the amulet back from Ares and somehow use their power, denying his ruthless plan without becoming forever his. I had made Hephaestus bring the sword; I had given Ares exactly what he wanted – just like he'd said I would. I had condemned Demi, Kadmus, Zenon and Melina and every mortal and god to a terrible fate. I was supposed to save them all, but instead I'd delivered them to their own kind of Tartarus. I had failed.

Anger rippled through me; anger with myself and with Zeus. Why didn't he heal me? His hand was still on my shoulder, yet he didn't take away my pain, or my wound. Why? Again I tried to talk but blood pounded in my ears and roaring darkness threatened to overcome me. My time in the mortal world was coming to an end. I could feel my life draining from me and the more I fought and raged against it, the faster I slipped away.

Zeus was not going to save me.

I raised my eyes to Hephaestus. His face mirrored my thoughts. The truth of my failure gripped my chest hard. Zeus bent down and kissed my forehead, then disappeared, leaving Hephaestus and I alone.

"Ares shall pay for what he has done," Hephaestus promised. I nodded, my head heavy and waves of pain rolling over me with the movement. Hephaestus drew me to his chest. "I am here. Close your eyes, Child. Your fight is done for now. Go, we shall see one another soon."

Relief washed over me with his words and I welcomed the darkness. My body was giving up and I couldn't stop it. I didn't want to stop it. My eyes fluttered shut.

I shall love you forever Demi. I silently promised. I wish I could see you one last time, to kiss you, to hold you. I'm sorry you will have to raise our sons alone, but know that I will be watching over you all somehow from my place in the Elysium Fields. One day we'll be reunited and you will meet my mothers. I love you.

Hot tears slid down my face as I closed my eyes and breathed my last breath.

PART III

After

1

I shivered. It was dark, more than dark, I knew I had my eyes open, but I couldn't make out a single shape. For a moment I just lay there, listening for the waves crashing onto the beach, the clash of metal as the soldiers fought, anything familiar or new, but there was nothing. No sound. No light. No smell of sea. Only silence and darkness. It didn't make sense. Where was I?

My tongue pressed against the small object in my mouth. Taking it from between my lips, I traced the raised patterns on either side of the round, flat disc. The coin Ares had dropped beside me. I squeezed it between my fingers and everything became obvious; I was dead. I had passed into the Underworld. I shivered again and rubbed my hands over my arms.

I rolled onto my side, expecting the pain of the wound Ares had given me to emerge but there was nothing. I pressed my hand to my stomach, the hole in the bronze of my armor was there, but the flesh of my stomach was no longer ripped open. No sticky, wet blood coated my fingertips.

I sat up. Where was I supposed to go and how would I find my way in the dark? I pushed myself to my feet and as I did, the complete truth of my death and what I'd been trying to prevent in my world sent me back to my knees.

I squeezed my eyes shut. I was dead. Ares had the jet and hematite. He was going to challenge Zeus for the throne. I'd given him everything he wanted. Arrogantly I'd presumed I would defeat him, just like I had last time. I'd believed the hind's blood would be all I needed. Hephaestus was right when he told me I should leave the sword where it was. I should have put the blood on my *new* sword and killed Ares with it instead.

I had failed everyone. I had failed Demi and my boys ... my boys ... Where were they? Did the mortal realm resemble its former self at all? Was Ares already ruler? Had all beauty and wonder ceased to exist? And what about Hephaestus and Artemis, were they also dead because of me? My head spun with questions and I slumped heavily to my side.

"Wake now child," a soft voice encouraged.

I opened my eyes, the immediate area now lit by flickering torches and a number of other people; the brightest of them took me by the elbow and helped me sit up. I was in a large cave, the roof high above, out of reach of the torchlight. To my left, a solid brown wall with jagged rock edges protruding out of the dirt stood. The bright man beside me wore a loose, white chiton held together at his right shoulder with a large pin. In his hand he held a short staff with two snakes carved around the length and a pair of wings at one end, his short, blond hair curled at his brow and ears just like Kadmus' did.

Renewed anguish at what my son and family might be experiencing began to rise beneath my breast but before I had even finished acknowledging the feeling, a deep sense of calm overtook me. It radiated from the hand at my back and flowed through my entire being. I had felt something similar before, but this calm was not like that – this feeling didn't flow through me to use for destruction and death. It wanted only to soothe me.

"I am certain you have questions, and I shall answer each as we journey together," the man said, standing and holding his hand out to me.

There were five souls milling about nearby, they held up their torches and led the way down a worn path. I allowed myself to be pulled to my feet, surprised at the warmth of the hand that gripped mine.

"I am Hermes, guider of souls to the Underworld," he told me.

"Are we not in the Underworld now?" I asked.

"We are in Erebus, the place of eternal darkness between the earth and the Underworld, far beyond the gates of the rising sun. I trust you know how you came to be here?"

I nodded. I knew only too well. I had left behind a terrible mess I had no way of fixing or intervening in now I was dead.

Hermes and I walked together and joined the others at a branch of two rivers. One of the rivers rushed noisily away into the darkness to our left, the dark blue of the water picking up the light from the twenty or so torches Hermes lit. The other was stagnant and dark, pungent with the smell of decay and topped with a slow-moving mist. I turned from it, watching instead the strong water of the first river. It wound its way around the bank and I became aware of other people standing at the edge not more than ten steps from me. They looked up with doleful eyes vacant of life or laughter as they shuffled about aimlessly and silently, their chitons old and dirty.

"We have reached the point where the Cocytus River flows into the Acheron and this is where I shall leave you." Hermes addressed us.

"The Cocytus River ... so those are the souls that were sent to the Underworld without payment for Charon and must now spend eternity walking the banks?" I asked, pointing to the miserable people.

"Mortals can be ever so dramatic," Hermes sighed. "The souls do not stay here for *eternity*, but for one hundred of your mortal winters, after which, Charon shall take them across the river for free. Here is Charon now," he added, pointing towards the dark, stinking river.

Out of the mist, a small boat appeared; its mast tall at its center, the sail tattered and torn. As it neared, I made out a single occupant standing beside the mast and holding a rope. He threw it to Hermes, who tied it to a round pole sticking out of the ground. The rotten smell intensified as the small boat cut through the water – and whatever else was beneath – and I covered my mouth against the stench.

"This is Charon, ferryman of the dead. He shall take you along the next part of your journey."

Charon stepped from his boat and onto the bank beside me. "Coin?" he asked in a sharp voice.

I nodded and handed it to him. He took it to the nearest torch and looked it over on both sides. Charon was not a handsome man, suffering a long, hooked nose and bow in his back. His beard was dark and knotted at his chest and he wore a conical hat and a tunic that had, perhaps, once been white. When his inspection of my coin was done, he put it between his teeth, biting down on the silver before taking it out again.

"You may cross," he announced, moving onto the next soul that had accompanied Hermes and me along the path. One by one, silver or gold coins were handed to Charon, his test the same for each until he had accepted them all.

He pushed past me and untied the rope from the wood, climbing back into his boat without another glance. He took a long, thin piece of wood and dug it into the bank, sending the boat backwards through the murky black water.

"Well, what are you waiting for?" he shouted. "Do you wish to stay here for the next hundred winters or are you ready to face the Judges?" The five other souls rushed to get onto the boat.

I turned to thank Hermes for getting me to Charon but he was gone, as were the torches he had lit up and down the bank. The darkness closed in again and I clambered aboard the small boat. Charon plunged his stick into the dark water again, steering the boat as I found a space beside a young man.

As the boat rocked gently over the water, I studied the other passengers. An older man and woman sat opposite me, holding each other's hands and looking neither curious nor afraid at what was coming or where we were. They paid no attention to the rest of us, preferring to gaze only at one another instead.

The young man next to me was covered in bandages, mostly around his head and neck and he nodded at me when our eyes met.

A young girl of no more than six or seven winters sat closest to Charon and she smiled at me and waved. Automatically I raised my hand in response, but I could not bring myself to return her grin. She appeared happy to find herself here and I wondered if perhaps the rest of her family had already come, perhaps she was looking forward to being reunited with them. After my mothers had been taken from me I would have welcomed the opportunity with the same joy.

The last young man in the boat was covered in blood and there was a large, red stain above his heart where it seemed he'd taken a spear. He looked furtively through the darkness around us and when his eyes locked with mine, I was startled to realize that I knew him – it was the Thespian soldier I had spoken to at the wall before we faced the Persians. I opened my mouth, but he looked away again, still searching the surrounding darkness. I realized he was waiting for Aphrodite to come and take him away, to keep him in her arms and care for him just like he'd told me she would.

I cast my eyes around the cavern but I could see nothing, there was only infinite darkness and thick water or mud that parted with a loud hiss as the bow of the small boat made its way across the Acheron River.

2

A flash of light lit Hades' dank palace deep in the earth. The God of the Underworld sat on his throne, dressed completely in black; boots, pants, himation. Flickering torches hung at intervals around the walls and cast a weak gleam across the brown dirt, rocks and weathered marble that formed his home. When he stood, the light picked up the single bright spot in the room – the golden crown upon his brow. In the muted light he smiled and raised his arm, his himation hanging almost to the ground.

He stepped forward and took Ares' outstretched limb, gripping it tightly. "Nephew, it is good to see you again," he said.

"And you, Uncle," Ares replied. "Ava shall be in your realm within a few candlemarks."

"You left her with someone to prepare her for the journey?"

"Hephaestus," Ares replied.

"Are you certain that is wise?" Hades frowned. "He has a deep fondness for her, would he not simply take her to Zeus and have her healed?"

"He cannot. I trapped them, he shall have no choice but to watch her life slip away," Ares smiled, dropping his hand from Hades' arm.

"But she has coin for Charon?" Hades pressed.

"Of course," Ares snapped, insulted at the implication. "It is not the first time I have sent someone to you here. She shall be able to pay her way, and once she arrives, you know what to do."

Hades bowed his head in acknowledgment. "And your plans to overthrow my brother, how do they progress?"

"Just as I hoped," Ares replied. "It shall not be long until I have what I have desired for so long."

"I look forward to our continued and prosperous agreement."

"As do I. Now, where is Aphrodite? We have many plans to make … after we celebrate."

"She awaits your return in Persephone's chambers. I shall find you once the mortal arrives," Hades nodded, returning to his throne.

"My gratitude," Ares replied. The god of war made his way through an arch and into the corridor he knew would take him to his beloved. He paused outside the door and knocked, waiting for his lover's admittance before he entered.

Her face brightened when she saw him and she leapt from the bed to kiss him fiercely. He kicked the door shut and held her. She had begged him not to face Ava again, knowing that the mortal still possessed the sword and quite possibly the power it had once held, but he had insisted he would be safe and had left her sitting miserably in that very room with only his promise to return as comfort.

Aphrodite pushed her fingers through his hair and over his arms and chest, no doubt confirming that he truly had returned safely to her.

"It is done," he told her when they parted. "In one moon I shall have the power to take the throne from my father and we shall rule in his place." He took the pieces of amulet from his vest, showing her.

Aphrodite cupped her hands beneath his, studying the jet and hematite. "One moon cannot come soon enough, then we can leave this awful place and I can see the beauty and openness of Olympos once more," she murmured.

"Persephone and Hades did not make you comfortable during your stay?" A frown marred Ares' forehead as he thought of Aphrodite suffering physical pain, as well as emotional, as she awaited his return.

"Oh they were as accommodating as can be expected given my surroundings," she sighed. "But you know how I yearn to be surrounded by beauty and light." She indicated the subdued torchlight in the room.

Ares smiled and nodded. "That I do, and I am certain that even Hades would agree – out of Persephone's presence of course – that you were the most beautiful creature in the Underworld and had brightened it so by being here."

Aphrodite returned his smile and wrapped her arms around his waist. "I have missed you, my love."

"As I have you, and I give you my word that we shall leave here just as soon as we can. But to return to Olympos before I have the power would be a mistake."

"We cannot return to the north lands after what you did to the Valkyrie, Odin and his people bay for your blood and it would not do to have come so far only to be struck down by them."

"Agreed," he said, pulling her close and kissing her again. "Besides one moon shall not be long enough for what I h–ah!" He clutched at his chest.

"What is it?" Aphrodite asked, concern crossing her face as her hands covered his.

Ares stumbled and sat heavily on the bed, attempting shallow breaths around the stabbing pain. Aphrodite followed him, her hands lifted towards him, yet not touching his skin.

His palm heated and he opened his fingers to find the jet no longer a solid black color – it was light orange and warmed his hand pleasantly.

He rubbed again at his chest as the ghost of a smile lit his lips. "The amulet," he whispered. "It begins."

Aphrodite's gaze dropped to his hand. "How shall you know when the power has been transferred fully to you? Is it safe?"

Ares met her eyes, his grin widening as he placed a hand on her cheek. "Do not fear. I expected discomfort, just as each in my line experienced when their wings emerged and they used the amulet for the first time. It is how it should be. When the power is mine, I shall know." His lover did not appear convinced so he drew her face to his and placed a gentle kiss on her lips. "I shall not allow small discomforts to keep me from making up for all the time we lost while my brother confined me to that cage. Trust me when I tell you that it shall be nothing but a pleasurable experience to spend the next moon here in the Underworld together."

Aphrodite smiled, hunger overtaking the concern on her face. He allowed her to push him onto his back, as she followed him down onto the plush bedcovers. Her breasts lay against his chest, and he wished to discard the layers from between them immediately, but instead he allowed her to lead their dance while he recovered his breath. She removed the parts of the amulet from his hand and held them up, the orange of the jet casting shadows of light and dark across her face.

"Perhaps I shall have to find new ways of distracting you from the pain that the returning power causes you," she grinned, sliding her finger up the front of his vest and separating the leather which held it closed.

"Perhaps," he agreed, gripping her thigh with one hand as he took the jet and hematite from her with his other.

He set them on the table beside the bed and found his lover's lips above him. The stinging surged beneath his skin again as their bodies entwined, but he concentrated on the feel of Aphrodite's lips on his, her warm breasts against his bare chest and the way she raked her fingers through his hair.

He closed his eyes as she moved above him, discarding his clothing with practiced efficiency, his breath shallow but painful. He frowned again. It was not only his lover's ministrations that caused his breathlessness but the gently glowing jet beside them. He willed the pain to quiet by squeezing his eyes shut. It intensified in response, spreading through his chest and back, high up on his shoulders and down his arms.

"When you have taken your father's throne, you shall be known as King of the Gods and I shall be honored to pleasure a king of such stature," Aphrodite murmured, moving lower as she continued her kisses.

Ares drew a halting breath and raised a hand to her face, caressing her cheek as she licked the hair at his navel. He smiled and opened his eyes, jumping at the face before him.

She straightened so her body was bared and exquisite before him. "What is wrong?"

Ares pushed himself to his elbows, scrambling backwards until his shoulders touched the wall. He opened his mouth, but could form no words. It was not his lover's lips that asked him the question. It was not his lover's body that sat before him in all its glory.

It was Ava.

It had been Ava's lips kissing him. Ava's hands caressing his body as he attempted to forget the pain at his chest. It would have been Ava that brought him to ...

He blinked and stared in horror at her. How was she there? It was not possible. Where was Aphrodite? She put her hand out to soothe him, but he recoiled in fear.

"My love, what is it? Why do you flee from me?" she frowned.

"You ... you cannot be here ... how are you here? Where is Aphrodite?"

She frowned and reached out to him again. "I am here, my love."

Ares shook his head and closed his eyes. "No. Do not touch me," he whispered.

"Ares, what is happening?"

He shook his head as agony engulfed his skull. He clawed at his temples as all sound outside his own body faded away. He could hear nothing but the beat of his heart and his blood as it surged beneath his skin.

*

A voice called to Ares through the darkness. It was different now. Familiar. He opened his eyes. Aphrodite was beside him, her hands cupping his face, worry etched across her features.

"My love, what happened?" she asked, helping him to sit up.

He blew out a deep breath and shook his head, grateful to find that neither action hurt to do so. "I do not know, but you ... you looked ... and I ..." he inhaled another breath, releasing it all the way before he spoke again. "It does not matter. I am fine and so are you."

"I am," she agreed. "Perhaps you should get some rest."

"But do you not wish t–"

Aphrodite placed her finger on his lips and shook her head. "I believe it is best if you rest. There shall be time for that later."

Ares hesitated only a moment before nodding his agreement. He was not certain he wanted Aphrodite's hands on him, what if her face became Ava's again? What if he was not able to make her go away next time? What if he enjoyed what she did to him?

He shook his head, clearing the thoughts from his mind and lay back down, Aphrodite joining him.

The fear that had taken hold began to subside and with it Ares' mind became clearer. His control returned. There was nothing to be afraid of. Clearly it had just been a reaction to the amulet; there were bound to be some side effects while the power transferred from Ava to him.

Eir had said she was not certain what would happen if he was able to separate the jet and hematite from the sword. Perhaps he would see each of the women of the Ker line – of his line – who had used the amulet. Next time he would not be caught unaware. He would be prepared and know that what he saw was not the truth. Perhaps in time he would even learn to dismiss the images when they first appeared for it would not thrill his lover if it happened each time they were intimate, and he intended for them to be *very* intimate over the course of the next moon.

3

"I have heard the gates to the Underworld are made from the metal of the gods," the young man beside me murmured as we drew closer to the opposite bank.

"Metal of the gods?" I repeated.

"Yes, it is known as adamantine and has been around far longer than our iron or bronze. It is said that when Zeus chained Prometheus to the rock as punishment for giving fire to the mortals, he used adamantine to bind him and not even the great Titan's strength could break it."

A huge silver gateway came into view, shining imposingly in the darkness. "The Adamantine Gates," I whispered.

Charon stood, throwing out the rope as the boat glided up onto the bank. There were more torches lit along the waterline but their light was almost dim compared to the gates. No souls walked mindlessly near the edge of the Acheron River but as my eyes adjusted I picked out six yellow, glowing circles high above us. I drew a quick breath as the rest of the picture emerged. The orbs were eyes and belonged to a giant, grey-black hound with three heads, each the size of a mature, bushy olive tree. One of its mouths held the rope Charon had thrown.

I shivered at the sight of the massive animal; reminded of when Ares had turned Damon into a similar looking creature.

"Everyone out," Charon barked, causing each of us in the boat to jump. One by one we stepped onto the sand, keeping our distance from the hound. "I leave these souls with you, Cerberus," Charon said, inclining his head towards the animal.

Cerberus lowered one of his heads in acknowledgement and flung the end of the rope back in Charon's direction. Charon caught it and within moments, the small boat which had brought us to the gates of the Underworld disappeared into the darkness, the faint slap as it cut through the muck the only indication there was something beyond the torch light.

The six of us looked at one another and I suspected that they, like me, wondered if we had to fight our way past the hound to enter the gates. I opened my mouth to suggest it, but before I had a chance, the gates swung inwards and Cerberus stepped back, slowly fading again into the blackness beside the glowing metal.

"You may enter. One at a time," a voice boomed.

I stepped forward but the young girl pushed past me and ran through the gates, the huge smile still on her face. She had been gone barely a moment when the voice rang out again.

"Next."

Again I took a step forward. This time it was the young Thespian soldier who bumped me and headed eagerly inside. When the voice called again, I didn't move, letting the young man enter. The old couple entered shortly after, their arms wrapped around one another, contentment written across their faces.

Finally, it was my turn. I stepped slowly through the gate and was no more than three paces inside when it swung shut with a crash behind me.

"Step forward," the voice commanded. I did as asked, wondering how I hadn't heard him speak when the other souls went in – his words bounced deafeningly around the walls.

Three bearded men on thrones of gold faced me, their red himatia shimmering. It was so much brighter this side of the gates, torch flames gleaming off shiny black rock, smooth and solid as any I had seen. The roof wasn't far above, carved from rocks and dirt and held up by marble pillars at each corner.

"Welcome to the Forecourt of the Palace of Hades. State your name and home," one of the men said, pointing at me with a long, gold staff.

I swallowed and held myself taller. "I am Queen Ava of Trachis, in the region of Thermopylae, home of the Malians."

"How fortunate we are to have a queen in our midst," the man on the middle throne smiled. "We are the three Judges of the Underworld. I am Minos, to my left sits Rhadamanthus and to my right, Aeacus. It is our duty to send those recently departed souls to their place in the Underworld where they shall spend eternity." I nodded, but said nothing, not that it seemed they expected me to, Minos continuing a moment later. "Our decision is final and you shall not change our minds, nor shall you be given the opportunity to do so. Do you understand?" I nodded again.

"You mortals believe there are only two areas of the Underworld – the Elysium Fields and Tartarus. But there are actually five. The Fields of Asphodel are where most of your kind spend eternity. It is where those who did not commit crimes, nor achieve great standing in their mortal lives go.

"The Elysium Fields are where those deemed heroic or virtuous by the gods are sent, and they are tended by Rhadamanthus. When a soul enters the Elysium Fields, he or she has a choice – to stay or to be re-born. If the soul chooses to be re-born and finds themselves in the Elysium Fields when their next life is done then they have the same choice. If they are sent to the Fields a third time, they may enter the Isles of the Blessed in the center of the Elysium Fields to enjoy eternal paradise.

"For those souls deemed to be evil or impious, we have far darker places. The Fields of Punishment are for those who have committed crimes against the gods, whilst Tartarus is for those who betray the gods. Both are most unpleasant and the souls trapped in either face eternal torment with no possibility of being offered re-birth."

I shivered with his words. I had done many good deeds in my life as a soldier, wife and mother but I had also betrayed Ares nine winters ago. I hoped that the judges would see that I had done so to keep mortals and the other gods safe from him. Perhaps I had kept *them* safe from Ares too.

"There are also five rivers named Acheron, Styx, Cocytus, Lethe and Phlegethon," Minos continued. "Some of those you have seen on your way to us, others you shall encounter as you travel to your eternal resting place. Once we have read your mortal deeds, we shall advise you of our decision and you shall be taken there." A rectangular slab of marble appeared in Minos' hand. "We shall be but a moment."

The three men huddled around the marble. I didn't think it was possible they'd spent as much time with the others from the boat as they were with me; they'd called the next soul so quickly. Then again, maybe like on Olympos, time moved differently here.

I stood, my hands closing into a ball, then relaxing as I waited for their answer. If I was sent to the Elysium Fields, I knew I would choose to be re-born. I would be just a child, and would not remember my previous life, but somehow I knew that if given the chance, I would find a way to change the mortal realm and wrestle it from Ares' grip. Hephaestus too would surely learn I had returned and would help me any way he could. Maybe I would get to see Demi and our sons too; not that I would know their true relationship to me.

A flash of light announced the presence of an immortal and I looked up, hoping it was Hephaestus coming to speak on my behalf, rather than an enemy like Ares.

It was neither. The man was handsome with short, dark hair and a neat, trimmed beard. His long himation was a brilliant red with flowing sleeves of black lined with gold. He bent his head to speak with the Judges, their conversation short and too quiet for me to hear. Minos asked urgent questions of his own, casting his eyes to mine several times. He didn't look happy but nodded to the newcomer, who promptly disappeared again.

Minos, Rhadamanthus and Aeacus faced me again, the latter two filing out through a small door to their right as Minos took his place on his throne.

"A decision has been made," he told me, his voice loud after the quiet consultation. "Queen Ava of Trachis, in the region of Thermopylae, home of the Malians, for your betrayal of Ares, the God of War, in his pursuit of claiming the mantle of King of the Gods, and for denying him the power he so deserved, we hereby sentence you to begin your eternity in the pit known as Tartarus."

"No!" I cried.

"For the greater crime of attempting to murder the same named god, we also sentence you to the Fields of Punishment, where you shall be removed to at a further determined time," Minos continued.

"You can't, you mustn't," I yelled, rushing towards him as fear and anger threatened to overcome me. Invisible chains instantly shackled my wrists and I struggled in their cold grip. "I have only ever done what was best for those I was entrusted to protect. It's true that I betrayed Ares in his quest, but you have to understand that no good would've come from his victory. I saved you. I saved gods and mortals from a fate they did not deserve, I–"

"It is done," Minos announced, bringing his staff down on the ground with a deafening crash.

I opened my mouth again, but no sound came and my feet moved of their own accord, taking me from the Forecourt of the Palace of Hades, back through the Adamantine Gates to the shores of the Acheron River.

The gates slammed shut behind me, control returning to my limbs. I slapped and shook the silver, but they did not open again. Voices caught my ear – my companions from the boat were being led away to the left by Rhadamanthus.

"Rhadamanthus, you know I shouldn't be sent to Tartarus," I screamed. Neither the Judge, nor the others acknowledged my words.

Cerberus towered above me, growling deeply, and I swallowed the rest of what I was going to say. I backed away from the gates, the hound following me. It dipped one huge head and sliced through the ties at my shoulder and waist. My bronze armor dropped to the dirt, leaving me in only my bloodstained chiton and sandals. I wrapped my arms across my chest to ward off the sudden chill.

"You shall not require such coverings here," Minos said, emerging from the darkness beside the gates.

"I don't belong in Tartarus, you know that."

"We did not come to the judgement lightly, nor would it have been our own, had we the choice. But we cannot undo it. Once the gods have spoken, we are powerless to stop their wishes."

"I don't accept that, there must be a way. If you could just grant me an audience with Hades."

"It is not in my power to grant such a request. As I told you, the decision is final and none are given the opportunity to alter it. There can be no exceptions."

"B–"

"Come," Minos insisted, holding up a torch and leading me in the opposite direction to Rhadamanthus and the others from the boat.

4

We walked down through a maze of tunnels which took us further and deeper from Hades' palace and the Acheron River above. Several times I tried to engage Minos in conversation but he wouldn't answer my questions or acknowledge my threats. I eventually gave up, determined to commit each turn and twist to memory instead. I would need to remember the way when I escaped from Tartarus. And escape was what I fully intended.

Finally Minos slowed and the dark rock walls that had accompanied us on our journey fell away, leaving us on a plain lit by hundreds of torches. It was warmer than it had been by the river, and quiet. I don't know what I expected to find in Tartarus, but I certainly hadn't expected the quiet.

"So, we're here. This is Tartarus?"

Minos turned and shook his head. "Not quite. Take my hand. Where the torches end there is only darkness, and my small light shall be no match for the utter thickness of the dark ahead."

I didn't fear the dark; gods knew I'd spent plenty of nights with the soldiers where we took watch without fire, relying only on the moonlight or our sharp hearing to warn us of approaching danger or an animal to take down for food for the coming days. But knowing that I was far from the mortal realm and the familiarity of that place, encouraged me to take Minos' hand as we journeyed forward.

We started across the plain and when we had passed the final torch, it went out, plunging us into complete darkness, just as Minos had warned.

The torch in his hand flickered but I couldn't see more than a pace or two in front and nothing on either side. I looked back towards the plain, but could see nothing there either. I was left in no doubt that one could easily get lost, which was perhaps the point.

We continued until a warm glow appeared in the distance. It was as though Helios himself was touching the ground with the first rays of his morning light. As we neared, I realized it wasn't light greeting us at all, but flames; long, orange flames that flickered and leapt high into the air above rich, red colored water.

Minos dropped my hand and stood by the edge, extinguishing his torch in the sand. "The River Phlegethon," he advised, even though I hadn't voiced the question. "On the other side lies Tartarus."

I swallowed and looked into the river. The flames were a few feet above the water, no, not water; it was flowing lava beneath them. Steam drifted off the bubbling red and mixed with the flames as the boiling mass wound its way around jagged rocks. Heat rolled off the river in waves and I took a step back, no longer feeling any chill.

Minos held his arms out in front of himself, the backs of his hands pressed together. As he moved them apart, the flames and lava in the river also parted and he nodded to the slightly glowing red dirt beneath.

"Walk across, I shall follow behind you," he instructed. I didn't move. He grinned. "It is quite safe, I give you my word. It would not do to bring you so far only to have you injured here."

"No, I'm sure Hades would prefer to do that in my new home," I muttered.

Minos laughed and shook his head. "Home ... I have heard Tartarus called by many names, but home has never been one of them."

I made no reply, but tentatively put my right foot into the opening he had made. The ground was warm beneath my sandal. It wasn't unpleasant but I didn't linger – for all I knew, I was already standing in the middle of Tartarus and Minos was going to let the lava and flames engulf me. I skipped across the dirt, relieved to find Minos only a step behind when I reached the other side. He returned the river to its position and it flowed on like there'd been no interruption to it.

There was no need for torches here; the darkness had been driven back by the flames from the Phlegethon River on one side and their reflection in a tall, brass wall on the other.

"Welcome to Tartarus," Minos said, banging on a small, wooden door set into the golden wall. It swung open and he waited for me to pass through before closing it again.

The walls that guarded Tartarus were two stones thick, plus the bronze layer, and equal to half my height, perhaps more. Any normal city that possessed such fortitude would've been almost impossible to breech. The fact I was in Tartarus made me think that the security here would be even greater.

On either side of the gate, towers of flat iron rose up, their tops lost to the darkness above. Beyond those, the stone wall returned, running further than I could see in either direction.

The atmosphere inside the walls was oppressive and a wave of finality took my breath away as I looked around. Dim torches stood at intervals within the main area. Blood-spattered dirt stretched out from the small wooden door and I couldn't see the wall of stones that marked the opposite side before the darkness encroached completely again.

Souls with lank hair wended their way aimlessly between the rocks and each other, their eyes as vacant as those on the banks of the Cocytus River had been. They were oblivious to the rats that scampered over their feet, and my arrival.

Silver chains hung from the wall to my left, some still claiming their captives with bloodied wrists and bare threads of clothing covering little of their flesh, while others dangled emptily, looking like they were waiting hungrily for their next victim.

I looked up at a sudden yell of alarm and saw a huge rock rolling towards me and Minos. I grabbed his cloak and dragged him out of the way, the breath knocked from me as I hit the solid stone wall.

Barely a moment later, a man with a long, white beard ran past us; his arms outstretched towards the boulder that continued unceasing in its journey away from him.

Minos straightened his himation and shook his head as he spoke. "That is Sisyphus, once the king of Ephyra, which you know as Corinth. Long ago, he toyed with the gods, incurring their wrath by enslaving Thanatos in chains, preventing mortals from their deaths, and for refusing to stay in the Underworld where he was sent upon his death. Finally Hades dragged him back and brought him here, where Zeus exacted the punishment you see before you."

"He is destined to chase a boulder through Tartarus for eternity?" I frowned.

"No, he must push the boulder up a tall hill. Time and again he gets it almost to the peak before its weight becomes too much and it rolls back down, where he must begin again.

"Why doesn't he just refuse to push it upwards again?"

"When you have been here as long as he has, you shall come to realize that it is impossible to deny. He feels an intense compulsion to continue at the task he has been set in the hope that *this* time he shall achieve what he set out to do. He cannot help himself; he must attempt it over and over again." Minos took a step forward, pointing out another man as I followed. "Tantalus is cursed to eternal hunger and thirst for divulging Zeus' secrets."

A small body of water lay in a perfect circle, deep enough that it reached Tantalus' thighs as he stood immersed in the clearness. A beautiful tree, full of large, ripe fruit stood at the edge of the water, its branches overhanging in such a way that, had there been any sun, it would have shaded him from it perfectly. As we passed, Tantalus bent down to cup his hands in the water, but as he did so, the water level dropped beneath his reach. He straightened again, reaching for the fruit above his head, but the branch rose into the air and he couldn't take it. He looked back to his legs, where the water was once again at his thighs and he extended his fingers to its surface, only to be denied again.

We kept moving, Minos extending his arm so I stayed out of the way of the flaming spinning wheel that rolled past us. "That is Ixion, fierce warrior king of the Lapith tribe in Thessaly. For a time, he was a favorite of Zeus' and shared a place at the god's table on Olympos. That was until one night, when Ixion attempted to seduce Zeus' wife. Zeus tricked Ixion by conjuring a cloud in the form of Hera, and Ixion could not resist when she came to his bed that night. The next day, Ixion foolishly boasted that he had spent the night with Zeus' bride, and for such treachery, Zeus killed him with a thunderbolt, ordering Hermes to strap him to the flaming wheel, which shall spin and burn for all eternity, stripping him of his flesh and regrowing it nightly so it can be burnt again."

I swallowed hard, not wanting to consider what punishments Ares might have in mind for me when he had the chance to exact his revenge. I was in no doubt he would come to me, and that his punishment would be just as prolonged and depraved.

Minos pointed to a group of women filling pots from a shallow, rectangular cistern. "The Danaides killed their husbands. In order to purify themselves, they must fill the bath and cleanse themselves in its water."

"But they can't," I said quietly, watching as the women pulled their jugs from the cistern. The clay containers had tiny holes up and down their lengths, making the task of getting enough water to fill such a bath, impossible. "But why are they in Tartarus, how was their deed a betrayal of the gods?"

"There are many reasons souls find themselves in Tartarus upon their death," Minos replied, refusing to meet my eyes.

Dread filled me as I considered that perhaps one day such hopeless, impossible tasks would be mine too. I would find a way to leave before I was unable to deny the continual attempts at the task that was set for me.

Minos continued across the sand, pausing when we came to the edge of a wide, dark pit. I hoped it was not where I was destined to spend eternity.

"This is the pit where the Titans once dwelled," he told me. "Some say they are still there, though I would not wish to descend the depths to find out." Before I could respond, a rumble of thunder rolled above us and a crack of jagged light broke the intense darkness somewhere beyond the walls of Tartarus.

"That would be for Salmoneus. When he was king of Elis, he forced his people to call him Zeus and worship him as they did the great god. For his acts of arrogance, Zeus struck him down with a thunderbolt and destroyed the town, forcing Salmoneus to suffer the same fate day after day in the Fields of Punishment. He has come to fear the rumble of thunder that announces Zeus' presence."

"I am not surprised," I murmured.

A flash of movement from my right caught my attention and I turned, finding three winged creatures touching down nearby; their thick hound legs a stark contrast to the womanly bodies above.

"The Erinyes," Minos said in a low voice. "Tisiphone, Megaera and Alecto stand guard, unsleeping, in the two towers beside the door we entered through." I swallowed loudly, forcing myself to look at them.

Their nakedness intensified their ferocity; skin black and leathery, only a shade lighter than their hair, which reached halfway down their backs in a tangled mess. Long, gnarled fingers with claws at the tips reached out, as though tasting the air through the nails. Snakes curled along their arms, the striped, white and orange bodies standing out boldly against the dark skin. Their breasts hung limply against their chests and aged, wrinkled faces stared as their bat-like wings fluttered gently behind them, fanning the smell of fetid decay towards me. I turned my head but the smell permeated the entire area.

The warmth of Minos at my side was suddenly gone, replaced by one of the Erinyes, her awful smell almost overcoming me.

"A new soul, how delicious," her voice rasped through her lips. As she made her inspection, her nails skittered along my arm, and I shivered. When she returned to stand in front of me, her eyes flashed, the bright red centers the same color as the Phlegethon River outside.

She smiled savagely, baring long, sharp teeth and reached out to trace her finger down my cheek. "We shall have much fun with this one, my sisters," she cackled.

The others circled me as the first had, running their claws along my skin and marking me with their putrid smell. I held my breath, but that only made them smile wider and stand closer and I didn't care for the way their snakes looked at me.

"I feel much within her and I ask you, sister Tisiphone, why we have not visited her before, when she was still mortal?" one of the Erinyes asked.

"She was put out of our reach long ago, but it appears we have pleased our master and at last he has given her to us to play with," the one named Tisiphone replied. I took a step back, but they followed, leering and baring their pointed teeth. "There is nowhere to hide, not from us."

"Nowhere to hide from yourself or your memories either," the second one added.

"I haven't committed any crime for which you punish," I said, breathing through my mouth instead of my nose. "I have committed no acts of murder against my kin, not my mothers, or any brothers or sisters."

"But we do not only punish for that which you speak of. Tell her, Alecto," Tisiphone directed her sister.

"We also punish those who do not respect the customs of hospitality," Alecto replied.

"I have never disresp–"

"We do not speak so you can deny your guilt," the third sister – Megaera growled, advancing on me. "You foolish mortals so often know little about why we appear to you when we are summoned."

I swallowed loudly again. "So why do you appear now before me if you don't think I'm guilty of what you punish?"

Tisiphone approached me again as her sisters drifted back. "Oh you are guilty. We also punish those guilty of breaking their oaths, and you have broken many." I opened my mouth, but a sharp claw at my lips silenced me. "You broke your oath to the God of War. You promised to rule at his side with your amulet and your immense power, to be his queen on the throne of Olympos when he took it from Zeus. He would have given you everything you desired, and more, if only you had allowed him to. But you chose mortals over a god and you broke your word."

"I don't know what Ares has told you, but I never promised to rule with him."

Alecto stepped forward to speak. "You need further proof of your guilt? Then perhaps we should speak of the soldier and his wife. Did you not give your word that you would always protect him? That you would return him to her arms when his time as a warrior was done?"

I drew in a pained breath as Lysistratos' body, cold and bleeding, rushed to mind. Eumelia's anger and utter devastation at her loss. The look Phaidros wore the day of Lysistratos' funeral. I was responsible for that pain, for that loss. I had known it then and I felt it acutely now. I closed my eyes, powerless to stop the images that flashed before me one after another.

"And what of your mothers?" Megaera asked. "How many times did you give your word that you would rid Greece of the Persian scum that sought to claim your lands? That you would avenge their deaths with all you had? Yet here you are, just as helpless as they were in their final battle. Just as dead as they are now, having broken your oath and failed in your strong words."

My knees gave out as their words engulfed me. Every pain, every doubt I had ever held rose to the surface as the Erinyes' voices became Mumma's. "How many times did you promise you would finish what we could not?"

"When the line of the Keres passed to you, it became your responsibility to defeat Ares, to keep him from taking Zeus' crown, yet you could not."

"You disappoint us with your death, we know Ares has won and has brought his destruction to the world we loved so much. We trusted you to bring about his defeat, but you failed. You are a hopeless failure and you have broken our hearts more than you can ever know."

I screamed, fighting against the truth of what they said. I knew I had failed. It flowed through every part of my being. I had broken my word and I had failed my mothers. I had failed Papou and Melina and Demi and our boys.

"Get out of my head!" I yelled, clutching at my temples.

The Erinyes laughed maniacally, crouching around me. Tisiphone's clawed finger lifted my chin until our eyes met. "But do you not see? We are not in your head, dear girl. You are not asleep, for only those in the mortal realm find themselves disturbed by us as they slumber with Hypnos. Here you shall never sleep and we shall never be far from you."

As if to prove Tisiphone's words, Alecto unwound the snake from her left arm and sunk its sharp fangs into my thigh. I screamed and they laughed again before disappearing into the darkness, taking my pain and the marks on my leg with them.

I shielded my eyes from a sudden light, pushing myself to my feet as a figure appeared nearby. I lowered my arm to find a man dressed from head to foot in black, the only break in his muted colors his bright green eyes and the golden crown which sat low on his brow. It was the man from the forecourt. No, not a man; a god. His hair, without hint of curl or wave, swept gently down his forehead towards his eyes, and his bearded chin was neatly groomed.

I advanced on him. "You. You told the Judges what my fate should be. You sent me here. I don't belong here. Who are you?"

"I am Hades, God of the Underworld," he replied. "But are you certain you do not belong here? Minos told you where souls go according to how they lived their lives in the mortal world. You cannot deny your guilt for the crimes you committed against the god of war, can you?"

"Ares put you up to this," I murmured, taking a breath before I spoke again. "The good deeds I've done far outweigh denying Ares an outcome that would've been of benefit to no one but himself."

"Careful now, Mortal. I am fond of my nephew and his plan to overthrow my brother. Should I perhaps bring the Erinyes back to remind you of the other crimes you are guilty of?"

"Your pets appear well versed in my past but I won't bow to their words, they will not break me."

"They are no pets of mine, but their master is one who cannot wait to watch the agony and pain they put you through."

"Ares doesn't have time to waste watching me. I'm so far from Olympos and he has a father to overthrow and a world to destroy, doesn't he?"

"He shall make time; I do not believe he is done with his plaything just yet, perhaps he has further plans for you."

"If that's true then why don't you take me to drink from the River Lethe so I forget my mortal life and my intense hatred of him? Then he could do whatever he wanted and I wouldn't fight or deny him like I have before."

"Oh no," Hades grinned. "Those sent to the Fields of Punishment or to the depths of Tartarus are not so fortunate as to drink from Lethe. You shall spend eternity remembering and reliving the worst moments of your mortal past. You shall sink to the greatest depths of despair you have ever known and your soul shall be crushed by the weight of your own thoughts … Now, what makes you believe Ares would want to miss a moment of that?" He laughed again and disappeared, leaving me alone to await the return of the Erinyes, or perhaps Ares himself.

5

I walked the entire length and width of Tartarus, following the stone walls by touch. Men wailed and screamed, but I saw no one, the darkness hiding them from view. In a way I was grateful for that, I didn't want to see what other cruel and futile tasks the gods had decided were fitting punishments for those kept here. Not yet anyway.

There were no breaks in the stone, apart from the wooden door we had entered, and no ledges or footholds in the large bricks where someone – like me – could climb to the top and escape. I realized the folly in that plan of course; if I couldn't see the top of the wall then there was no telling how tall it was and I didn't relish the idea of jumping off something so high. I didn't think the fall would kill me, after all, I was already dead, but I would most likely break both my legs and endure torturous pain when I hit the ground, which would hinder my plans for escape.

There was also the Phlegethon River to consider. There was a bank and sand between the lava and the doorway we'd entered, but I didn't know what lay on the other three sides of Tartarus' walls.

I returned to where Minos had left me, the torches illuminating those he had pointed out. They paid me no attention, going about their tasks without thought for anyone else. I'd welcomed their ignorance as I made my inspection of Tartarus but now it was time to make myself known to them.

I wondered who to approach first – from the stories I'd heard of the men Minos pointed out, they'd all been sent to Tartarus long before I was born, long before my grandparents were born. They'd been suffering for hundreds of winters.

I chose the closest man and introduced myself. He didn't reply or acknowledge me. Neither did the second, or the third but I kept at them, imploring them to respond, to help me find a way to escape, even taunting them to see if that made a difference. It didn't.

"Come on," I finally yelled. "Have you all been here so long you've forgotten that you once wanted to escape? Didn't you once want to escape?" I added a little quieter.

They remained silent but Tisiphone's voice carried down to me from her place high up on the tower. "Escape is impossible," she cackled. The flutter of her wings announced her arrival and she floated down, coming to rest on the dirt nearby. "Many have attempted it, all have failed. In time they forget such silly desires, getting so caught up in their little tasks that they have no time for such plans. It is how Hades safeguards his realm."

"I will never forget. I will never stop trying to get free. I don't belong here and you won't keep me," I spat.

Tisiphone laughed, exposing her blackened teeth. "Ah, the determination of a new soul. It has been a long time since we have had one and I had almost forgotten the sound of defiance." She took a step forward and I took one back. "All souls succumb to the despair and uselessness of their eternity here. You shall be no different. You carry much guilt inside and it is a delicious feast for me and my sisters to experience.

"Your soldier friend blamed you just as his wife, your half-sister, blamed you. You broke your word and did not stand and fight side by side as you had promised. Of course he was angry with himself for a long time after he came to the Underworld too. Angry that he had put his trust in a mere girl, who after all those winters training to be a soldier, turned out to be as all the others were – having a child and putting something other than her training first. He could not do that, he did not do that, he was a true soldier; he left his wife and son and lived in the barracks as all the other men did, the strong ones who did not allow parenthood to change who they were."

"No," I shouted. "You're wrong. Lysistratos knew I would've been beside him like I always had, but my children w–"

"You tell yourself all the lies you wish, but you know you failed him."

"No," I repeated, putting my fingers into my ears like a child.

Tisiphone continued but I screamed, drowning out her voice with my own. Alecto appeared beside us, her snake sliding from her arm and onto mine, its tongue darting out to taste the air, its smooth body moving up my arm and over my shoulders to lay across the nape of my neck.

I wriggled my shoulders, trying to dislodge it. It didn't work and I knew I'd have to use my hands. I removed one finger from my ear and tried to grip the snake. I couldn't get a tight enough hold with only one hand so removed the second from my head and grabbed on, trying to pull it free. I had barely placed both hands around its body when the beast whipped itself around and caught my hands, pinning them with such force that I cried out.

"You are no match for us, Mortal. Our master warned that you would be defiant, but he trusts that we shall get the job done, just as we always have."

"I would tell you to go to Tartarus, but we're already here," I growled.

Tisiphone laughed a deep, throaty laugh and flapped her wings, hovering a few feet off the ground. "We are certainly going to have some fun, you and I." She turned and flew back to her iron tower.

Alecto retrieved her snake and I took two quick steps back, rubbing at my wrists. She too flew back to her post.

The few souls still stood nearby. Still none of them paid any attention to me or to the Erinyes. I wondered if they'd even seen or heard them. Tisiphone's words swum in my head. Had Lysistratos really thought those things? Had he hated me for falling in love with Demi and not living with the soldiers like I always had?

I shook my head to clear the thoughts. I could not let the Erinyes get in my head and have victory over me.

"You must stay strong, Child," a familiar voice said. I turned to the flash of light to my left finding Hephaestus beside me.

I looked him over warily. "Are you really here or are you just another game the Erinyes want to play?"

"I am here," he assured me, placing a warm hand on my arm.

I took a deep breath and nodded. "You were right back in Thermopylae." I lowered my eyes from his. "About my sword; I should have never asked you to get it. I gave Ares everything he wanted."

"Hush now, it does not matter," he said, drawing me against his larger body. "I am doing all I can to help you get out of here, but it may take a little time."

I pushed off him and started to pace. "There's no time, Ares has the pieces of the amulet. He's got everything he needs to defeat Zeus. He will destroy the mortal world."

"So it would appear," Hephaestus murmured.

"Has it already happened? Is that why you're here now?" I circled him, looking for evidence of wounds.

"Ares has not carried out his threat to harm me. In truth I have not seen him since you and I last saw one another."

"What about Demi, Melina and the boys?"

"They are all safe and well, though they miss you terribly."

"Then take me with you, reunite us. Help me find Ares and take back the jet and hematite. The hind's blood broke your protection over me when it touched the sword, so what if I could use them again and Ares' hold over me – through them – is also broken?"

"It is not in my power to simply take y–"

"What about Zeus?" I cut him off.

"I must go, but I shall return soon," Hephaestus said, disappearing as quickly as he had appeared.

"No? Don't leave me here. Take me with you." I called, but he was gone.

"Stay strong. Resist the Erinyes and all shall be as it was meant to very soon," his voice echoed off the walls.

Sisyphus' large boulder rolled by and when the old man ran past, I followed, catching up to him when his rock came to rest against a tree.

The Erinyes had the power to get inside my head, but I would not let myself believe anything they told me. Not about Lysistratos or anything else. If I did, I would be no better than Sisyphus and his fruitless attempts to roll his rock to the top of the hill. I had to deny them, and by extension Ares, until Hephaestus returned to take me away. Or until I found my own way out of Tartarus.

"May I assist you?" I asked, placing a hand on top of Sisyphus' rock. He looked up, his light blue eyes almost grey around the dark center. He shrugged and moved to the opposite side, heaving the boulder from the tree trunk and back in the direction of the hill.

I joined him, rolling it over the dirt and sand, finding it moved easily across the flat surface. "How long have you been here?" I asked. Sisyphus didn't reply. "Do you remember why you're here?" Nothing. "Do you even remember who you are?"

"I remember everything," he murmured.

"Good because I need your help."

"Help, ha!" Sisyphus snorted, his features momentarily breaking from the lifeless mask. "No one can help us here. We are the damned, worthless souls who have committed acts of betrayal against the gods. We do not deserve help." His eyes darted as he spoke as if he expected to be punished for speaking the words out loud.

"Yet I'm helping you now and look how quickly we've returned your rock to the base of the hill," I said, indicating the rise in front of us. Sisyphus cast his eyes in the direction we had come then laid them briefly on me, before resting them on the hill ahead of us.

I put my hand on his skinny arm and squeezed it just slightly. "When Hades brought you to Tartarus, you didn't give up your quest for freedom easily, did you?" Sisyphus shook his head. "Then tell me all the ways you tried to escape."

He shook my hand off and dropped his eyes to his task. "I cannot."

"Sisyphus, please, help me."

"You should leave now. I must get my rock to the top," he insisted, rolling the boulder back up the hill.

"I *will* find a way to escape and if you help me, I'll take you with me."

Sisyphus paused, turning to me with a frown. "I do not want to leave, this is where I belong. I deserve to be here and each time I fail to get my rock to the top of the hill, I know it is Zeus' way of telling me that I have not yet paid for my betrayals. You would do well to get back to your own task, lest they find further painful ways to punish you for disobedience. They are fond of that here you know."

I shook my head in reply. "This *is* my task," I murmured.

6

I couldn't bring Demi's face to mind, the attempts I made never quite right – her eyes the wrong color or her face not entirely her own. I had no idea how much time had passed since I'd arrived in Tartarus but with each moment, my beloved wife's features slipped further from my grasp.

Time had become fluid and I measured it by the times when the Erinyes invaded my thoughts and I wished them gone, and when I desperately wanted them with me so I wasn't alone in the dark with only my mind for company.

Hephaestus had told me to resist the Erinyes, to stay strong against them, and I was, I had. For a while. But the longer he stayed away, the harder it became.

I closed my eyes and thought of Demi again. I could still picture her lips, pink and soft as she pressed them to mine in that familiar way. I ached that I would never hold her again.

"Demi," I whispered into the darkness.

"Your lover did not wait for you. She took another and they raised your sons until they became men. None of them mourned your death for they knew the truth; you chose Ares." Tisiphone's words taunted me.

There is a bed. Ares lies on top, eyes closed, as I kiss his stomach.

"When you have taken your father's throne, you shall be known as King of the Gods and I shall be honored to pleasure a king of such stature," I tell him, moving lower.

He draws a shallow breath and finds my face with his hand, caressing my cheek as I lick the hair at his navel. He smiles and I push into him, feeling him rise beneath me. Ares and Ava. The Chosen One and her Master. Lovers. Confidantes. Rulers. Destiny, fate, whatever you want to call it. All is as it should be and I welcome it.

I shook my head to clear the image, a wave of sickness passing over me. "That is just a fabrication Tisiphone. Ares and I have never been lovers. Would never *be* lovers. He has Aphrodite for that. I have … had Demi."

"Perhaps it is not your past that I show you, but your future."

"I will never belong to Ares, not like that. Not in any way."

"You cannot be certain of that. You cannot know your future path, not even what awaits you here in Tartarus. You may find yourself welcoming the arms that you claim to despise. How many times have you wished to be kissed? For a lover's embrace? To feel more than just emptiness?"

"I never wanted Ares to be that lover, it has always been Demi. Ares knows that. I will never be his, I never was. It makes no difference that he called me his Chosen One, my heart never belonged to him."

Tisiphone cackled and I pressed my head back against the rock I had come to call mine. Had Demi taken another? The thought of it pierced me to the deepest reaches of my soul.

"It's not true," I told myself firmly. She wouldn't. She would've asked Hephaestus to bring her to me when he told her he'd visited me, even if it meant entering the Underworld.

But what if she was telling the truth? I would never deny Demi the chance to be happy again. Perhaps that was why Hephaestus hadn't come back. Perhaps he couldn't bear to tell me, or lie to me about Demi and her new lover. Perhaps they had got married. Did my sons call her mother as they once had me? I shut my eyes tight, letting the tears come.

Demi's new lover is beautiful and kind, laughing at the joke she whispers in her ear. They hold hands as they walk through the agora, heads bent together as Demi shares her past. The other woman's tone is gentle yet firm with Zenon when he rushes through the streets, almost upending a basket of pomegranates. He returns to her side, holding her other hand, looking up at her with such adoration. Kadmus walks beside his brother, smiling and waving his hands about as he describes a particular color he wants to find at one of the stalls. My boys. They have forgotten me. They have forgotten that she is not the one who raised them until their eighth winter … or was it their tenth? I cannot recall that either.

Demi looks upon her with joy and love, the smile never leaving her lips as days turn to moons and moons to winters. Her skin glows as she throws a stick to Damon, laughing as he leaps high in the air to catch it and when she turns to look at me, the raven haired beauty who has captured my wife's heart, rests a hand on her rounded belly. Demi approaches, putting her arm around her and kissing her cheek as she places her hand on top of her stomach, just as she did so many times when I was carrying Kadmus and Zenon. They are happy. They are a family and I will never be a part of that. My time with Demi and our sons is long past. I cannot breathe with the truth of it.

The images change. Demi is an old woman. Her eyes and mouth have small lines around them and her hair has faded to grey. But underneath the changes, she is still my Demi. Voices emerge and I swallow as I recognize them; Mumma Skylar, Mother Alexis, Papou, Agrias and Melina. Somehow I know they're together in the Elysium Fields. They smile at one another, sitting on a patch of bright green grass, drinking wine from a large amphora, talking and laughing. I smile, yearning for Hephaestus to return and take me to join them in that place of eternal happiness.

"She does not show you the truth," Ares' familiar voice startled me and dispelled the image. He leaned against a small tree, the ball of light in his hand the only illumination around us.

I couldn't stand, my body weak, as it always was after the Erinyes had visited me.

"She shows you what you want to be true," he added, voice thick, as if he'd just woken from a long sleep.

"Not always," I countered, remembering only too well what she had put into my head about him and me. I studied his features, wondering why he didn't come any closer; he was paler than usual, a light sheen of sweat beading on his forehead and dark marks beneath his eyes. "Why are you here?"

"The Erinyes tell me you have spoken with other souls about escape."

"They weren't useful in the matter."

"Then why do you persist with your questions?"

"Because I don't belong here."

"We both know that is not true. Besides, these walls are well guarded by the Erinyes and if by chance you were able to get past them, you would find your way blocked by the River of Fire."

"Odysseus and Orpheus both entered the Underworld on occasion and returned safe and well to the mortal world afterwards. I don't wish for that, only to find my way to the Elysium Fields."

"Odysseus and Orpheus were not already dead when they visited the Underworld, nor did they ever find themselves in Tartarus. You shall never find yourself outside these walls."

He stepped towards me, a hand outstretched to steady himself. I awkwardly pushed myself to my feet, keeping my back pressed firmly against my rock.

"You and I shall be together for a very long time." He reached out and caressed my cheek. My eyes fluttered closed at his warm touch and I leaned into him ever so slightly. "The power of the amulet binds us, even here, and perhaps it shall still bind us once the power becomes fully mine. I know you feel it too." I nodded, feeling his lips graze my temple. "We were always destined to be together. Once I believed it was with you by my side, but your life in the mortal realm was not as it should have been. Demetri … Demi denied you of your true path. They wanted to change who you truly are." As Ares spoke, something shifted deep within me.

I open my eyes, finding his flashing red ones so very close. "Demetri did not approve of me using the amulet. He said it changed me."

"You belong here, far from his reach, far from anywhere. You desire the simplicity of your days and nights here."

I nod. "I do. I can do what I want, when I want. I practice with my sword, well it's only a stick, but in my mind I see it and feel that it's my own sword, with its leather across the handle helping me to grip it firmly." Ares smiles and nods in return. "Demetri's sword had leather around its handle as well."

"He was nothing more than a slave. He was not the one for you."

"No. After he left me in Konitsa I was relieved. I enjoyed our time in the wind. I had never felt that before but …"

"… there was no future for the two of you," Ares finishes.

I shake my head. "He was just a runaway slave and I was the Chosen One. *Your* Chosen One. He would have wanted me to change, he would have wanted me to stop using the amulet and to deny you of what you wanted with it. He would have asked me to marry him, to have a family and give up my soldier ways."

"But instead you chose to be with me, you used the amulet and we conquered Zeus and took Olympos for ourselves, do you remember?"

I nod, the battle he speaks of clear in my mind; Zeus lays, defeated, at my feet. The other immortals stand in what remains of the palace of the gods, some cheering our victory, others lying bloody and dying beneath our sandals. Ares is beside me, his cheeks flushed and chest heaving as he throws one of our rivals into the abyss below. We conquered many towns and cities before challenging Zeus. Our Keres had stood beside us, reveling in the carnage we created and sending soul after soul to Hades in the Underworld.

The power Ares and I hold between us with his immortality and my amulet is incomparable. We destroy enemies old and new and he has never looked as glorious as he does at this moment. His body, his power, intoxicates me and when our eyes meet, his reflect my own desires. With a flash of light he clears the crumbling room of all others and we consummate our partnership and triumph in the most primal of ways. His hands tear the armor from my body, his lips replacing it. The mark on my ribs glows hot as I writhe atop him. He holds me, watching as I rise above him time and again. Our lovemaking is fierce, as fierce as the battle has been and I wish for it never to end.

Brought from the vision, tingling desire floods my veins. I trace the dark whiskers of Ares' beard, recalling how it felt at my throat up on Olympos. We are an unstoppable force. I want to feel his hands on my body again, for him to take me to the brink of consciousness day after day just as we did after we took Zeus' throne. I want to feel the hairs of his chest against mine, to fist my hand in his perfectly groomed hair, to …

Ares clutches his chest. He staggers away from me and disappears, taking the desire I had felt with him and leaving me with a deep ache.

7

He is gone. My Ares is gone and I need him. Panic rises within me. Where is he? Why did he leave me? Why did he clutch at his chest? Is he ill? I run, searching the dirt covered area, but find only shabbily dressed figures stumbling along.

I call to them, but they take no notice of me. I stop the nearest man, grabbing him by the shoulders. He cowers from me.

"Where is Ares? Have you seen him?" I scream. He doesn't answer, even when I shake him hard, his head rocking back on forth on his neck like it's made of thin reeds rather than bone and muscle and skin. "You must have seen him. Why won't you answer me?"

Still he doesn't respond. I push him to the ground and he scrambles away into the darkness.

My skin prickles. I claw at my face, my arms, my thighs. It itches. It hurts. Why does it hurt? My hair falls over my eyes and I twirl it around my finger, tugging until my scalp burns, all the while scratching at my legs.

My eyes drop to my tunic and the blood stain spread across the front.

Ares.

That deep shift rolls inside me again and I am drawn from my panic.

Ares did that. We were at Thermopylae. He held me inside that shield and we fought. He drove my sword through my stomach. He killed me.

I don't love him. I hate him. None of what he said was true. He wasn't real. None of what I saw with us being together on Olympos was true. It was the Erinyes. Again.

I screamed, clutching and tearing at the material above my stomach, driving my fingers deeper until I tore it from my body. I ripped and shredded my tunic until there was no evidence of the blood left, until the material hung in shreds above my skin.

Exhausted, I dropped to my knees, crawling across the dirt until I found my rock. I pressed my fists to my eyes, great sobs bursting from my chest.

I remained there until footsteps pounding the dirt nearby made me lift my head. I couldn't see anything – the torches all but extinguished again in the pit of Tartarus.

"Who's there?" I called.

No one answered.

The endless dark was full of noises; of screaming and wailing and running and laughing. I put my hands over my ears, rocking back and forth. Tears streamed down my face as I curled up on the ground, fresh dust sticking to my cheeks as I drowned out the sounds with my own wails of anguish.

8

I woke. Somehow I knew it would be different to yesterday. I felt more like my old self, not that I looked like it. Yesterday was a bad day. Yesterday the Erinyes visited me and I believed everything they told me.

Yesterday I laid in the dirt for candlemarks. I writhed and cried, wailing and screaming just as the other souls in Tartarus did. I tore at my tunic and my hair. I reached up, the long, dark strands knotted and dusty between my fingertips. Clumps were scattered around me on the ground.

My chiton was no longer white but that wasn't because of yesterday – it had started to lose its natural color before then. A crudely ripped section was missing above my stomach. There had once been a bloodstain there. I removed it, not wanting to be reminded of Ares and how he sent me to Tartarus.

The more I thought about it, the more I didn't think it was yesterday that I tore at my clothing, or saw the Erinyes. It may have been the day before, or the day before that. Perhaps that piece of material was never there at all.

I frowned. Why couldn't remember when – or if – I tore it off?

Was it darker? No. Torches were lit throughout the area, there were plenty of them. It was brighter than before.

I shook my head, rubbing at my arms.

No, the material was there once, I am sure of that.

I placed my hand against my stomach, feeling the rise and fall of my breathing. The sensation calmed me. I had to fight those fears, those thoughts. I had to fight to stay in the place where I remembered my life from before. I knew who I was, and I had to get out of Tartarus and save the earthly realm from Ares. It didn't matter if those I once loved were long gone. I was destined to save the mortals and the gods from Ares.

I was the Chosen One. I am Queen Ava of Trachis, in the region of Thermopylae, home of the Malians. I must keep reminding myself of all that I was, all that I am and all that I must be. I *am* going to escape. Ares will not keep me here.

9

They have returned, I see them, in the distance. They approach, their eyes of green and blue twinkling even in the low light around us. I smile, but they do not return it.

Mumma Skylar slaps me hard across the face. "You are a failure. You did not protect your family, our family. My father is dead because of you, because you did not kill Ares when you should have. You had help from another god and still you failed. You were chosen, yet you were weak," she pauses, breathing hard as she spits the words at me.

When she continues, her voice is softer. "We entrusted you with the amulet and for what? To see you here in the Underworld while Ares takes what he has always wanted and destroys everything you should have protected? You disgust me. I am ashamed to call you my daughter."

Mother Alexis steps forward. I cower from her, but she does not raise her hand. "When you were still in my belly, your Mumma wanted to kill you, to stop you ever having to choose whether you would join Ares when your time came, just as she had to. I would not allow it, convincing her that you would not carry her curse inside you. But I was wrong and you have disappointed us greatly. Perhaps I should have allowed her to kill you after all."

Then they're gone. I slump to my knees, wanting to call them back, yet hoping to never see them again. How could they speak such words? They don't care about me anymore. They hate me. But they're not wrong; I despise me too.

I surrender to the dark thoughts, swaying back and forth as I chew my dirty nails. I was the Chosen One, but I lost that title, along with all my others. I don't have Mumma's amulet, or the pieces I broke it into. I couldn't defeat Ares with the hind's blood that Artemis gave me. My family doesn't love me, and why should they? I'm a failure and I have disappointed them with my continuing misguided actions. I was arrogant and believed that because I'd defeated Ares once, that I would do it again. I was so wrong. I thought too much of myself, of my abilities and my past and now I'm nothing, stuck in this place forever.

I no longer harbor thoughts of escape, what's the point when I know that escape from Tartarus is impossible? Even if I still held such a wish, where would I go? No one waits for me, no one wishes for my return. Hephaestus' continued absence is proof of that. He said all would be as it was meant, yet I remain in Tartarus, alone and lonely. Clearly this is where I am meant to be.

I am cold. I wrap my arms around my waist where some of my chiton is missing. Where is it? I don't remember how that happened. When it happened. My hand is warm on my stomach and I remember that I haven't eaten. Why don't I feel hungry or thirsty? I don't even remember the last time I ate. Where can I find something here? Do I even want anything?

I get to my feet. There's a tree with a man standing beneath it. He has fruit on his tree and water at his feet, but it seems he can't reach either. Strange. I don't want anything to eat and my body has warmed again. I sit in the dirt, my back against a large rock I have found and I wait, but for what I do not know.

10

"We have been here over a moon, and still you say we must stay. Why?" Aphrodite asked, brushing out her long hair. Her eyes settled on her lover on the bed. His were closed and he had not moved for a long while, though she knew he was not asleep.

"I have told you, the power from the amulet has not returned to me yet."

"Perhaps it shall never return," she murmured.

Ares squeezed his hand into a tight ball, the movement sending pain up his arm. He wished for the thousandth time the discomfort was over. "What did you say?" he asked through gritted teeth.

Aphrodite turned, putting her brush aside as she spoke. "Do not deny that you have not thought it too. Day after day we wait, and yet nothing changes, nothing happens. You lay there, barely moving, your pain denying you of your strength. If you had not killed the Valkyrie, then perhaps we could have returned to them for answers."

Ares' eyes opened and he rolled his head to the side to meet hers. "They called into question my power, my godliness, would you have preferred that I left them unpunished for such insults?"

"Unpunished? No. But kill them? Why did you not wait until you had the amulet, why did you not wait to see if it would do as you hoped?"

He had asked himself the same questions, over and over again. He had the answer – his rashness had overcome his sensibilities – but he would not admit that to his lover.

"You were not there, you cannot understand," he said instead.

"I was not, that is the truth, but I do not enjoy who you have become. You are different, you are not my lover. You do not look at me the same way."

"I still adore you."

"What then of the promises you made me, that I would barely notice the moon we had to spend in this awful place flying by as you loved me with passion unequalled and unbridled? It has been weeks since you even touched me."

Inwardly he sighed, knowing he could not deny the truth of her words. With effort, he pushed himself to his elbows and held his hand out to her. "My love." Aphrodite crossed the small room and perched beside him on the bed. "It shall not be forever, I give you my word. I shall regain my strength and I shall be the god I always have for you. I wish for that more than you can know."

Aphrodite ran her hand down his bared chest, the hairs springing back into place when her palm moved on. She continued lower, and he saw the disappointment cross her face as her touch failed to bring more than only the slightest movement to his once barely-restrained body. How he longed to feel something, anything, when she touched him.

"I am beginning to believe there is another who holds your heart," she said, removing her hand and lowering her eyes from his.

He looked up, startled. "Aphrodite, no," he insisted, taking her hand and returning it to his body. "You wound me with such words."

"There is no proof to what you say," she said, squeezing and stroking him the way he had always enjoyed as if to emphasize her words.

"*That* is what you wish to base your assumptions on?" he asked, nodding to her hand.

"With you, it is all I have ever needed," she replied, a frown creasing her forehead.

"Why is it you accuse me of such things?"

"When you sleep, you often speak another's name. You do not say it in anger or through battle. You speak it as you once spoke mine."

"That cannot be, I have not dreamt for a long time," he said, knowing that he had barely met Hypnos the past moon, much less Morpheus. "Who is it you say I speak of? Who do you believe you have lost me to?"

"Your *Chosen* One," Aphrodite replied in disgust.

"No," Ares was adamant. "If it is her name I am speaking then it must be the amulet's power working through me, cleansing me of the blood of the line."

"I hope it is so, for I do not relish another's on your lips."

"As I would not wish for another's to be on yours."

"There never shall be," she whispered.

175

He nodded, searching her eyes for a sign that she kept the truth from him. He had heard whisperings, but he was afraid to ask, lest they were true. Perhaps now was the time to set his mind at ease or to aid him in formulating his next plan. Perhaps another goal would assist in his recovery.

"I heard you had taken Adonis as your lover whilst I was gone," he said.

"I did not know you were given to believing rumors," she said, snatching her hand away.

"So you deny it?"

"Of course. There are those who are jealous of the close friendship the boy and I have, but you know that I raised him as a son and no matter the fame of his beauty or the perfectness of his body, I have never wanted him in my bed. He does not possess the skills to satisfy me, not as you can."

"Then I should say that he is lucky, for I would not have allowed him to live had you said it was so," Ares said, trailing a finger down Aphrodite's side, the slightest thrill touching his insides.

"And if you had not already killed *your* young charge, then perhaps I would have done the same," Aphrodite said.

Heat ignited in his veins and with it, a surge of his former strength. He smiled and lifted Aphrodite from her place beside him on the bed, sitting her atop his thighs. She was as naked as he and the feel of her filled his blood with fire. He raised his body so their chests touched, her breasts peaking against him and exciting him.

"Do not ever accuse me of having given another my heart. It has only ever been your hands, mouth and body I have craved. Ava meant nothing to me. I would never have taken her to my bed. Not ever," he said, running his hands up her thighs and possessing her breasts with his lips.

"Then why did you kiss her in Kierion?" she asked, arching her back and pressing into him, eyes closed.

"It was only ever to get her to use the amulet, please you must know that," he replied, his breath shortening at the feel of her around him.

"Prove it," Aphrodite said, quickening her movements.

Ares pulled her onto his hard body, pushing up into her. He had feared he had lost the fierce passion he once held for her, that they had lost the very essence that was 'them'. But as he moved inside her, he felt it all return and he closed his eyes, relieved they had not lost what he treasured, that the power of the amulet had not taken it from him.

11

"You don't really exist," I told him. "You're nothing more than the work of the Erinyes, of Ares. You left me here. You don't care about me. You've turned from me just like the rest of my family."

"I have a way for you to leave this place," Hephaestus replied, ignoring my words.

"There's no way for me to leave. Besides, I don't deserve to. I failed everyone who ever relied on me, everyone who ever put their trust in me. I failed the mortals I swore to protect. I failed the gods that helped me. I belong here reliving my failures and knowing I can never atone for what I did."

"There is no truth to your words. Please Ava, you must fight those thoughts."

"Even if I could, I would not wish it."

"You must, if not for yourself, then for Demi. For Kadmus. For Zenon."

I turned my back on him. "They don't wait for me, they're long grown. Ares has destroyed their world, their future happiness. *I* destroyed that with my arrogance and the belief I would triumph like I did before. I was selfish. I was wrong."

Hephaestus spun me to face him and slapped me hard. I stumbled with the force; my head cleared by the pain that ripped through me.

"Apologies," he said as the echo of his strike quieted.

I worked my jaw open and closed, wiping at the tears that dripped down my cheek. I was still in Tartarus, but I no longer felt the full weight of my failure against Ares. Anger at my inability to resist the Erinyes flowed through me instead, followed swiftly by relief that Hephaestus had finally returned.

"Take me from this place, please. I'm so confused, I don't know what's real and what's not. Take me to the Elysium Fields where I belong."

"I do not have the power to remove souls once they have been judged. I can come and go in the Underworld if I so choose, but it is Hades' domain."

"Then how can I leave?" I frowned.

He drew me to his chest, hugging me tightly and lowered his voice to reply. "I have what you need, but there is much we must do." He pulled back. "I come for many reasons, though it is Hades that I seek first," he said, louder than I would have thought necessary.

"And I am here, Nephew," Hades' voice greeted us a moment before he appeared in a flash of light. The two gods stared at one another, Hades with his head cocked slightly to the side, Hephaestus meeting his eyes with a cool stare. "Please, tell us both why you have come," Hades said conversationally.

Hephaestus released me. "I came to request that you allow Ava into the Elysium Fields, or at the very least the Fields of Asphodel. She does not belong here with you and she has suffered enough."

Hades smiled. "Ah, my dear nephew, you know it is not at my request that she is in Tartarus. I am only the keeper of the souls; I do not pass judgement on them."

"Ares had no righ–"

"Ares has the same authority you do towards those that offend or betray you, though I note that you never subject them to a fate such as he does. Instead you allow them to live far from you with no true consequences befalling them,"

"I punish them in my own ways," Hephaestus corrected.

"You are weak," Hades sneered.

"No, I just do not share your, or Ares', particular taste for revenge."

"You attempted to have your revenge once," Hades reminded him.

"It was not well received, as you may remember."

Hades laughed. "No, you were humiliated in front of all our kin, but then no one expected anything less from a lame god."

Hephaestus drew his arm back, a ball of light sitting in his palm. "Now, now," Hades grinned. "You know how Zeus feels about us fighting each other."

"Zeus is still alive?" I asked, standing between the immortals as they stared each other down.

"Yes," Hephaestus confirmed.

"So I never … Ares hasn't … we didn't …" I struggled to put into words what the Erinyes had shown me. None of it was true; I hadn't helped Ares against Zeus. There was still time to deny him.

"Demi?" I asked.

Hephaestus lowered his arm and the ball of light disappeared. "She is still safe, as are your sons."

"For now," Hades said. "But it shall not be long before Ares is strong enough to take Zeus' throne. I shall be at his side when he does, whilst you cower before us and Ava suffers under the weight of her own mind."

"We shall see," was Hephaestus' only reply.

Hades started to pace back and forth, his hands linked together behind him as I had seen Ares do long ago. "You have visited Ava many times, yet you did not appear to her. I watched you, watching her, as she succumbed to what the Erinyes showed her," he smirked.

"You were here and you didn't save me from them?"

"I could not. I cannot interfere with what they do," Hephaestus replied, turning to Hades again. "Ava should be with her mothers and grandparents in the Elysium Fields or the Fields of Asphodel. None of them would be a threat to Ares and his plans there. If you wanted to, you could make it so."

"You assume that is where her family is to be found," Hades said, his smirk now a wide grin.

"Where are they if not there?" I asked.

"Do you truly believe Ares would have allowed them to have such peace after what they did to him? Your grandmother, your mothers, they all defied him in his quest for Zeus' throne just as you did," Hades replied.

It had never occurred to me that *their* afterlives may not be peaceful. "Where are they?" I repeated. Hades only grinned as a thought hit me with force. "Are they here, in Tartarus?"

I'd scoured the lengths of the walls when I arrived but I'd seen no one who resembled my mothers, not that I'd thought to look for them; I'd been too intent on finding a way to escape. I didn't think the few souls I'd seen and spoken to before the Erinyes started visiting me were the only ones in Tartarus, there was so much darkness and so many voices, had I simply missed my mothers? Had they fled when they saw me?

I had to find them. If Hephaestus had a way to get me out, then we would all go; I wouldn't leave them behind to suffer as I had.

"I have enjoyed our chat so very much, but I am afraid that I am required elsewhere," Hades said, his grin widening.

"Tell me, are they here?" I yelled, but he was gone.

"Do not waste your breath, we have much to discuss," Hephaestus said.

"I won't leave without them. We have to search Tartarus, all of it, they don't deserve to be here anymore than I do and I cannot leave without them."

"I cannot feel them as I could feel you when your sword was protected with my blood. But I do not believe they are in Tartarus."

"You could search must faster than me, can you do that?"

"Of course," he replied, disappearing instantly.

My mothers. My grandmother. I could have been so close all this time and I never knew it. If there was a way for us to leave Tartarus, if we could get to the Elysium Fields, or even into the Fields of Asphodel perhaps we could find some way to stop Ares from taking ... I paused as a thought occurred to me. It wasn't enough to simply find them and take them from Tartarus; we needed to escape the Underworld entirely.

I started to pace, sending up puffs of dirt as my sandals scuffed over the ground. Each of us, individually, hadn't been able to defeat Ares, but what if we were all together? It was true that Ares had the pieces of the amulet, but what if it was our *line* that gave us power and the amulet was just a vessel able to release that power?

I needed to trust in my family, my history. I needed to trust that something important could come of the Ker line that did not bring about the destruction of the entire mortal world. I had chosen to put my faith in gods, goddesses and hind's blood rather than the mortals of my family. Papou and Demi had been at Kierion and helped me alter the amulet, but I'd battled Ares alone at Olympos. And in Thermopylae with the Persians approaching, I had sent Demi away, facing Ares alone once again.

I knew that the next time I faced the god of war I could not do it alone; I had to do it with my mother and grandmother alongside me.

Hephaestus returned. "They are not here."

"Maybe they're at the Fields of Punishment, we should go there to look for them," I suggested, adding my thoughts about the Ker line and what we might achieve together.

Hephaestus nodded. "What you suggest may be possible, but for now, we must concentrate on getting you out of Tartarus."

"And how do we do that?" I asked.

"With this," he replied, pulling a small bronze helmet from beneath his chiton.

"What is that?"

"Hades' Helmet of Invisibility."

12

"**Y**ou *must* be at our meeting point by the time the sun goes down tomorrow otherwise our plan shall fail and I do not wish to think what would happen to either of us if it did," Hephaestus said. "Time here is confusing, you know that, but once you emerge from the pit of Tartarus you shall experience night and day just as you did in the mortal realm. Now, you are certain you remember which way to go once you are through the gate?"

"Yes," I nodded. "And when I reach the Fields of Punishment?"

"There are no walls around the Fields, but you must act quickly. I do not know how often Ares, Hades or the Erinyes visit your family, if indeed they do at all, but I cannot do for them what I have done for you."

"I understand."

"Follow the paths and cross the rivers on your way up to the surface as I suggested and your days in the underworld shall be at an end."

"And I will really be alive? Not just that shadow of my former mortal self you and Zeus spoke of when we visited him on Olympos?"

"Yes. Your life thread is to be restored in the Moirai's weave. You shall be yourself. Zeus wishes for it to be so," he assured me.

"Then I will be there in time."

"Good. I believe we are ready," he said, reaching out to hug me carefully around the helmet hidden beneath my ripped tunic. "When you have everything in place look for me by the wall to the left of the door; I shall disappear, returning momentarily to the same place. The moment you see me return, you must put the helmet of invisibility on. If you put it on too early or too long after I have returned ..."

"I know. I will watch for you."

He nodded. "I shall see you where the rivers of Styx and Cocytus meet at Lake Acherousia before the sun sets tomorrow."

"Till then," I agreed with a tight smile. Hephaestus laid his hand on my shoulder, squeezing briefly before moving off to take his place near the door.

I blew out a deep breath and squared my shoulders, striding towards Tantalus, Hades' helmet bumping against my hip as I walked.

Hephaestus' plan was risky and there was no guarantee it would work. I was supposed to create a distraction with the other souls who resided in Tartarus, which in turn would distract and occupy the Erinyes long enough for Hephaestus to leave, take a soul from the banks of the Cocytus River, give that soul my memories, and alter their entire being so that for all intents and purposes they were me – in looks, memories and actions.

At the exact moment he and the new me returned to Tartarus, I had to put on Hades' helmet which would effectively remove me from Hades' sight and feel, though he and Ares would still believe I was where they had put me.

There was so much that could go wrong and if I'd been forced to drink from the Lethe River, it would have been near on impossible for Hephaestus to do what he planned. He'd told me that once memories were consumed by the Lethe, they were much more difficult to retrieve. I took another deep breath. I had a lot of ground to cover before sunset tomorrow; leaving Tartarus was only the first part of my journey.

I located Tantalus beneath his tree and approached, stepping into the warm water. He raised his eyes, surprise written across his face to find me in front of him. I bent down, cupping my hands together and filling them. His surprise grew when the water did not recede as I reached for it. I brought it up to his lips. He grabbed at my hands greedily and groaned when the liquid touched his tongue.

"More?" he croaked.

I nodded and reached down again, bringing another handful to him. When he'd emptied my hands a third time, his eyes cleared, the vacant look disappearing.

He looked down at the water and drew his foot out. It came up easily. "I have not thought of doing that for so long," he smiled.

"Can you get out?"

He pulled his leg up again, triumphantly stepping out onto the sand as I joined him. "My deepest gratitude to you," he said, reaching out and taking hold of the fruit beside him. He took a bite, groaning again as he savored the taste.

"I'm pleased I could help you, Tantalus. And now I need you to do something for me."

"Anything," he immediately replied.

"We must free everyone, just as I have freed you. You must assist them with whatever task they are attempting. We cannot stop until all the souls in Tartarus are broken from their useless tasks."

"And we shall feel as we did when we first arrived here?"

"Yes, and we will find a way to escape. The wooden door between the Erinyes' towers is the weakest point, but we cannot break it down unless everyone works together."

"I shall not fail you," he promised, rushing off excitedly to find a soul to help.

I smiled at his departing form and joined Sisyphus as he pushed his boulder along. Just like before, he didn't acknowledge me as I helped him roll the stone up the hill. We were almost to the peak when he started to lose his grip, the boulder threatening to overwhelm him and roll back down as it always did.

"I've got this," I assured him, gripping the rock at the base to steady it.

"I can never get it further than this," Sisyphus panted.

"You will today," I told him, pushing the rock end over end until I reached the top.

It stood for a moment, balancing precariously at the top of the hill, before falling forward and racing down the other side with a speed far greater than it had ever done when Sisyphus lost hold of it.

Sisyphus took me in a hug which crushed the helmet against my ribs and when he released me I repeated my request to help with the others, to which he agreed without hesitation, just as Tantalus had.

I found the Danaides nearby and realized they held two different sizes of amphorae. I smashed the tops off the larger ones and placed the smaller amphorae inside the bases, demonstrating how the water would not drain away when they took it from the cistern.

I passed Tantalus and Sisyphus several times as we moved around the large walled area, each time a new soul regained their old demeanor, they joined us and soon there were close to four hundred men and women gathered near the doorway.

I stood at the base of the hill Sisyphus had spent so many winters rolling his rock up and watched as the crowd started to move toward the door. Tantalus led them in their attack, although he made no battle speech like Moeris had the day before we had faced the Persians. The crush of men and women met the wooden door, kicking and pounding their fists against it, screaming to be set free and cursing whichever god had sent them to the deepest place imaginable.

Hephaestus was in place to the left of the chanting mob and I took the helmet from my tunic as he nodded and disappeared. I'd asked him what would happen to the memories of the soul who received mine and he told me they would still be inside them, remaining hidden unless I failed to get out. I had no intention of failing and sent a silent prayer of thanks, knowing that they would face an eternity of punishment for crimes that were not their own.

When the light that would announce Hephaestus' return began, I gripped the helmet tightly between my hands. The top of the bronze was patterned as though it had been made from the scales of a fish and I placed my fingers into the slight dips in the metal, waiting for him to re-appear.

The light brightened and he was there, along with another perfect version of me. I didn't hesitate, slamming the helmet on and hoping I was hidden, as I could still see myself perfectly when I looked down.

13

Ares sat on the edge of the bed he and Aphrodite had shared for so many moons, staring at the jet and hematite in his palm. He did not know how long he had been there, staring, but Aphrodite had not returned from her visit to Persephone, and normally she was gone several candlemarks.

The dense black of the jet appeared to mock him with its continued coldness and dark color. The pains in his chest had returned with renewed force and he saw Ava more and more often in both his waking and sleeping moments. He barely kissed or touched Aphrodite, for when he did, he saw Ava's face, he felt Ava's hands on his body and he feared he would utter her name as he reached his release.

He could not understand why the power had not returned. The Valkyrie had said it would only take a moon. It was not because Ava resisted the madness the Erinyes invoked, he had seen her with his own eyes – she had succumbed to them far quicker than he had believed she would.

His palm warmed and he pushed himself to his feet. This was it, he could feel it. Finally the power was his. He would challenge his father for the throne and he would be unstoppable. He would take Aphrodite from this dank, dark place where she would shine radiantly at his side. He would make her his wife and no one would part them again. They would rule Olympos for eternity.

The jet began to change color; the faintest orange to dark orange, to light blue then darker, from blue to swirling silver, heating all the while until it singed the flesh of his hand. He kept as still as he could as the hematite slid towards the silvery gem, drawn by unseen forces.

A bright light leapt from the re-joined pieces and Ares turned his face from the intense heat. Simultaneously, pain lanced through him, as though a sword had been thrust into his chest, piercing his heart and flooding his veins with heat.

"Ah!" he cried, sinking to his knees and clutching at his skin. As quickly as the light had appeared it disappeared and Ares slumped forward, the pain too great even for the god of war.

*

"Help me get him to the bed," Aphrodite directed. Ares felt himself lifted up and placed on soft covers. With effort, he opened his eyes, finding Aphrodite and Hades standing over him. "What happened?" Aphrodite asked, her fingers stroking his face.

He swallowed, attempting to remember. Pain … heat … the amulet. He pushed himself to his elbows, agony clenching every muscle as he moved. His palm stung where the amulet had burnt his flesh, but the jet and hematite were not there, replaced instead by the image of the double three-sided shape of the Keres.

"The completed mark," Ares murmured. He looked up at his lover. "The amulet, where is it?"

"I do not know. On the table?" she replied, frowning.

With help from Hades, Ares swung his legs over the side of the bed. "They are not here," he said, scanning the top. "I was holding them. They changed. And there was light and …"

"Perhaps you do not need them, Nephew," Hades said, indicating the mark on Ares' hand.

"No. Something is wrong. I must search for it," Ares insisted, attempting to disappear. Nothing happened and he slumped against the table.

"You must rest. Come lie down," Aphrodite pleaded.

Ares nodded and allowed her to guide him to the bed, his eyes still fixed on his hand. The sign of the Chosen One, what did it mean? Was he the one now? Had the amulet's power finally become his? He did not feel power. He did not feel as though he could challenge his father for the throne. The discomfort he had felt since he returned to the Underworld had not disappeared with the amulet, if anything, he felt weaker. Perhaps she …

"Is Ava still in Tartarus?" he asked.

"Yes. I was just with her and Hephaestus," Hades replied.

"Hephaestus? Why was he there?"

"He wanted me to move her to the Elysium Fields. Of course I told him I would not."

"He cannot do it himself, can he?" Aphrodite asked.

"Of course not, the Underworld is mine. He cannot take her anywhere without my knowing it, and he shall not attempt such a feat for he knows that my punishment, and Ares', would be swift and cruel."

"Did he break her from the Erinyes' grip?" Ares asked.

"For the moment, but she shall not attempt escape."

"How can you be certain of that?"

"Because I implied that her mothers were in Tartarus and she shall exhaust herself searching for them, which shall give the Erinyes plenty of time to put her back into her former state."

"Good. Return to her often and ensure it is so. As soon as I have regained my strength, I shall join you," Ares said, adding in a quiet breath, "and I shall find out what I can do now that I wear the Chosen One's mark."

14

Hades' helmet of invisibility was nowhere near as large or as heavy as the Corinthian style helmet I had favored during my days as a soldier. It more closely resembled the open Thracian style our men wore, but didn't have the long cheek pieces on either side. It sat comfortably around my head, the back reaching almost to the base of my neck. The front came down over my eyes where two half-moon shaped holes had been omitted from the bronze cast for the wearer to see out of.

Hephaestus searched the immediate area and when he nodded, I knew the helmet had done its job. I was hidden from him and everyone else in Tartarus. The 'new' me rushed to the crowd of bodies at the wooden door, grabbing each by the shoulder and scrutinizing their features before moving onto the next one. It took me a moment to realize that she was searching for Mumma and Mother. Hephaestus had said he would only give her my memories up to when Hades told me that my mothers were not in the Elysium Fields. He was sure she'd search for them, just like I'd wanted to.

Over all the noise of the souls yelling and banging against the wooden door, another piercing sound began. One of the Erinyes floated towards the ground, dragging her long claws against the iron tower she called home. I covered my ears, as did many of the other souls, their shouts immediately quietening.

A flash of light announced another presence and I drew a quick breath as Hades appeared not more than a few feet from me. "What is the meaning of this?" he roared. "You!" He pointed to the face that resembled my own. Tisiphone dragged her from the crowd and pushed her towards Hades. "What have you done?"

"I would've thought that was obvious; I seek my mothers. You told me they weren't in the Elysium Fields, so I sought help in leaving this place so I could find them. For that I needed the trapped souls here to remember who they were, who they are."

It was strange to see her gather herself up, straighten her shoulders and confidently answer the god of the Underworld in such a familiar way, but I grinned – she resembled me in every way.

"You aided her once again, Nephew?" Hades asked, turning to Hephaestus.

"I did, but I am certain that neither she nor they shall remember how it happened once you are through with them."

Hades worked his jaw angrily, but he did not dispute Hephaestus' words. Instead, he grabbed the doppelganger by the arm and pulled her towards the door. "If you are all so desperate to take your leave, then we shall go. Tisiphone, gather the rest and bring them to the River of Fire. We shall see how eager they are to follow her once they have experienced its wrath."

The souls looked at each other, no longer certain of their wishes, but before they could change their minds, Tisiphone captured them in a bubble similar to the one Ares had often used.

Hades blasted the wooden door open, dragging my copy out as Tisiphone followed with the other souls, and me following her. Hephaestus breathed out audibly and nodded before he disappeared.

I was once again on the outside of Tartarus' walls and beside the Phlegethon River, the flames from the River of Fire leaping high into the air above the swiftly running liquid. I slipped past Hades, Tisiphone and the other souls, keeping close to the large bronze wall of Tartarus until I stood twenty or so feet from the gathered party.

Even though I knew I had to hurry, I stopped, unable to take my eyes from Hades and the other version of myself. Hephaestus had told me I would have to cross three of the Underworld's five rivers on my way back to the mortal realm and with Phlegethon being the first; I had to know what it would do. Would I burn, my flesh eaten away until I was merely bones? How quickly would it regrow? *Would* it regrow?

I didn't have to wait long to find out, Tisiphone had no sooner brought the souls in the bubble to stand next to Hades, than he threw the one that looked like me into the flames.

She hit the water with a splash, resurfacing almost immediately, her screams piercing the quiet around us. Her body thrashed; arms and legs flailing wildly as she tried to get back to the shore. I knew when it came time for me to cross, I would experience everything she was, for she held my memories, my thoughts, my loves and hates.

A shiver ran the length of my spine and I sent out another silent word of thanks to her. I didn't know yet how I could repay her, but I vowed that one day, somehow, I would.

Tisiphone threw the rest of the souls into the river, their howls of pain drowning out the first. I backed away, turning and running as fast as I could to my right, following the flaming river as it took me down the long side wall of Tartarus.

When finally I came to the corner of the bronze, I knew I had to cross the Phlegethon. The path on the other side would start to curve upward and after a time I'd meet the deepest point of the Acheron, which I would also need to pass through. The Fields of Punishment were on the other side of that.

I believed I would find Papou and my mothers in the Fields. It was the only place that made sense if the Judges hadn't sent them to Tartarus. Minos had said that souls who'd committed crimes against the gods were sent there and I was sure Ares would've seen their denial of teaching me who I was, and Papou cutting off Mumma's wings, as a crime against him. I couldn't be as sure about Zita, after all Papou had said she'd betrayed her family and the Ker line by being with him. But if she wasn't in Tartarus then there was nowhere else for her to be either.

I paused at the side of the river, inhaling deeply as I squared my shoulders. Heat rolled off the forbidding mass as I tentatively stepped forward. At first, the warmth reminded me of the hot springs back at Thermopylae. I smiled as I remembered all the time I'd spent there as a child, and then with my own children these past winters.

I waded through the thick, thigh-deep water, finding a large rock to hold as I reached the middle. I lifted my leg again and stepped forward, my foot barely meeting the ground before Ares' laughter echoed around the river. I fell against the rock, agony ripping through my body. Flames rose around me, their licking heat searing my stomach and flooding my blood. I looked down, finding the end of a sword poking out through the hole in my tunic. Blood dripped from the end and fell, mixing with the flowing water around me.

I squeezed my eyes shut, willing myself to remember that Hephaestus had said that nothing I saw in the rivers could hurt me. Nothing I saw would be true; no matter how realistic it seemed. Only if I succumbed to the visions and the pain would I truly be lost to the waters and unable to get out. I had to press on.

I pushed off the rock, and stood unsteadily in the buffeting water. A rope appeared next to my head and I took it, trying to see what it was connected to above. My eyes travelled high along the braided surface, but it disappeared into the darkness. I gave it a firm tug, inflaming the pain in my stomach, but it didn't give way. I started to make my way forward again, holding tight to the rope.

The water swirled around my legs, getting stronger the further across I went. I gripped the rope in both hands, the wound at my stomach protesting with every movement. The water got faster still, gushing noisily over the rocks protruding from the water. It slammed into me, stopping me from getting a good grip on the rope. It slipped through my hands, the course fiber dragging painfully across my palms, stripping the skin until they were raw and pink.

I stared at them in disbelief; the jagged layers of torn skin the same as I had suffered after days of dragging Demi on a litter to find help for the spider bite. Just as I had in Konitsa, I tried to bend my fingers, but the movement sent shooting pain through my hands, up my arms and around my body.

I stumbled on through the water, crashing painfully into unseen rocks beneath the surface and recalling more of the journey to Mount Smolikos all those winters ago. The walk up the mountain had seen me slip and fall, finding hidden rocks beneath the snowy path to bruise my shins and cut my thighs. The trip down had been just as painful, often with Demetri's weight joining my own on the ground as he suffered with the effects of the spider's venom.

I continued across. I was going to make it; I could see the bank on the other side. I was almost there. I smiled despite the pain in my body. If I could just make my way to that rock to my left, I would be able to reach it.

As I altered my direction, my right foot caught between two rocks beneath the water and I lurched, twisting my knee painfully. I cried out, clutching at it as I caught myself on the closest rock. Mount Smolikos again, I could see it; Demetri and I had fallen back inside the mountain when the ground collapsed during our descent. I had thought him dead when I woke, and had twisted my knee when I found our passage up the steps blocked by hundreds of rocks. I blew out a long breath, trying to dispel the pain at my heart when I thought of Demetri lying somewhere cold, barely breathing, alone.

I took a tentative step but a blinding pain hit me high up on my shoulders and I fell forward, plunging into the heated river. My palms stung as they hit the sandy bottom. My wings pushed and tore at the flesh on my back, fighting to be released, until finally the skin gave way with a loud rip and they emerged, long and pointed, dropping fine black tendrils towards the flickering flames of the river. My head pounded in time with my chest as the weight behind me grew. I turned to look; a pair of large, full grown wings flapped slightly behind me, just like they had on the Thessalian Plain.

Determined to reach the bank of the river, I pulled myself through the water on hands and knees. The edge seemed suddenly further away. How was that possible? It wasn't, I told myself; it was just another trick designed to impede me. The pain of my hands and twisted knee compelled me to get to my feet, but I'd barely managed to straighten when an arrow shot out of the water, lodging itself in my left arm. I grabbed at it, recognizing the Persian arrow that had pierced my flesh the day Demetri had first kissed me. I ripped it from my shoulder, the diamond-shaped wound fresh and bleeding, the rich red staining my tunic as it leaked out.

With one hand covering the newest of my wounds, I inched forward. Something massive and unseen crashed against my left side. My limbs cracked loudly, sending a new wave of agony through my body. I tumbled into the water. I could no longer feel either my leg or my arm and I was swept along with the current, struggling to keep my head and the helmet on it, above the boiling water.

I managed to catch hold of another small rock not far downstream, my fingers screaming as the jagged surface cut into my raw flesh. I rested my cheek against its warmth, inspecting my limp appendages. They floated like tree branches in the wind and refused to obey my commands for movement, just like they had when I was six winters old.

Pain ebbed and flowed through my wounds in time with the warm water that poured downstream over me and the other rocks, hiding and then revealing some while finding a path around the base of others. I took a deep breath, willing myself on, I was only four or five body lengths from the edge of the river. I couldn't give up. I wouldn't.

Ignoring the intense pain the actions caused, I reached my right arm through the water as I kicked off the bottom with my obedient leg. The peaks of several rocks formed a line across the water and I half-swam, half-dragged my body towards them, using each to propel me towards the next as I closed in on the far bank.

When the gritty sand met my tender fingertips, I gathered my last ounce of strength and pulled myself out onto the bank, rolling over onto my back as my wings disappeared.

I lay there, drawing in deep breaths as slowly the pain flooding me subsided and feeling returned to my left side. I felt for each wound. They were gone; no raw hands, no arrow wound in my shoulder, no bruises or cut on my legs and no sword sticking out through my stomach. I exhaled and sat up, readjusting the helmet on my head. One river down, two to go, I told myself. At least I would know what to expect next time.

I pushed myself to my feet, wondering which way I should go. Hephaestus had said there would be a path, but the darkness here was so complete that I didn't know how I would find it. I hadn't asked him to provide me with a torch for my journey, and I didn't know if it would be made invisible by Hades' helmet if I held it or if it would be seen by anyone who happened along my path.

As if in response to my thoughts, the area was immediately lit, although I couldn't see by what. I stepped forward and the light moved with me. I looked left and right, both times the area I faced lit up, showing the slabs of dark rock pressing in from either direction. I could no longer see the bronze wall of Tartarus on the other side of the Phlegethon River so I made my way to the left where, after a few moments, my light revealed a gap and a number of steps cut into the rock.

I walked steadily upwards until I emerged from the rock stairway, finding myself on the banks of yet another river. It had to be the Acheron, and just beyond it, I would find the Fields of Punishment. I was so close to seeing my mothers for the first time in almost twenty winters, and perhaps I would meet my grandmother Zita for the first time.

But first I had cross the Acheron River or, as Hephaestus had called it: the River of Woe.

15

The section of Acheron River I stood before was just as stagnant and pungent with the smell of decay as where Charon had met us with his small boat. The floating mist shrouded the opposite bank in shadow and I wondered how far across it actually was. I'd crossed the Phlegethon with lamed limbs, but now they ached from the activity, and the subsequent climb up the steps. I didn't want to think how much the Acheron would weaken me or how it might prevent me from getting to Hephaestus' meeting place in time.

Instead, I took a deep breath and sank my foot into the muck. The disturbance released rank odors that swirled about, mingling with the mist. I covered my nose as my foot slid in further, warm mud slipping between my toes and covering my ankle within moments.

The dark goo reached to my thighs but as I crossed, the bottom dropped away and I found myself submerged up to my waist. I was grateful at least that the waters in the Underworld were not cold, having always preferred the warmth of the hot springs to the cold of the rivers Melas and Asopos outside Trachis.

I waded through the river, waiting for the pain to start but nothing happened. I started to move quicker, wondering if maybe I could reach the opposite bank before the memories of past pain surfaced ... or perhaps all my pain had been dealt back at the River of Fire, perhaps once you crossed *one* river, there was nothing more to endure except the feel of the waters themselves. Whatever the reason, I didn't hesitate, almost losing my sandal as I squelched quickly through the quagmire. I was over halfway across, drawing my hands and arms through the stinking mud when the far bank emerged from the fog, bringing Lysistratos with it.

He stands before me, his tiny son in his arms and a proud smile gracing his lips. I stop, frowning at the sight. What is he doing here and why is Phaidros still just a tiny baby in his arms? He did not die as an infant; he is not dead at all that I know.

Lysistratos hands the tiny bundle to me. I reach out, taking Phaidros in my arms, the brown mud of the river dropping back into the water as I do so. Eumelia joins us, wrapping her arm around Lysistratos' waist as he settles his own across her shoulders.

"I cannot thank you enough for bringing Lysistratos here, Ava," Eumelia says.

"He would not have missed meeting his son for anything, I assure you," I reply without hesitation, the words familiar, yet long past. "But we must leave today, Moeris shall send men after us if we are gone too long and I would not wish for our lie to be exposed."

We have been in Trachis for two days already and I am anxious to return to Athens. Five days ago, Lysistratos asked me to return home with him so we could meet his son. He could not wait the moons or winters until we returned with the rest of the soldiers. Though I was eager to see off the Persians where we had fought them at Marathon, he was my best friend and I could not deny him his wish, nor did I want to.

"I do not wish to leave yet," Lysistratos says, stroking his son's head. "Moeris shall not miss us one more day."

"We must go," I tell him.

"You should," Eumelia agrees, laying her head on her husband's chest. "It is your responsibility and I am proud to know that you keep our town and all of Greece safe from enemies. I am certain you shall return soon and when you do, we shall visit you every day at the barracks and watch you train."

"Perhaps Moeris shall allow me to visit you at home as well," Lysistratos says, embracing Eumelia.

"If that is so then it is indeed time you returned to he and the other soldiers. I do not want you to get in trouble and have such privileges revoked."

Lysistratos takes Phaidros from me again and Eumelia steps closer, hugging me warmly. "Keep him safe," she whispers.

"I shall always have his side in battle and when he celebrates his thirtieth winter, you shall have him at your side again to keep. Your family shall be whole and you can add more children to your home if that is your wish," I reply.

"Six winters sounds a long way off at this moment, but I trust you.

Please come, share a meal at our table when you and the soldiers return to Trachis."

"I shall look forward to it," I reply.

As I release Eumelia, she disappears, as does Lysistratos and Phaidros and I find myself in a small, dark room. Lysistratos lies on the bed, his face pale, his undamaged eye closed. His face and arms are clean, the bandages not yet soiled with his blood.

I speak, my voice barely above a whisper, though that is too loud. "You must fight, Lysistratos. Fight your wounds. Please. Recover for Eumelia and Phaidros and for me," I say, squeezing his hand.

The silence between his breaths lengthens and I can feel him slipping away. We have spent the best part of the last eight winters together and I cannot lose him as either my friend or a fellow soldier. "You must look upon your wife and child again. Do not leave us. Stay, I beg it of you."

My words rouse him. His eyes crack open as he speaks in a rasping voice. "Ava ... You must remember ... to gift Phaidros my necklace."

"And I shall, when it is time. It cannot be so yet."

"It is ... Please, you gave me your word." I close my eyes, nodding. "Ava, we have known each other ... so long ... and I have always been proud to ... call you my friend," he gasps. "I could always rely on you when we ... faced our enemies ... and when your time here is ended ... I shall look for you ... in the Underworld. Tell Eumelia I love her... and ensure Phaidros knows who I was ... and that I loved him." Lysistratos closes his eyes again, his final breath breathed.

"I am sorry," I whisper.

Eumelia enters the small room, tears pouring down her cheeks. "You! This is your fault," she screams.

"Eumelia, no," I cry, dropping Lysistratos' hand, knocking over the chair in my haste to get away from her as she advances.

"You promised you would keep him safe, that you would always be by his side in battle, and yet you allowed him to go to this fight without you. Where were you when he was being speared to death? When his limbs were being chopped without care from his body?"

"I could not ..." I start.

"You chose not to. Your belly is swollen with your children so you have forsaken all previous promises, but what about my child? You destined him to grow without his father for more than just the four winters it was supposed to be."

I can't catch my breath but I have no reply for her. She speaks true. I made promises that will no longer come to pass. Except for the necklace, I have to ensure Phaidros receives it. I must.

"Eumel–"

"No! You promised he would return to me for good in his thirtieth winter."

"I …"

"I shall never forgive you. You have taken a father from his son, how should I explain that to Phaidros when he is old enough to ask after him? You shall never be welcome at our table again and though we have only just learned of it, I shall call you sister no longer. Take your leave."

I have failed her. I have failed Lysistratos. Because of me, Phaidros will grow without a father, without ever knowing the kind and gentle side of the bravest soldier I have ever known. I may not have wielded the weapons that took him from this world, but I'm still responsible for his death, I know that.

She picks up the chair, dropping heavily into it and taking Lysistratos's hand as she wails for her loss. I swallow around the lump in my throat and nod, even though she doesn't see it.

I swallow the lump in my throat. "As you wish," I whisper. I silently vow that Eumelia and Phaidros will never want for anything and I pray that in time Eumelia and I will speak again and she will let me give Phaidros the necklace like Lysistratos wanted. "I am sorry," I add, leaving the darkened room.

When I looked up again I found myself sitting in the muddy depths of the Acheron River. The thick waves lapped at my chin, the stench hitting me with its full force as tears dripped down my face, silently hitting the waters below.

Regret beat in time with my heart, a gnawing ache settling in my chest denying me of a full breath. I was responsible for Lysistratos' death, I'd known it then and I wouldn't deny it now. I wondered what had become of Lysistratos' necklace; I'd left it at the palace before I faced Ares. I wondered if the palace still stood. Had the Persians taken it for themselves? Did someone other than Phaidros now wear the necklace?

The ache in my chest increased as I acknowledged the truth of my failure against the Persians – the consequences had been or would be far greater for more than just my family and friends. And that was to say nothing of the failure I'd had against Ares. Every mortal, every god would be forever changed. I had to keep going.

I had to find my mothers and Zita. We must defeat Ares and …

Papou appears, standing in the thigh-deep water, his face young and smiling. He leans forward, his hands set in a way I recognize immediately; he's going to catch a fish. I smile. How many times did he taken me to the water's edge to teach me to do the same? How many times did I scare the fish away by laughing at his wild flailing as they swam by and he grabbed at them with his bare hands? Papou puts a finger against his lips and I cover my mouth with both hands, just like I did when I was a child. He watches the water, waiting for the right moment. He plunges his hands into the river, pulling out a long, silver fish that thrashes and fights for freedom. He holds it up triumphantly for me to see before throwing it onto the bank and wiping his hands on his chiton.

He straightens again, his eyes finding mine, but there's an odd demeanor to his stance. I realize it's because Ares is here. He holds Leonidas' sword in one of his hands, the other bunched in the front of Papou's chiton. I push myself through the muddy water. He can't take Papou from me again. I will not let him. I've barely taken one step when Ares raises the sword, slicing it across Papou's throat before disappearing.

"No!" I cry as Papou slumps into my arms.

My knees tremble and we sink into the stinking water, Papou's life draining from him as we fall. I have failed him again. I have not been able to stop Ares from killing him even here. I am not worthy to be called Queen. I can't keep my people, my family, or my friends safe from my enemies. Ares and Phaeops were in Thermopylae because of me, because I had once wronged them, because I didn't kill them when I had the chance. Now Papou and Lysistratos are both dead, taken before their time and in the cruelest of ways, leaving behind loved ones who don't deserve such pain.

I should take Hades' helmet from my head and let him or even Ares find me and take me back to Tartarus or to the Fields of Punishment where they can punish me for my crimes for eternity. If my mothers are there they won't want to see me; perhaps they truly are ashamed of me for my failures.

Papou disappears and I find myself in my chiton, the freezing marble of the statue of Artemis numbing my hands and thighs as I crouch in the courtyard. The Persian pushes Mother into the hands of another soldier and grabs Mumma by the throat.

"You shall do what I tell you to do, when I tell you to do it," he says.

"Go to Tartarus," Mumma says, drawing her legs up and kicking him in the stomach. The soldier doubles over, gasping, but she is held firm in the grip of the two other men that accompany him.

"You shall regret that," he says, looking up at her, his breath coming in bursts.

He staggers to his feet and places a hand on Mother Alexis' shoulder, drawing the knife back with his other.

"No," I cry, but my vision is darkened.

I stand on the beach, looking out over the water. I am wearing a plain white chiton, my hair swept back into a long plait down my back. It is cold, but I do not care. I refuse to wear my long himation.

My mothers are gone, sent to Charon in the Underworld with a coin on their lips and the largest piece of my heart. I turn from the crashing waves, the remnants of the funeral pyres still evident further up the sand. Half-burnt laurel branches litter the ground and a single twig of rosemary tumbles end over end past me.

I stand in the courtyard, my gaze locked on the Throne Room floor with its dark stain. I want them back. I have questions I cannot get answers to. Papou Leandros has gone, banished from Trachis by Yiayia Melina and told never to return. Yiayia and Papou Agrias do not love me anymore, when they argue I hear them speak my name and when I enter the room, they turn, refusing to look at me, answering none of my questions. Thaddeus would tell me why the Persians were here, but he too is dead, taken by the enemies who took my whole world and turned it upside down. His wife could not bear to be without him, jumping to her death on the rocks far below the west gate.

I do not understand why the Persians were here, they were gone by the time I woke the morning after they took my mothers. They did not take coin or drive us from the palace so they could call it their own. They do not appear to be regrouping to attack us again. I do not understand anything, least of all why Yiayia sent Papou away. She blames him for Mother's death, but how can she? It was not Papou who drove the knife into her, he did not hold her in that room and demand that she and Mumma ... what? The Persian, he wanted something from them, something about ... me? I cannot remember. As much as I want them to, his words do not come back to me but I have thought of them, and the man, every night since it happened.

I need my mothers to come back for I cannot go on without them. No one here loves me and I do not want to stay. Perhaps I should fetch Philo. The two of us could find our own place to live, somewhere far from the palace and the memories. Somewhere I am free to be someone other than the princess who lost her mothers when the Persians came to Greece. Perhaps it is distance from here that shall give me peace. Perhaps somewhere else I shall feel as if I belong. I can look for Papou, he still loves me and would allow me to stay with him. We shall spend his banishment far from Trachis and we shall be happy. I close my eyes, the rich ache of my wishes coursing through my small body. My knees find the hard marble as pain and torment flow out of my heart and away on the wind.

Thick mud filled my mouth and I opened my eyes. I was no longer a child of nine winters mourning the death of her mothers, though the familiar ache burned inside my chest, suffocating me with its presence just like it did the night I received Mumma's amulet.

I spat the foul mud out, wiping my face with the only clean patch of material at the shoulder of my tunic. My heart weighed like a stone in my chest, heavy and unmoving. I closed my eyes as the slow moving waters buffeted me gently from side to side. My mothers had died because of me, because of who I was destined to become. They'd fought Ares and his soldiers and he'd killed Mother so Mumma would tell me who I was and where I'd come from. She'd refused, thinking she was protecting me, but she should've taken his advice.

She should have taken his advice. I blinked. The weight in my chest lessened ever so slightly. She should have told me, they both should have. The pain of loss loosened its grip, replaced instead by anger. There was no need for them to die that night. Fury with the Persians, my grandparents and with Ares charged through me. Only it was not just anger flowing and pulsing in my blood.

It was pure rage.

Beneath the sadness, vengeance drove me on. It had been rage that spurred me on when I was ten, twelve, sixteen, eighteen winters old. Anger and revenge were the motivations I had always taken into battle when I faced a Persian soldier. Until I had met Demi, until I had learned that I was the Chosen One.

If only my mothers had told me. We could've faced Ares together then, or when I turned nineteen winters old, when my powers began to surface. If only they'd trusted me, trusted themselves enough to teach me to control the power or to resist Ares then perhaps they wouldn't be dead and neither would I.

Adrenaline surged through my veins and the fatigue that had settled in my legs and arms disappeared. I pushed myself to my feet, seeing that the far bank of the Acheron River was within reach.

I took an unsteady step, my sandal catching in the mud at the bottom of the river. I pulled at it firmly and with a gurgle, it reluctantly released me. I half-walked, half-fell towards the edge, landing painfully against a small rock protruding from the dirt. I grabbed at one of the green bushes lining the side of the river and pulled myself out onto the bank, puffing slightly as I rolled onto my back.

16

The Acheron River had not claimed me. I had not allowed it to drag my body beneath its dirty waters by the weight of my memories. I had crossed two of the rivers of the Underworld, and when I finally found my mothers in the Fields of Punishment, we would help each other to cross the final river. It would not be long until we were all free of Hades' realm.

I lay on the bank, regaining my breath and strength as the first long fingers of Eos' dawn spread across the sky. I'd stopped being angry with my mothers for leaving me a long time ago. I knew that they'd been trying to protect me. I still wished they'd had the chance to warn me and teach me about who I might be, but I didn't hold their reluctance to share such truths with a mere child against them. If I'd ever thought that Zenon or Kadmus held that kind of power, I wasn't sure I'd have spoken of it to them either, not until they were older.

The acute sense of loss and the rage at the secrets and betrayals of my family I'd felt slowly dissolved like a dream.

I rolled onto my side. The Acheron lay silently behind me, flowing in its slow way as though I hadn't disturbed it. Reeds on tall stalks lined the bank and through their gentle swaying I made out a flat field. I pushed myself to my feet again and trampled through the reeds and undergrowth, my eyes darting left and right.

The Fields of Punishment. It didn't look like a place of punishment. As Hephaestus had said, there was no wall but in several places blood pooled in a straight line along the ground. I kept moving past them.

Blood flecked the ground, not as much as in Tartarus, but drawn along flattened blades of grass and the occasional bush. It was quiet. No screams of pain. No wailing. No one chasing rolling stones or reaching for food and water just out of arm's length. There didn't seem to be anyone there at all. Maybe the field was like the immense darkness just outside Tartarus – impossible to traverse without a guide. Perhaps I would get lost, destined to walk without purpose forever.

I shook my head. I wouldn't let such thoughts in, nor would I succumb to them. I'd made it so far already; rising against what the rivers of Phlegethon and Acheron had shown me. I would not be undone when I was so close to finding my mothers.

I pushed aside a large bush heavy with bright pink flowers and saw them standing not ten feet from me in the middle of the open area. The ground beneath their sandals was dusty, the blood less prominent. My heart soared.

Mumma's black hair lifted in the light breeze as Mother reached for her hand, lifting her chin towards the sun that peaked over the horizon. The two of them stood as though they were back at the palace in Trachis, greeting the day together as they had so many times when I was a child. It was such a comforting, familiar sight that for a moment I forgot where I was and why I had come to find them. I didn't call to them or announce my presence, I just watched them like I used to. Perhaps just as they had once done, they prayed for a good day, for a day that, come the setting of the sun, would see the two of them still together with those they loved.

I swallowed loudly, I didn't want to imagine the punishments and pain they'd had to endure all these winters. Maybe the Erinyes visited them and only when they remembered themselves they continued their ritual of greeting the day together.

Today will be your last in the Underworld, I silently promised. I will free you and together we'll free all gods and mortals from Ares' grip. We'll find Demi and be together again as a family.

After many long moments, they opened their eyes and stepped towards two other figures, their hands still entwined. Arms opened and in the brightening light, I realized that one of the figures was Papou Leandros. Just as I expected, he hadn't escaped Ares' wrath either. Had it not been for his and Zita's coupling, perhaps the Chosen Ker would have been born sooner to Ares' line, and without the want to deny her master what he wanted.

The fourth in their group was a woman with long, dark hair in the same shade as Mumma's. I didn't need an introduction to know she was my grandmother, Zita. They spoke together in quiet tones and even though I couldn't hear their exact words, I recognized the lilt of Mumma's voice amongst the others. Zita's holding the same familiar tone.

I took another deep breath. I needed to reveal myself to them.

Hephaestus had said time moved differently outside the mortal realm and I didn't know how quickly the sun would stay in the sky above; it had already moved quite a way across the dark blue as I'd crossed the Field and stood watching my family. Hephaestus had also warned that I couldn't remove Hades' helmet altogether when I revealed myself to my mothers. I could push it up off my forehead like I used to do when I was a soldier, but I had to ensure it still covered the majority of my head. If it was knocked free or someone took it all the way off I would be exposed and our plan would be lost.

I blew out the breath, praying that what the Erinyes had shown me was not true, that none of them despised me or would turn in disgust when I showed myself. I stayed where I was, but slowly pushed the nosepiece of Hades' helmet up.

It was Papou who saw me first. He gasped, stumbling backwards as he groped for Mumma's arm. "Ava," he whispered.

My mothers turned, their mouths dropping as their eyes found mine. Mother immediately approached; her face a mixture of joy and despair.

"Sweet girl," she whispered her hands finding my cheeks. "Is it truly you?"

"Mother," I nodded, my throat constricting around my words.

She gripped my neck, my shoulders, my hands, checking for herself. "You have grown so much, were it not for the torturous visions we have witnessed all these winters, I would not have recognized you. Well, that and the truth that your eyes are still the exact mirror of my own."

"Our eyes have seen much Mother – some we'd rather wish we hadn't," I murmured, swallowing around the lump in my throat.

She wrapped her arms around my shoulders, drawing me into a tight embrace. I put mine around her waist, noting that we were the same height. She planted a kiss in my hair and I breathed in the faint scent of cinnamon and rose I remembered from my childhood.

"I have missed you so much, Mother," I whispered.

"As we have you. What happened to your tunic?" she asked, releasing me.

"I had to cross the Acheron River to get here, it's more marsh than river, and I wouldn't like to spend time in it again."

"And the missing section, did you lose it there?"

"No, that happened on a dark day here in the Underworld."

She nodded, reaching up to touch the helmet at my head. "This is aiding you?"

"Yes. I couldn't be here without it."

"Hades helps you?"

"Not knowingly."

"Oh," she said, stepping aside as Mumma joined us, her eyes scanning every inch of me, just as Mother's hands had.

She took my hands in hers. "You are such a beautiful combination of the two of us," she smiled. "You have always had your mother's deep sea-green eyes that hide and reveal so much, and your raven colored hair is reminiscent of my own. It saddens me to see you here, and yet I cannot deny the joy I feel that we are reunited after so many winters. Tell me, what of Ares and his plan to defeat Zeus for the throne of Olympos, did you deny him that wish, did you break the line of the Ker as we were led to believe?"

"Or were the visions he showed us of your death true?" Papou added, stepping near and taking me in a crushing hug. "Did he truly take the jet and hematite from your sword? Does he now have the power to take what he has always wanted?"

When Papou released me I hung my head, unable to face them as I gave my answer. "He has everything he needs."

"Then we must do something."

I raised my eyes, finding Zita at my side.

"How?" Mother asked.

"I do not know, but it must be the Moirai that see us here together in the Fields of Punishment," she put a warm hand on my arm and smiled. "I am very pleased to finally meet you, Egoni,"

"And you, Yiayia Zita," I replied, giving her a tight smile. "But I was not sent here to the Fields like you were."

"What do you mean, my darling? Are you still alive, did the Erinyes lie to us when they showed us your death? Who has aided you in entering the Underworld?" Papou asked, his questions pouring out.

"No, what you saw was the truth; I died at Ares' hand, just like you all did, but Ares didn't have me sent here."

"Where did he send you?" Mumma asked.

"There will be time to talk about that later. For now, we must stand against Ares," I replied. "I believe I have a way but we need to leave this place, we must leave the Underworld, quickly. Together we have to stand against our oldest enemy and harness all the power we can from our strong Ker line. We must combine our love for one another and the power of us all being in one place at the same time, against him."

"How can you be certain it shall work?" Mother asked, her brows drawn together.

"I can't but we have to try."

"Ares is weakened. I feel it as deeply as I have ever felt anything. Ava may speak the truth; certainly together we would be far stronger than we could ever have been alone," Zita said, placing her hand on Mumma's arm. "Skylar, you told me what happened at Ava's birth, you saw how powerful a group of Keres could be when they put their minds to it. Her plan has merit."

"Then it is decided," Mumma nodded. "I gather you have been given directions to make our way out?"

"Yes."

"Then we leave immediately." Her voice left no room for argument and reminded me of the commanding presence she had always exuded when I was a child.

17

I led my mothers and grandparents across the Fields of Punishment in the opposite direction to where I'd come from. Hephaestus had told me we'd know we had left the Fields behind when we reached the juncture of the Lethe and Cocytus rivers. We wouldn't have to cross either of the rivers – at least not in the same way I had with the Acheron and the Phlegethon – there would instead be wooden bridges we could use. He spoke of Rhadamanthus using the bridge to lead souls from the Palace of Hades to the Elysium Fields.

As we made our way toward the mortal realm, the only river we'd have to physically immerse ourselves in would be the Styx. On the other side of it, the Cocytus ran close and we'd have to follow the two rivers until the Cocytus branched off into the darkness and the Styx turned upwards. We would continue with the Styx and enter the Nekromanteion to find ourselves in the land of the living.

The five of us spoke little as we walked, I kept Hades' helmet up on my forehead, my hand poised to pull it down quickly if needed, but we saw no one. Ahead, small pools of blood were gathered every few feet between bushes and flattened grass. I recalled seeing the same patterns earlier and slowed my pace until I was shoulder to shoulder with Mumma.

"The blood seems concentrated here, I saw the same when I entered the Fields on the other side beside the Acheron. Do you know what it's from?"

She shook her head. "We do not see many others, though sometimes we hear their screams, as I am certain they hear ours." I drew a deep breath, uncertain how to reply. I wanted to ask her what her punishments had consisted of, how often the Erinyes had visited her and if she and Mother had travelled to the Judges together in Charon's boat, but I was afraid. Afraid of the answers she would give and afraid that she might keep them from me like she'd kept her knowledge of what I could become when I was a child.

"I often heard rather than saw others when I was in Tartarus," I offered instead.

Her eyes met mine, holding them for a long moment as her mouth opened several times. No sound emerged, but when Mother joined us, Mumma gave me a nod, signaling that our conversation on the subject of the blood, and everything else, was over for the time being. I inclined my head in return and lengthened my strides until I was several paces in front of them.

I passed the blood and continued on, the shrubs and grass thinning to reveal darker patches of dirt and small pebbles. A crack of thunder suddenly split the air and I spun around, looking from the sky above to where Mumma lay flat on her back among the bushes.

"What happened?" I asked, rushing back to her.

"I do not know," she replied, taking my offered hand and pulling herself to her feet. "Something hit me. I did not see what it was, did any of you?"

Papou and Zita shook their heads.

"You are bleeding," Mother said, raising her hand to Mumma's face.

"Could we have been discovered?" Papou asked.

"I don't see how, but we should hurry," I replied.

The four of them scanned the Fields as they inched forward and it took all my strength to keep my hands at my side and not pull them along faster. If Hades had somehow learned that it was not the true me in Tartarus then it wouldn't be long before he began looking, and I had no doubt he'd begin his search in the Fields with my mothers.

I backed up, passing the point at which Mumma Skylar had been stopped. She approached, but Papou put his hand on her arm and strode forward instead. He barely got a step more before he too was swept backwards by an unseen force, landing heavily on his back, his nose bloodied.

"I don't understand," I said as Zita helped Papou to his feet. "There's not supposed to be a wall here. There *is* no wall here."

"There is no *visible* wall," Papou corrected. "But that does not mean we can simply leave if we want. You did not believe it would be so easy, did you?"

"But Hephaestus ..." I started, knowing that I *had* believed it would be that easy. "I don't understand how I'm supposed to defeat Ares if we aren't together. That was the plan I made. Hephaestus agreed. He told me how to get here and where we have to go to leave the Underworld."

"Can you call him? Ask him for assistance again?" Mother asked, wiping the last of the blood from Mumma's face.

"No, he can't appear here again," I replied, pacing back and forth.

Zita stepped towards the unseen barrier, reaching out to touch whatever it was. A moment later found her on her back, Papou rushing to her side. She waved him off and I noticed that the mark on her left shoulder stood out brightly on her skin. I crossed to Mumma, inspecting her mark; it also glowed black against her bronzed skin. I placed a hand on my ribs where long ago my skin had held the completed mark. It was slightly warmer than the flesh around it and I pulled roughly at the torn fabric. My mark had returned.

I gasped. "This is not possible," I murmured.

Ares had the jet and hematite from the amulet, so what did the re-emergence of my mark mean? Did he intend to somehow use me? To use us, even from the Underworld? Did he intend to recall us and use our line back in the mortal realm? Did he have the power to carry out such an action? Before my panicked thoughts could overwhelm me completely, Zita spoke again.

"You must go, Child. He approaches," Zita warned.

"Who?" I asked, even as I realized I knew the answer. Barely a moment later, Ares appeared in a flash of light and I dropped the helmet over my face.

He staggered to his feet, one hand at his chest, the other clenching and unclenching beside his thigh. His eyes darted to the four faces around him and he suddenly straightened. None of my family moved and I wondered briefly how often they'd seen Ares in the Underworld; how often Zita had felt when he was going to appear.

Ares circled the small group, looking them over, his lips mouthing unspoken words. When he got to Mumma, he turned her so her left side faced him.

"She has the mark," he muttered, crossing immediately to Zita and turning her also. "They both have it. It is as if the line is re-emerging, yet Ava does not bear her mark, I have it instead. Finally her death has given me what I seek."

"You have seen our daughter? Where is she?" Mother asked, grabbing at his arm.

Ares shook her grip as he replied. "She is there." He turned his back and started to pace like I had. "But she has no mark. That now belongs to me. *I* am the Chosen One now. The Ker line has been restored. These marks are proof of that," he muttered. "Finally I am gaining the power, but why do I not feel the strength? Perhaps I must wait until the entire line has been re-established. These two are only the end of it. I must find the others, the true Ker people. But where? They are not to the north and I cannot go to Olympos, but I do not expect they would go there. Where would they go to find me? How can I call them to me? Can they feel me and return from wherever they have been since I was imprisoned? And what of the jet and hematite? Perhaps when the Keres find me, they shall bring the pieces with them." Ares continued his quiet questioning, ignoring my mothers and grandparents, who exchanged confused looks.

"I *must* now truly be the Chosen One. I must prepare my allies and search for those of my line. Together we shall bring about my father's defeat and I shall finally rule the gods."

"Wait, Ares, please, if you have the power you need, bring Ava to us so we can spend eternity together," Mother said, her fingertips touching the god of war's arm again. He jumped and backed away as though he had forgotten that she and the rest of my family were even there. "Please?"

He looked down at his palm with a frown, the dark shape standing out boldly against the light pink of his hand.

It was indeed the mark of the Chosen One, the completed mark, my mark, and I didn't understand how we both wore it.

Suddenly Ares laughed, but he didn't give my mother a reply, disappearing again in a flash of light.

18

Zita was the first to speak, and only when she did, did I push the helmet up onto my head again.

"Something has happened to Ares. He suffers from madness and delusions, as though the Erinyes have turned their ways to him. I have never seen him in such a state, but I feel his power waning, he does not possess the Keres' power, nor the power of the amulet, and I do not believe he ever shall."

"How are you so certain?" Papou asked.

"When I lived with the Ker, we had the ability to feel one another; we could feel each other's arrival and departure, just as the gods do amongst themselves. When one of us died, we felt that too, it was as if part of us died with them. When a new Ker was born, our power was strengthened, as it was when we fed. But though I felt his arrival just now, I did not feel his strength, not as I have before when he appeared to me. He is weakened not only in mind, but in body also."

"He did not exude his usual controlled demeanor," I agreed. "And it sounds like he doesn't have the parts of the amulet anymore. But if he doesn't have them, where would they go?"

"I do not know. Perhaps by killing you, he destroyed the power the amulet had over the line instead of transferring it to himself as he expected," Zita replied.

"But he wears the mark, just like I do, how is that possible?"

"I cannot explain that either, but your life force is strong, I feel that.

You continue to get stronger whilst he begins to fade. There has been a shift in power. You must return to the mortal realm. This may be your only chance to defeat him."

"I can't do it without all of you."

"It appears you must," Mother said. "We cannot leave these Fields as you can. You must return to face him before he finds a way to regain his strength."

"I won't leave you here. I can't say goodbye to you again," I said, taking her hand between my own.

"My sweet girl, for now we must continue to be apart. I do not wish for you to be trapped here as we are. Your young family needs you, your wife must long for your return and if you have such a chance, you must go back to her."

"You know about Demi and me?" I asked, surprised.

"Leandros told us of your pairing," she nodded. "We are happy you found someone to love, and to love you in return as we did."

"There has to be a way to set you free. I'll speak with Hephaestus and Zeus. I will make it so."

"If you are able then we shall be grateful, but for now you must concentrate on leaving the Underworld and facing Ares," my grandmother said.

"Zita speaks the truth. You may only have one last chance to deny him what he wants," Papou added, placing his hand on my shoulder.

"And you cannot do that from here," Mumma agreed. She stood several feet from us, her hands held out in front of her like she was feeling her way along an invisible wall. "I too can feel Ares' weakness, perhaps his hold over us here shall be lifted."

Papou shook his head. "You felt the intensity of the power when you were repelled. You understand it is not just Ares' will that holds us here. This is Hades' domain, Ares is a mere visitor and we shall not be able to escape our prison."

"Ava escaped from Tartarus, Father. I am certain between us all we can do the same here," Mumma said as a gasp escaped Mother's lips. I hadn't wanted Mother to know I'd been in Tartarus, at least not until we were far from the Underworld's clutches.

"She did not work alone; she wears what I assume is Hades' Helmet of Invisibility and had the aid of Hephaestus," Papou countered.

"Why then does Hephaestus not come here and help us to escape also? He sent her here to find us…"

"You talk about me like I'm not here," I frowned.

Mumma turned to face me, her face unreadable. "Apologies, it was not intentional. But I am not prepared to sit here and allow you to face Ares alone. Not if there is a way for me to accompany you."

"Your father speaks the truth. Yes Ares is weakened, but the unseen walls that keep us here are not. Ava must return to the living without us," Zita said.

"No," Mumma shouted. "She has walked without us for long enough."

"And she shall have to walk without you for some time yet," Zita replied calmly. "She is the Chosen One. She always has been, no matter how you wished it was not so. No matter how many times we all had to sit here, unable to help her as she learnt about the amulet and its power from Ares. We all suffered as we saw how it filled the dark places of her being with calm and clarity, with the intoxicating power and thoughts of revenge that Ares had planted in her heart so many winters before. But this is how it must be, Skylar."

"I cannot accept such an answer. I am her mother, I should have protected her, but I have known for many winters that I played into Ares' hands when he came to Trachis. He incited me to defy him. He knew I would."

"Sky, what happened with Ares was not your fault," Mother whispered, laying her hand on Mumma's arm.

Watching them, hearing their words, I understood how it had to be. My belief that we had to stand together was wrong; I must face Ares alone. I had to finish what he began in Trachis so many winters ago. He'd come for me when I was barely nine winters old and had taken my parents instead. He'd returned a second time and taken Papou from me in his same callous manner. I wouldn't let him take those I loved again. Somehow this time he would die at *my* hand. I would take him from those who loved *him*. This time I would not fail.

"Mumma," I said, crossing to her side and taking her hands in mine. "It's time I left you. I will face Ares again, alone. But do not fear for I shall not be truly alone; I carry you and Mother in my heart today, just as I have every day since you died. I may not be able to feel Ares like you and Zita do but I carry your strength and determination. The strength of the Ker line runs through my blood. I will not fail you again."

"You have never failed me my dear, sweet Ava. Never. I am so proud of who you have become, of what you did, how you denied him when he came for you. It is true that I never wanted you to carry the burden of Ares and the Keres and the amulet, but instead I left you to grow without something far more important; your Mother and me. I was blinded by my own arrogance when I faced Ares, believing that I could out-smart him, that by defying him he would respect me and leave you alone, but he shall not stop until he sits on Zeus' throne."

"I will never let that happen," I replied. "I understand what it is to be blinded by arrogance, when I faced Ares back in Trachis I got Papou killed, then myself. When I faced him on Olympos I was protected by the God of the Forge but this time I will take the strength of the Keres with me. I have always taken you with me; I remembered the story you told me about Artemis and her hinds and when I last faced Ares I used their blood against him.

"You used the blood of Artemis' hinds on Ares?" Mumma repeated.

"I tried to."

"What happened?"

"You said Ares showed you how I died. Didn't he show you that too?"

"No," Zita replied. "Tell us. Quickly."

"I put the blood on my sword but it broke Hephaestus' protection and Ares was able to call the sword to his hand. He wiped the blood off and took the pieces of the amulet from it before killing me."

"Did the blood touch his skin at any time or did he use a cloth to remove it?" Mumma pressed.

"He wiped it off with his bare hand. Why?"

"It would explain his strange behavior. What do you remember of the story?"

"You said hind's blood was the only thing able to kill a god. It's why I suggested it to Hephaestus in the first place. But it didn't work."

"I believe it did, it is just taking longer than you expected. When Ares touched the blood with his hand it would have immediately begun to seep into his skin and eventually it would have got into his blood."

"So the effect isn't immediate, but it *is* weakening him," I finished.

"Exactly," Mumma nodded.

I looked up, noting that the sun had moved further across the sky. "I should get going. I have to meet Hephaestus before the sun sets and I don't know how far I still have to travel."

"Go," Mumma said, pulling me into a hug, her lips at my forehead. "Always remember that we are so proud of you and that we love you."

"I love you too, Mumma," I replied, squeezing her tightly as I struggled to take a full breath. She released me and Mother wrapped her arms around me.

"Be safe my sweet child. We shall be together again one day," she whispered.

"We will and I hope it is not in this place."

Mother kissed my cheek. "I love you."

"I love you, Mother."

"You shall stand proudly and with strength against our enemy and you shall be victorious. I know you can bring about what we could not, Chosen One," Zita said, hugging me quickly.

"Thank you," I smiled.

Papou was the last to approach, but he enfolded me in his arms like I was a small child again. "When we met in Konitsa after so many winters apart, I told you that you had your Mumma's fire and Alexis' beauty, but you have far more than that. You also have Skylar's desire to protect those who cannot – or do not – realize they need protection, Alexis' determination and Zita's strength. You are a perfect combination of them all and I am proud to call you granddaughter."

"Thank you, Papou. I miss you so much."

"As I miss you, Child." He released me and I turned towards the path I had believed, until so recently, I would walk with my mothers and grandmother on my journey from the Underworld.

I took a deep breath, straightened my shoulders and gave a final nod to them all. I stepped across the dirt toward the final rivers that would take me far from the Fields of Punishment, from four people I loved so dearly and, I hoped, back to four people I loved just as much.

19

It wasn't long before I reached the wide wooden bridge that spanned the Lethe and Cocytus rivers. I had walked quickly, Hades' helmet pulled low over my face once again.

I'd resisted the urge to look back to see if my mothers and grandparents still stood at the edge of the Fields of Punishment. I knew if I did, my strength to leave them behind would waver and I knew I couldn't let that happen. As desperate as I was to remain in the Underworld with them, I couldn't – there were so many more families that needed my protection. I had to go forward, upward to the surface of the Underworld, back to Demi, Kadmus, Zenon and Melina; back to the living members of my family. I had to face Ares and finish what I'd started with the hind's blood.

The sun obediently stayed high above me as I crossed the bridge, the water of the Lethe hidden beneath a thick layer of mist, which didn't clear even when I brushed my hand through the topmost part of it. I continued on, passing over the dark blue of the Cocytus, which bubbled away noisily on its way over the submerged rocks and through the green reeds.

The knowledge that, while the hind's blood hadn't killed Ares outright, it had bought me time to return to the mortal realm and face him again, ensured my steps continued quickly. Maybe the next time I came face to face with the god of war, I would have the advantage. I hoped that was the case as I had no idea how else I could hope to defeat him. I couldn't ask Artemis for more hind's blood, yet running Ares through with a sword was not the answer either.

I followed the Cocytus River to the left until the path beside the flowing water narrowed and I glimpsed the River Styx for the first time. In contrast to the previous rivers, the water in the Styx was almost clear. Light colored sand which looked as soft as the grains on the beach back home lined the bottom, intermittent pieces shimmering when they picked up a ray from Helios' light above.

I drew a deep breath and dipped my foot into the tepid water, surprised at the swift current that swept past my ankle. I entered completely, the water reaching my waist even though I was still beside the bank. I began to wade across, disturbing the grainy sand and occasional pebble, sending them rushing down the river on the current.

I didn't know what to expect from the Styx – so far none of the rivers had been what I expected – I only knew I had to keep moving. I had to remember where I was and what was true. I couldn't believe what it might show me. I'd seen my mothers; I knew where they were and what they truly thought of me, and of everything I'd done. I entered the River Styx with clarity and truth in my mind, as well as my heart.

The further I went, the darker the grains of sand swirling in the water became. They danced about my ankles, my thighs, my waist, reminding me of the amulet when I'd harnessed its power in Konitsa and brought destruction down on the Persian army Ares had conjured. The jet had turned orange, then a cloudy grey, and the grains now swirled beneath the water like they were smoke drifting into the air from a hot fire.

I ran my fingers through them, but they were no more solid than the water they played in, splitting apart and reconnecting as they weaved about my hands. The strands began to form shadowy pictures; swords, helmets, shields, spears, battle formations. I watched as the outlines became solid forms with more detail. Persian soldiers with yellow caps. My mothers held captive in the palace. The face of the Persian who had taken them from me.

I feel the heat of the sun at my back, my sword between my palms. It trembles above my head, my arms aching with the strain of holding back Lysistratos' attack. It is three winters since my mothers passed into the Underworld and I no longer feel lost or abandoned. I feel anger and hatred towards the Persians and I train all day, every day, so when I get the chance for revenge, I do not fail.

I am a hoplite in the army of Trachis, the only female soldier, but not the only one who seeks revenge for losing parents, siblings or friends. Lysistratos is my favorite sparring partner. Moeris oversees us during training, pushing us to our limits and beyond as he shapes and molds us into elite fighters. He took over as head of the army when Mumma passed and though he has known me since my birth, he did not show me favor, telling me I must earn my place, just as the other epheboi had to. I was not prepared for many of the challenges of a soldier's life, but I welcomed them anyway, thriving on the conditions and hard work, and the knowledge that if I was successful, it would take me far from Trachis.

I hate the Persians with a passion that runs so deep and so fierce it is almost painful. They shall pay for killing my mothers, for turning Agrias and Melina's hearts so cold that they abandoned me when I needed them the most, and for driving papou Leandros from Trachis. I only wish I had been able to join the soldiers when they marched with the Ionians and burnt Sardis to the ground. I would have killed as many Persians as I laid eyes on with nothing short of glee. But I would not have allowed them a quick death. No, I would have ensured they died slow and painful. That they had time to remember all they had done, all those they had loved, to regret their actions. I can still bring to mind the face of the Persian soldier who held the knife at Mother's throat, the one who had sliced her face and, eventually, driven his knife into her stomach.

Lysistratos disappears and it is the Persian that takes his place, his sword against mine, his face only inches away.

Heat floods my blood. "I have waited for this day," I tell him, my chest constricting with long held grief and anger.

He smiles and steps back, taking his sword from mine. He sneers and re-sheathes his weapon, as though he doesn't think I will harm him. He thinks he's in control, that he will get what he wants, just like he did in the palace. But I promised myself that when I finally found him, it would be my sword that brought about his death.

I take a deep breath and grip my sword tighter. I slash at him, cutting a long line across his cheek. He laughs again, folding his arms across his chest. Red tinges my vision, rage infusing my blood. I charge, driving my sword through his stomach, pulling it out and thrusting it back in, then into his side and his throat. He continues to laugh, though it is now a silent mockery he makes of me. I stab at him until my arms ache. He doesn't fall. I don't understand. He can't still be alive, his blood drains from his many wounds. But he does not sway, he continues to stand and laugh.

I scream and cut his head from his shoulders. It falls into the water, his hair fanning out, swishing back and forth. Exposed bloody muscles and bone glare up at me from the cut across his neck until his head floats away on the current, eventually disappearing from sight, along with his body.

"No," I shout, my breath coming in pants. I'd promised myself that the Persian who killed Mother would suffer a painful death, slow and calculated. I would not allow him mercy for what he'd done to me and my family. I promised myself that when I had my revenge I would take my time, I would not lose myself to my anger, to his words or taunts, or anything he might use to dissuade me from taking his life. But I hadn't done any of that, I'd killed him as quickly as any other Persian, I couldn't control myself, I would never feel that I'd avenged them, I had not made him suffer, I had not …

My revenge … No, I left those thoughts of revenge for Persian blood behind long ago. I knew the truth – it wasn't Persians who killed my mother, it was Ares and, I could only presume, Mumma and Thaddeus. The soldiers were his own, their clothing and faces made to resemble Persians so I had an enemy I could easily name. An enemy that I could fight when I was older, when it was my time to prove I was the one he'd waited so long for.

"No," I growled, blowing out a deep breath. I would not allow the Styx River to incite me to fight old battles, to believe I hated the Persians for crimes which were not their own.

They were still my enemies but not for killing my mothers and turning my grandparents against me when the pain of the loss of their daughter was too much for them to bear.

The sword vanished, along with the adrenaline of the fight. I staggered the rest of the way across the river and pulled myself up onto its bank, noting that the sun had crossed the sky at an alarming rate while I'd been preoccupied with the visions in the water.

20

"I must find it again. As the Chosen One I need it to conquer my father and take his throne," Ares murmured.

"Please, my love, you need to rest. You grow weaker each moment and when you disappear I worry that you shall not return again," Aphrodite said, laying her hand on her lover's arm.

"There is no time for rest. Do you not see the mark on my hand? It is done, the power is mine."

"If the power was yours then you would feel it, you told me that yourself moons ago," she countered.

"It *is* mine! Do you d–" He could not continue, the pain gripped his chest again and he fell to his knees.

Aphrodite took his arm and helped him to his feet. "Ares, please, you must rest, I am certain the amulet shall return to you when its power is fully restored, your Keres too. Please, I am worried for you."

"No, I must find them. I must find the amulet," he insisted, pushing her away. "I have looked everywhere I dare, yet I cannot find them."

"Perhaps they no longer walk in this world, did you ask Hades if they had been received at his palace?"

"Who would have buried them, who would have provided the coin for Charon? You told me they vanished when I was sent to the cage. Perhaps my father hides them. But how can I be certain of that? I have no allies that can simply ask him without raising suspicion and you are too afraid to return to Olympos, so tell me, what am I to do?"

"I do not know, but wait for them to find you. I beg it of you."

Ares paced slowly back and forth across the dirt of the small room, his teeth gnawing at his fingernails. "I know where I have to go," he suddenly said, halting his steps. "I have heard the mortals speak of a great temple – the Nekromanteion of Ephyra. They believe they can speak to their dead ancestors there. The chosen line of my Keres are akin to my descendants, but if they are truly dead they could tell me so and I could attempt to find them wherever they are. They shall know where the amulet has gone. Perhaps they have it and are waiting with it for me to find them. Yes. Yes, I must go to the Nekromanteion."

"Ares, no, rest first and then I shall take you myself. You cannot go alone."

The pain resurfaced beneath Ares' breast and he nodded, allowing Aphrodite to help him across to their bed. "Just for a little while, then we shall go." He smiled as he lay back, pulling her to his side. "We shall soon have the amulet, my Keres and the throne of my father. You shall see. All shall be well for us again, I give you my word."

"I can only hope you speak the truth, my love," Aphrodite whispered.

21

I started down the rounded corridor of the Nekromanteion of Ephyra. Hephaestus told me the River Styx would lead me up through its corridors to the main entrance, where I would be able to see Lake Acherousia; our meeting place.

A cool breeze ruffled my hair as I wended through the passages, around and over rocks that pushed up through the dirt, determined to trip me as I made my way over the uneven ground. It was dark outside the light of the helmet at my brow, but when I directed it either side or above me, I could make out the smooth slabs of stone that formed the archways and walls. I raised my hand above my head, caressing the solid, cold masses as I passed beneath them.

When I arrived at a branch, I took the left path where the River Styx continued to flow along the edge of another, wider pathway. A pale light appeared up ahead soon after and I stumbled over more small rocks in my haste to exit the cold corridor. I pushed through a series of large iron gates and stepped out into the warm evening air. The scent of a recent storm greeted me; the stone of the Nekromanteion had obviously been warmed by the sun before the rains came down, sending up a rich, almost solid aroma. I drew the smell into my lungs, noting the drying patches of dirt beside muddy puddles.

The Nekromanteion was at the top of a hill, the lush green of the Thesprotian Valley spread out below. The River Styx flowed out beside me, following the gentle arc of the hill down into the valley where it met a second river before arriving at a large lake.

A bird screeched overhead, pulling me from my observations. I raced down the hill, following the line of the Styx and jumping over the stones littering my path, desperate to reach the lake before the sun set behind the forest on the other side of the water.

Breathless, I arrived at the Acherousia Lake, the gentle breeze that lifted my hair barely causing a ripple across the surface of dark water before me. I doubled over to recover my breath beneath the towering plane trees standing proudly around the lake. Their leaves whispered in the gentle breeze, but it was a larger movement that caught my ear.

I looked up, expecting to see Hephaestus standing before me, but instead a huge crane settled itself on a boulder, its red beady eye looking directly at me. I still wore Hades' helmet but there was no doubt it could see me.

The crane hopped down from the rock, stepping towards me on long, thin legs no wider than my finger. Its three black toes left impressions in the mud between the reeds and I straightened, realizing it held something in its pointed pink beak. It paused a couple of feet from me, its eye still focused on my face, as it extended its wings. They were the same light grey as its body but darkened to a deep black at the tips. Dark grey feathers clustered at the front of the crane's long neck and a tuft of bright white downy feathers at the back of its head reminded me of Papou's wispy hair atop his head. A light grey stripe drew a line across the top of the crane's head, separating the darker grey just as the River Styx parted the green of the Thesprotian Valley.

I took a cautious step forward, extending my hand to the bird. It came toward me again, opening its beak and letting me remove its gift. I gasped at what I took out. Mumma's amulet. It looked just like it had when I found it in my palm at the Pass of Coela in my nineteenth winter; a black gem as long as my first finger but not quite as wide, two thin lengths of silvery-red iron winding their way from top to bottom in a downwards swirl, holding the jet safely inside. A second piece of looped iron was attached to the top where once a soft length of leather had kept it around my neck.

I cradled the amulet in my hand, wondering if its power had been restored just like its pieces had. In a sudden flurry of movement, the crane elongated the feathers either side of its neck, raised its long wings and sent itself high into the sky above with nothing more in the way of a goodbye. It circled the area then flew off in the direction of the Ionian Sea, the farthest point west of Greece's lands.

"Thank you," I whispered to the disappearing form.

I looked down again at the amulet in my hand. I had so many questions and I was impatient for Hephaestus to arrive. If I spoke, he would hear me and I would see him before he saw me, but I didn't dare take Hades' helmet off before he arrived; we hadn't discussed when the removal of the helmet would take place.

Two things happened simultaneously and without warning: the renewed mark on my ribs announced its presence with a blaze of dark light beneath my torn tunic, and a blinding flash announced the presence of an immortal being.

I lowered my hand to find not one, but two people – two gods – standing before me. I recognized Ares immediately, the other, who held the god of war by the waist, I assumed was Aphrodite. Wavy, golden hair framed her face and trailed down her back, not one strand stood out of place even though she struggled to hold Ares upright.

Ares looked up, our eyes meeting, and I knew that just as the crane had before him, he too could see me. But how was that possible? I raised my hand, confirming I still wore the helmet.

"You … I killed you … you cannot be here," he stammered, dropping to his knees.

Aphrodite followed his gaze, her brow furrowing as she searched the area. "Who do you speak to, my love?" she asked.

"Her," Ares replied, pointing at me. "Do not tell me you do not see her."

"Who?" Aphrodite asked again. "We are alone here, with only the trees and the water to keep us company. Please, love, begin the ritual you believe shall allow you to speak to your Keres."

"How do you have the amulet? It was in pieces. I took them from the sword, you saw me, it was just before I killed you," Ares continued, ignoring Aphrodite's pleas. I remained silent.

"Ares, there is no one here. Please, you are not well. Perhaps we should return when you are feeling better," Aphrodite suggested, putting her hands beneath his arms once again.

He wrenched himself away from her grasp. "No. You cannot see her, but I do. Ava is here, she has come to speak to me from the Underworld. There is no need for the ritual. She must know where the Keres are, where the rest of our line is."

"Ava is in the pit of Tartarus where you had Hades put her. You have seen her yourself. This illness you feel, the things you see, they are not your precious amulet returning its power to you, it is the three winters we have spent in the Underworld. You have been too close to the damned souls who grow weaker of mind from the punishments and torments you and the Erinyes torture them with each passing day. How many times did I beg you not to go down there? But you did not listen and now I fear the Erinyes have turned their madness and delusions on you."

"It is no delusion! She stands not six feet from us," Ares yelled.

"Where, Ares? There is no one else here. We are alone," Aphrodite insisted.

"Not entirely alone," Hephaestus said, materializing to my right. He eyed the immediate area, but it seemed he couldn't see me either.

"What do you want, Hephaestus?" Aphrodite asked, her mouth set in a grim line.

"Oh I just wondered if the rumors were true; that the great god of war had lost his powers. That he was weakened," Hephaestus replied with a grin.

"I should have known you would take pleasure in belittling him, that you would take pleasure in such cruelty."

"As if you and Ares have not been cruel to me all these winters; you made me look a fool to the other gods, the way you flaunted your affair. How quickly you appear to forget what *you* have done."

"Perhaps if you had been a better lover, she would not have returned to my arms," Ares panted, raising his palm.

Hephaestus laughed at the sputtering light that appeared in the war god's hand. "It appears that perhaps you are the impotent one now, Brother. How long shall the goddess of love wish to have you in her bed when you cannot raise ev—"

"Enough," Aphrodite shouted. "Ares is sick, Hephaestus. It is cruel to taunt him when he is so unwell."

"And yet he would gloat and dance if it were me sitting pathetically on my knees, unable to raise a fireball, unable to appear without assistance."

Ares growled, pushing himself to his feet. Aphrodite tried to help him, but he shook her off. "I do not need you to speak for me, Aphrodite. I am not so unwell that I cannot spar with my brother as we have enjoyed so many times before."

Hephaestus smiled. "Tell me what you see, Brother. Do you see Ava's face? Does she appear to you now? You know that you do not see the truth. You killed her. We have both visited her in the Underworld. You know she cannot escape from Tartarus, so why do you deny what you know to be true?"

"She *is* here, it is not a delusion of the Erinyes. Ava stands beside you. She holds the amulet. Sh—" His eyes found my mark, glowing through the hole in my tunic. "It cannot be," he murmured, looking down at his palm and the image that matched the one on my ribs. "She has the Completed Mark, just as I do. I do not understand. I thought I was the Chosen One now. But she has it and the amulet. But it was in pieces, it cannot be whole again."

"You see a memory, Ares. That is all it is. Do you not understand that? Ava is dead. You took the jet and hematite from her sword. The mark on your hand I cannot explain but she does not have it any more, she has not had it since her sons were born, since she broke the line of the Ker."

Aphrodite was adamant but Ares shook his head. "No. I shall prove to you she is here." He frowned and staggered toward me.

I froze in place, unable to decide what to do. I couldn't run in silence and if I moved, Aphrodite would be alerted to my presence. I might also lose the helmet and then I really would be exposed. But what would happen if I stayed in place? Would Ares try to take the helmet from me? Did he know what it was I wore? And how could he see me when Aphrodite and Hephaestus couldn't?

I closed my palm around the amulet, ensuring Ares couldn't simply take it from my hand. We stood face to face, barely a foot separating us. I wished I had my sword, or a dagger, with Aphrodite unable to see me it would be so easy to run it through Ares' heart, to finish what he began so long ago and take my revenge for what he'd taken from me. But would it be enough? Ares was weak and I wanted to believe it was the blood of Artemis' hinds that caused him to be so, but I couldn't be sure that a sword to the heart would finish a god still blessed with immortality and some powers? I tightened my grip on the amulet as Ares raised his hand.

"You are here, I feel it," he whispered.

I didn't dare to breathe. He didn't reach for the helmet like I feared he would, instead he clasped his hands around the one of mine that held the amulet. I bit down hard on my lip, imploring myself to stay quiet as the amulet warmed against my flesh. Ares smiled, never taking his eyes from mine as familiar heat flooded my veins.

There was no pain at my shoulder blades like there'd been when I previously wielded the amulet. My wings didn't fight to be released from my skin but the calmness and deep feelings of power, invincibility and that certain truth that went with the heat, filled me completely.

The amulet's heat increased beneath my hand, burning me. All at once the lake and valley around us disappeared. Aphrodite, Hephaestus, the last rays of Helios' light all vanished until only Ares and I stood, his hands still clasped over mine, in a place I didn't recognize.

22

Hundreds of Keres with long, dark hair and brilliant black wings watched as nine fair-haired women gathered around a large fire. A cloaked figure stood in the midst of the group, arm outstretched above the flames. I strained to see the face and gasped when I made it out.

Ares.

I looked to the god whose hands still held mine. He seemed just as surprised as I was. I tried to remove my hand from his but couldn't; wherever we were, whatever the amulet wanted to show us, we had to experience it together, linked as spectators to the happenings. One of the women took a sword from her belt and the cloaked god of war held his arm in her direction.

"With the addition of your blood to the blood of your Keres and the elements of jet and hematite, a powerful amulet shall be created," the woman started. "There shall be one specific line within the Keres who shall bear your mark. They shall be your Chosen ones. They, and they alone, shall carry your mark through every generation born hereafter. One day a great warrior shall be born to this family. She shall not be as the others are. She shall be powerful. A force not to be taken lightly. A force to be reckoned with. She shall be the only one able to control all four of the amulet's elements of fire, water, wind and earth."

The Valkyries, I realized.

"How long must I wait for this warrior?" Ares asked.

"When the time comes, you shall know," the woman replied. She reached out, gripping Ares' wrist and dragging her sword across his forearm. A single drop of blood fell from his flesh into the fire below, sizzling as it touched the flames.

The woman re-sheathed her weapon and Ares took back his arm, the gash already healed. She reached into the fire, seemingly immune to its heat, and pulled out a familiar shape; Mumma's amulet. The jet glowed, the silver of the hematite picking up the flickering oranges and yellows and reflecting them onto the faces of the women nearby.

As the jet cooled and became the black I had first known it to be, a number of the gathered Keres reached for their left shoulder. The black of their eyes flashed, turning the centers darker, as brilliant red replaced the colored outers. One by one, they were marked with Ares' symbol; Δ like I knew their descendants were destined to be.

"Every female in this line, your line, must be tested and by doing so, the amulet's power shall be strengthened. When you find your Chosen One, the two of you shall bring about your father's downfall and you can rule as King of the Gods just as you wish. Go now, Ares, God of War, and begin your quest to create your Chosen One."

"But how–"

"We have no more answers for you," the woman said, the scene darkening before us. The blackness was as complete as the plain outside Tartarus and I waited, heart hammering beneath my breast.

The amulet's power flowed through me, warming my skin as image after image flashed before me. Child after child appeared, always female, dark-haired and certain they were the one. They all knew of the Valkyrie's words, all believed they held the power Ares desired. They yearned for it, wanted it above all else. I could feel their desire, the intoxicating certainty the amulet pushed through their blood. The power they held in their hand when their wings emerged. I also felt their disappointment when Ares tested them a second time and they could produce no power over the water they stood before.

Faster and faster the faces appeared, winter after winter they stood, wanting to prove to Ares that they were the one, failing time and again. I felt Ares' frustration grow each time until I saw Mumma. She lay on a small bed, her face pale and eyes closed. Bandages covered her back, blood seeping through them at an alarming rate.

Once again Ares and I stood just out of reach of the Ares of that time and his companion; a Ker with bright red eyes and powerful wings. She stood by Ares' side and they spoke in hushed tones. The Ker seemed to be trying to convince Ares that the broken body was one of theirs, that she was the one they'd been waiting for.

"See what is inside her, feel her blood running through you. You see how she differs from all the others of our kind as it was said she would."

Ares checked Mumma's arm for himself. "We cannot allow her to die, Master. Not when you have waited so long."

"Why did we not know of her when she was first born? How was she able to live without our knowledge all those winters?"

"I cannot say for certain, though perhaps the mortal bloodline masked what we feel each time one of our line is birthed."

"There can be only one to whom she belongs," he said coldly.

"Yes, Master," the Ker said, hanging her head.

Ares looked hard at her. "Your daughter."

"Yes, Master."

"And the Bessoi tribesman; he is also alive. He hid this child all along."

She nodded again, raising her eyes. "I should have gone myself that night but I ... I was weak, sending my mother to do the job I could not. I beg your forgiveness, Master, if I had known ..."

"It matters not now," Ares replied, dismissing her words with a wave of his hand. He crouched down beside Mumma's bed, leathers creaking. His eyes searched the features of her face. After a moment he reached out, laying a hand over her mark. Bright light lit the area and Mumma gasped in her sleep.

"We shall know soon enough," he murmured, disappearing from the small room and taking the Ker with him.

The darkness came again. When the light returned, Ares and I found ourselves in a room I recognized; my mothers' bedroom at the palace in Trachis. The room had belonged to Demi and I too, but not at that time.

Mother sat in the middle of a circle, her face scrunched up in a grimace of pain. Mumma was bound to a chair between two Keres, chin touching her chest, her dark hair covering her face. Two Keres each had a hand around her upper arm, their other in the palm of the Ker beside them, a perfect unbroken circle. Ares stood behind them pacing, waiting, as they chanted and spoke a language I could not understand.

Mother screamed.

"It is almost time. I can feel it. Bring my Chosen One into the world, Alexis. Do it now."

"You cannot have her, Ares ... she shall not be who you believe," Mother panted.

"I can feel it. My Keres can feel it, she is exactly who I have waited for so long for."

"Skylar! Wake up!"

"Skylar cannot hear you; she belongs to the Keres now. With her strength she shall aid in the birth of your daughter, and when it is done, she shall die and the child shall be ours."

Mother threw her arm out desperately, digging her nails into the exposed flesh of Mumma's arm. "I have only just found you, you changed my life. Do not make me walk alone in this world. I cannot do it again. Come back to me, Skylar. Please, I beg it of you. I cannot do this without you."

Mother's words roused Mumma and she bucked against her restraints, shaking the Keres' hands from her shoulders. Mother screamed again as Mumma broke free. She pulled her sword from its sheath, driving it into the nearest Ker. Ares was instantly at Mother's side, his voice adding the Keres' chants.

Mumma slashed at the Ker around her, felling them until Mother's voice halted her. The Ker woman held me, staring in disbelief at the bare patch on my shoulder. Ares took me, inspecting my tiny body for himself. I cried and Mumma snatched me away, hugging me against her chest.

"She is not one of you. Leave this place. Do not return. Ever," Mumma growled.

"She does not carry your mark. She is not your Chosen One," Mother breathed, reaching her hand out to Mumma.

Mumma helped her to their bed and handed me to her as she settled us on the covers.

"She does not wear the completed mark," Ares murmured.

"It must be there. Eir told you she would," the Ker said.

Mumma turned and drew her sword on Ares. "Get. Out," she snarled.

"She is powerful, Granddaughter. With your tainted blood and lack of wings, you may not have felt it, but she is of the line. She *is* the one," the woman insisted.

"No!" Mumma screamed, charging the Ker and running her sword through her stomach. Blood spilled from her mouth, as well as the wound in her stomach as she grabbed for it.

The blackness came again and when the light returned I saw myself in that same room, Zenon and Kadmus suckling at my breasts. They were no more than a candlemark old. Demi sat by my side, her face shining with joy. There was another being in the room; the Valkyrie who had created the amulet. Her deep blue eyes shone in the dim light, golden wings picking up a draft. She had not been there that night, at least I had not seen her, but she stood, watching me with my family, her brows drawn together on her forehead. She turned, pinning Ares and I with her stare.

"Eir," he whispered.

"The line was broken this night; when she birthed sons," she told us. "The Ker blood was tempered in Skylar by the mortal blood of Leandros. It was further tainted with the introduction of Alexis and Thaddeus. When Ava made her children with Demetri, not even the blood of the god within him was enough to reignite the line."

"Where are the rest of my Keres?" Ares asked, his hands tightening around mine.

"They are long gone, just as I told you. When your Chosen One defied you and altered the amulet, she destined them to die, just as she has destined you to the same fate."

"I cannot die, I am a god," Ares insisted. I remained silent.

"You shall die. You *are* dying. Can you not feel it?"

"It is the amulet's power coming to me that is all."

"No. You shall not be long for this life." The Valkyrie swept her hand across the image, changing it before our eyes. Ares held me captive in the purple bubble, my sword in his hand. He grinned, running his palm along the blade, removing the drops of hind's blood I had placed there. "When you took the blood from the sword, you doomed yourself," she said. "It seeped into your skin, your blood. It is what kills you."

"No, it cannot be so," Ares murmured.

"It is. There can be only one who wears the mark of the Chosen One and it is not you. The amulet has always protected the line. It continues to protect Ava, even now. You cannot harm her. You are dying and she has won, you shall never rule the gods as you wished."

"I shall tell Aphrodite it was Ava who poisoned me. She shall take revenge if I cannot. She has escaped Tartarus, Hades must also be informed. I—"

"Your time is done, God of War. Ava's part in your death shall not be known by Aphrodite, neither shall Hades ever learn she is not held in his realm. Her future is with her family."

"No," Ares murmured.

Eir's eyes captured mine. "Yes," she said.

In a moment of perfect clarity, I knew the Valkyrie spoke the truth; my future would no longer have me fearing Ares' return or a battle between gods that I must end. I would be free to live with my family until Demi and I were old and our sons were long grown.

The amulet scorched my palm, but still I could not shake Ares' hands from mine. Eir and the image of Ares and me in Trachis turned red before me. Ares frowned, his breath catching suddenly.

"It is done, the line is gone. The amulet shall hold no more power. It shall be only a piece of fine jewelry to be handed down the line of Ava and Demi. You feel the end coming, you know my words are true," Eir said.

"It cannot be, I shall not allow it," Ares growled.

The red colored everything around us, Eir herself the brightest area. Ares cried out, but his hands remained around mine. The image disappeared and we stood once again on the banks of Lake Acherousia. Eir remained with us, her body glowing ever brighter. I closed one eye, but she continued to shine until suddenly she exploded in a shower of sparks and flames.

I turned my head, squeezing both eyes shut, the shockwave tearing Ares and I apart. His hands were ripped from mine and I opened my eyes as he flew backwards through the air, clutching at his chest. His eyes closed before he hit the ground with a thud at Aphrodite's feet. She rushed to his side.

The red was gone, Helios' light too, the area now lit by the two immortals who had remained by the lake. I opened my hand, the amulet cool. The deep black of the jet was infused with red sparks, flashing inside the gem as I had seen Ares' eyes flash when he first appeared to me in Konitsa many winters ago.

"Ares, no, you cannot leave me," Aphrodite cried, clutching her lover's chest. "Please, I cannot be without you." Her words echoed Mother's but I knew they would not bring Ares back to her. She buried her face against his clothing, sobbing.

Ares' arm flopped outwards, his palm upturned, revealing the mark of the Chosen One. It started to disappear, his chest rising and falling with far slower regularity.

I looked back to the amulet. The red inside the jet spluttered and sparked, burning out moments later.

Ares too breathed his last breath.

23

The power and warmth the amulet sent through my blood cooled and the finality of Ares' death hit me. He and I would be enemies no more. We would never again battle for the power the amulet held. He would never invade my dreams or my waking candlemarks, trying to get inside my head and do what he wanted, or use me for his own endgame. He was no more, and though I was relieved I would no longer have to fear him and his plans, I was saddened by his death, the way his demise had panned out and I hadn't expected that.

"Zeus!" Aphrodite screamed, tears staining her cheeks as she lifted her head to call the king of the gods.

"What is it, Child?" Zeus asked, appearing beside Ares' crumpled form.

"You must heal him, please. The Erinyes, they have driven him to his death, they planted thoughts in his mind. They weakened him. He believed that the mortal was here, that she no longer resided in Tartarus with Hades. He spoke of such nonsense."

"He did indeed believe Ava was here, Father," Hephaestus added. "When he attempted to prove it to us he collapsed and now ..." he indicated Ares' unmoving body.

Zeus knelt down, bending his ear to Ares' lips and placing his hand over his son's heart, his face stoic as he listened.

"Please, return him to me. You are the only one who can," Aphrodite whispered.

"I am afraid I cannot," Zeus replied. "His immortality has been lost. His heart no longer beats beneath his chest."

"But how is that possible? Was it the Erinyes? Did they do this? So often the mortals take their own lives after the Erinyes have visited them, but Ares did not, he did not throw himself from a cliff or drive a dagger through his own heart. Besides, neither of those deeds would have harmed him. There is no way for us to die, not unless …" Aphrodite's face drained of its color. "Did you strike him down? I saw no light b–"

"I did not. I give you my word," Zeus said, taking his hand from Ares' chest and placing it on Aphrodite's arm. "My son and I had our differences, but I did not take him from you with my thunderbolts."

"I cannot spend eternity without him. I shall not," she cried.

"I cannot bring him back."

"Then send me to him. I understand we shall not be found in Hades' realm, but I wish to leave this world."

"Aphrodite, no," Hephaestus said, crossing to her and taking her hand.

"Yes," she insisted, snatching her hand away. "The only god I ever loved is gone and I do not wish to walk in this world without him. He was everything to me."

"I know. I have always known it to be so," Hephaestus nodded. "But I ask you to reconsider. Do not take your love and light from the world; the mortals need it in their realm, just as we gods need it in ours."

"Eros can carry on my legacy."

"Eros does not follow in your footsteps, his knowledge and sense of what true love is, is not the same as yours," Hephaestus countered.

"He may not embody all that I do, but if Zeus asks it of him, he shall do what he can to ensure that my legacy of love lives on in my worshipper's hearts." Aphrodite addressed Zeus again. "Allow me this, Father. Allow Ares and me to be together for all eternity."

"Are you certain this is what you wish for?" he asked.

"I am," Aphrodite replied.

Zeus was a quiet a long moment. "How do you want to be joined with Ares for all eternity?"

Aphrodite drew a deep breath and I briefly considered removing my helmet and appearing to the gathered gods to stop Zeus from allowing such a request. As much as I'd wanted Ares to die, I didn't want the world to lose the goddess of love and beauty. I didn't want more immortal lives to be lost than was necessary. Preventing the death of many gods was why I'd tried to kill Ares in the first place.

I remained hidden. Perhaps with a great evil *and* a great love removed from our world, the balance would not be harmed and we mortals would continue to live as we had before.

"I want you to turn me into the most beautiful bright red-rose bush and for Ares to be changed into Selinon, planted beneath me in Artemis' sacred grove where we can grow together for eternity."

A flash of light announced another presence and I was surprised to see

Artemis join us. "When Selinon is planted with a rose, it protects the plant from insects and weeds, allowing the flowers to bloom strong and beautiful," she said, placing a hand on Aphrodite's shoulder. "That would please Ares – to him it would appear that even in death he protects your beauty from any who would seek to harm it."

"I once loved you, Aphrodite, and though you could not return my affections I shall ensure that the rich red of the rose you become forever symbolizes deep love and devotion, just as you have for Ares," Hephaestus said.

"Thank you," she said, reaching out to rest her hand on his forearm, acknowledging that their past was not quite resolved, but would not end acrimoniously. "Would you care for us in your grove, dear Artemis?" Aphrodite asked.

"I shall, for all my days," Artemis replied.

"We must leave this place and I must announce to the other gods what has transpired here this evening," Zeus said, gathering Ares' lifeless body in his arms.

In a flash of light, four of the five gods at the Lake of Acherousia disappeared and I wiped at the tears that fell across my cheeks.

Hephaestus stood, staring at the place Ares had laid. "I am sorry it ended this way, Brother," he murmured. "I shall mourn your death, but I shall also rejoice in it."

"As shall I," I agreed, pushing the Helmet of Invisibility up off my face.

Hephaestus turned, smiling with relief. "I had hoped you were truly here. You finally ended Ares' life?"

"It was the hind's blood, and the amulet, I believe," I replied, opening my hand to reveal the restored gem.

"Ah." He reached out for the helmet and I passed it over. "You shall have no need of this any longer. Wait for me here, I must return it to Hades' palace before he realizes it is missing, but I shall not be gone long."

"Do you have to go?" I asked. "I don't feel safe alone here."

"You are not alone," he replied with a smile, pointing to the outline of the crane circling high above us.

"Promise me you will be careful. Hades was fond of Ares."

"I know," Hephaestus said.

"It was Aphrodite who freed Ares from the cage, she got you drunk and you told her where to find the key," I added.

"I know that as well," Hephaestus said, dropping his head. "But that is in the past now. When I return, I shall take you to Demi and your sons."

I smiled, my heart lightening immediately at the thought. "The boys will have grown much in three winters," I said.

"Three winters?" Hephaestus asked, frowning.

"Aphrodite said that she and Ares had been waiting in the Underworld for three winters for the amulet's power to return to him."

"She meant three winters to a *god*. In the mortal realm you have only been gone nine moons. It is Skirophorion, the last moon of spring. You return from the Underworld two moons after Persephone, and just as she brings joy and renewed life to the world, you too shall gift those closest to you with the same."

"Oh," I murmured, grateful I hadn't missed my sons' growth as much as I thought I had. My smile faltered as another memory surfaced. "Has Demi ... does another warm her bed?" I whispered.

Hephaestus crossed to my side, lifting my chin with his finger. "Do you truly believe she would discard you so quickly, so easily?"

"No, but the Eriny–"

"Lied to you. Demi would never take another. She shall be overjoyed at your return. She was devastated when I told her of your death at Ares' hand."

"You did not tell her about your plan to free me?"

"No," he replied, disappearing before I could question him further.

24

"Come, it is time you were reunited with my daughter," Hephaestus said, offering his hand. I put my palm against his, closing my eyes as my feet lifted off the ground.

"We are here," he announced moments later.

"Where is here?" I asked, opening my eyes again.

"Gitani, on the southwest slope of the Vrissela Mountain in the Epirus region of western Greece. Demi feeds your family by fishing the waters here, she is surprisingly talented," he smiled.

"My wife fishes? When did she learn to do that?" I asked, unable to keep the smile from my own face.

"I believe Leandros was teaching her in secret before Ares returned, it was to be a surprise for your birthing day celebration." Hephaestus pointed to a small house up ahead. "That one is theirs."

I drew a shaking breath as I stopped before the door, suddenly nervous at the reunion I longed for so desperately. I raised my knuckles but Hephaestus stilled my arm, indicating my tunic.

"Wait, you do not wish to frighten your family."

"No. They don't need to know what I endured in the Underworld," I agreed.

Hephaestus nodded and ran his hand alongside my body, swapping my dirty, torn tunic for a clean white chiton. "Better," he nodded. "Shall I take the amulet, for now at least?"

I nodded, handing it to him. He put it into his chiton as I knocked at the small wooden door. Soft footfalls neared from the other side and it opened.

"Ava?" Demi whispered. I smiled and nodded. Her deep brown eyes flecked with yellow filled with tears. "Are you really here or does Morpheus taunt me again with dreams of your return?"

"I am really here," I assured her.

She reached out, pulling me into a tight embrace. I wrapped my arms around her neck, breathing in her familiar scent as the tears fell.

"I missed you so much," I whispered.

"And I you," she replied, her voice thick. "We heard there were no survivors at Thermopylae. Hephaestus sa—" I silenced her with a fierce kiss.

"I know. I was," I replied, pulling back so I could take in her face again. Her high cheekbones were a beautiful bronze, as was her nose and strong chin. Her pink lips looked as soft as ever and I could not resist running my finger over them. She closed her eyes as I trailed my finger along her jaw. My beautiful wife stood before me, just as alive as I was. I took her face between my hands, pulling her lips to mine again, gently this time.

She increased the pressure at the small of my back, drawing me against her body as our mouths met. We spent many long moments reveling in the feel of one another, pausing only when Melina's soft voice spoke.

"Who is at the door, Demi?" she asked.

I released Demi and she stepped aside, revealing me and Hephaestus. Melina gasped, reaching for a nearby chair to steady herself. I crossed to her as Hephaestus closed the door.

"Melina," I smiled.

Tears slipped down her cheeks as she grabbed my shoulders and pulled me to her chest. "I have spent these past moons believing that the next time we met would be in the Underworld, and yet here you are, safe and well. I cannot tell you the joy I feel knowing that you are here."

"Are you here … for good?" Demi asked.

"I am. I will never leave you or send you away again. I give you my word," I replied, taking her hand and squeezing it. "Where are Kadmus and Zenon?"

"Sleeping, but I can wake them," Melina replied.

"No, leave them. Let them share the joy of my return in the morning. I'll just look in on them, then we'll sit and talk. I want to hear everything you've been doing since you left Trachis."

"There is much to discuss," Melina agreed with a nod.

I made my way to the room Melina indicated. Kadmus and Zenon lay side by side on a bed big enough for the two of them and possibly one more. I sat on the edge beside Kadmus, my heart filling with joy that I could be with them once again.

From the moment I'd woken in Erebus, I hadn't really believed I would ever see my sons alive again. Even when I started to make my way out of

Tartarus I wasn't entirely sure, especially when I was crossing the rivers. It would've been so easy to let their visions detain and devour me. But I had fought them, I had fought myself, I had fought to return to the mortal realm so I could watch my boys grow, just as a mother should if she has the opportunity.

I wrapped one of Kadmus' curls around my finger, twirling it gently before placing it behind his ear. He murmured, but didn't wake. I bent down, placing a kiss above his temple.

"Sleep well, Kadmus," I whispered.

I walked around the other side, pulling the blanket up over Zenon's shoulders. His hair stuck straight out at the crown and I tried to push it down, but as soon as I removed my hand, it popped up again. I smiled, leaning over and kissing his cheek.

"Sleep well, Zenon."

I straightened, folding my arms across my chest. The murex shell Mumma had given me sat on the table beside the bed, the two sections beside one another, exactly how I'd kept them in my room in Trachis. I smiled, glad Demi or one of my sons had thought to bring the last physical link I had to my mothers with them to their new home.

"I'm back and I won't leave you again," I told them, before returning to Demi, Melina and Hephaestus.

Demi took my hand and the four of us settled ourselves at the table. "Does Ares know you've returned? Are we safe from him here?" she asked.

"It's over between me and Ares. We have no more battles to fight," I replied.

She frowned. "How so?"

"Ares is dead," Hephaestus supplied.

"Dead? How? I did not believe gods could die," Melina gasped.

"Before I faced him in Thermopylae, I went to Artemis, asking her for the only thing I believed could kill a god; the blood of her golden hinds. After some convincing, she let me take five drops. I put them on my sword, intending to drive it into Ares and poison him but instead it broke Hephaestus' protection over me and Ares was able to take the pieces of amulet from my sword. He believed that by killing me, the line of the Ker and the power of the amulet would be given to him."

"But it did not," Hephaestus added. "When he wiped the blood from Ava's sword, it soaked into his flesh and, though it was far slower, it eventually killed him, we witnessed his death ourselves."

"Thank the gods," Demi whispered. "I've longed for the day we're free of him forever. But what of Aphrodite, of Hades? They were always loyal to Ares, you told me that yourself, will they seek revenge on you?" she added, her brow furrowing.

"No. Neither of them know it was the blood that killed Ares and they'll never find out."

"Are you sure?"

"Yes."

"What then of the jet and hematite? Where are they?"

"The amulet has been restored, but it holds no power," I replied, recalling the spluttering colors inside the jet as Ares had died. "When I returned from the Underworld, Mumma's amulet was given to me, the jet and hematite back together, just as they were before we separated them in Kierion."

Hephaestus handed me the amulet and I held it up for Demi and Melina to see. "Before Ares died, we were both holding it and it filled us with clarity and a surge of power, as it has several times before for me. We learnt the future, the truth, we learnt that Ares would die, that I'd won and my part in his death would not be known by his allies.

"Ares collapsed and when he died soon after I … I cannot explain it, but I somehow *felt* that the amulet and the power it held died too. I never believed I'd see the day when I thought of it again as just a piece of jewelry, but I sit here tonight, and I know it is so."

"But I don't understand how you were able to leave the Underworld. Was it with your help? And if so, why didn't you tell me of your plans?" Demi asked, addressing Hephaestus.

"I kept it from you for your protection. I could not risk Ares finding out what Zeus and I had planned."

"Zeus?" Demi asked.

"Yes, it was my father who suggested what we do."

"If the intention was for me to leave the Underworld anyway, why didn't he simply heal me before I even ended up there?"

"He could not. We had to allow Ares to believe he had won. I had to allow you to die in my arms and go to the Underworld. You had to cross the Acheron River in Charon's boat and be judged. I suspected that Ares may play a part in where you ended up, but I hoped he would be too preoccupied with the amulet and the power he wished for to worry about what I was doing."

"Hades said Ares always made time for his *playthings*," I said sourly.

Hephaestus nodded. "Indeed. But it was important that he and Hades knew where you were, so that when the time came, our plan would work."

"What was the plan you and Zeus devised?" Melina asked.

"After Ava died and we sent her to the Underworld with her coin for Charon, Zeus and I went to see the Moirai. I asked them to restore Ava's life thread in their weave, telling them she must continue to live so Ares could not carry out his plan."

"You didn't think the blood from the hinds would kill Ares?" Demi asked.

"We could not be certain as it had never been tested before. When my protection over Ava was broken, Zeus spoke with Artemis. She believed the hinds' blood *would* kill Ares, it would just take longer. She felt it had lost some of its potency when it broke the hold I had created with Ava, but it was still strong enough. Zeus decided the time for him to sit idly by and allow Ava to fight Ares on his behalf was over."

"So you visited the Moirai?" I prompted.

"Yes. Atropos – the one who cuts the threads of life – told us that Ares too had come, though he asked her to cut the thread we wanted restored. Lachesis, who is in charge of the threads and their allotted lengths, told Ares what she would have told me, had Zeus not been at my side: 'the line is not for lesser gods to decide when it is cut or how long it is woven for.'

"As king of the gods, and the only immortal the Moirai had agreed to obey, Zeus commanded Clotho – the spinner – to do what I asked of them. She was reluctant, but agreed to spin Ava's life thread back onto her spindle. There was a condition though; if Ava was not able to escape the Underworld by the time the sun set the following evening, her thread would burn up and she would remain stuck there forever.

"Thankfully you made it to our agreed meeting point and your life thread continues strongly on Clotho's spindle as though the battle with Ares and your subsequent death, never happened," Hephaestus said, laying his hand on my arm.

"But doesn't Hades know Ava is no longer in his realm?" Demi asked.

"No. The second part of our plan included me swapping Ava's soul with another, though how I did that is a longer story and one I shall share with you on another night."

"When my time in this world is done again, how do I explain to the Judges how I've returned?"

"Their knowledge of you ends when they place you where you have been sent, the next time they see you they shall not know you."

"And what of the soul who took my place? It's not fair she suffers my fate instead of her own. Can you return her to the banks of the Cocytus so when it's time, Charon can take her to the Judges and she can be placed where she should've always gone?"

"Zeus intends to speak with Hades, telling him that you are to be moved at his wishes. With Ares gone, Hades shall realign himself with the true King of the Gods and shall do whatever Zeus asks to show his commitment. She shall find herself in the Elysium Fields, as herself, for the aid she has shown to Zeus during this time."

"I want my mothers, Zita and Papou to be sent to the Elysium Fields as well, can you ask him to do that?" I asked.

"They will be resettled there," Hephaestus nodded.

"You saw your mothers?" Demi asked.

"I did, but we only spent a brief time together. Ares sent them to the Fields of Punishment, but they're together and are as well as can be expected."

"Why didn't you bring them out as well?" Demi asked Hephaestus.

"The realm of the dead is not a place I hold power over," he replied firmly.

"But Zeus could, why didn't you ask him?" Demi argued.

"No. It's enough to know they'll be in the Elysium Fields where they belong. As much as I miss them, I know we'll be together again one day and I promised them that I would get out of the Underworld and return to you, where *I* belong."

Demi cupped my cheek, kissing me firmly on the mouth. "It's where you have always belonged," she agreed.

"I know that now," I replied.

"How did you know you could trust the Moirai's words? Immortal beings do not always keep their promises," Melina asked Hephaestus.

"Lachesis spoke of a sign appearing, something that linked Ava and Ares, though she did not say what it would be."

"The mark of the Chosen One," I murmured.

"I believe so," Hephaestus agreed. "Both you and Ares wore the mark towards the end. Lachesis spoke also of an item Ares deemed important finding me, which had to have been the amulet. When the Moirai were convinced to re-weave your life thread into their tapestry, the jet and hematite left Ares. I cannot explain how the individual parts were reunited or how it then knew to come to me, but it did. I sent my crane on ahead, in case you should need the amulet's power before I arrived."

"I'm curious how Ares could see me even though I wore the Helmet of Invisibility. Perhaps it was because we both wore the Chosen One's mark?" I mused.

Hephaestus shrugged. "That is the only explanation I can think of also. You were as hidden to Zeus, Aphrodite and me as you had been to Hades and the rest of the souls in the Underworld."

"I'm curious about something else too," I said, turning to Hephaestus. "Once Ares was dead, why didn't Zeus insist I be returned to the Underworld? Why did he allow me to return to Demi? Ares is no longer a threat to Zeus or the throne, Aphrodite is also gone and Hades will realign himself. He has no further use of me or the supposed power of the amulet."

"Father has grown fond of you. He saw how you were prepared to put your life in the Moirai's hands once again in order to keep him safe and on his throne. He knows all you had to sacrifice – those you lost to Ares' hand. Artemis too spoke on your behalf, citing the instances when your mother and grandmother had done the same. She requested as a favor that you be allowed to live a settled life with your family, without threat to your sons or their descendants from the god of war. So here you are."

"I believe we should be very grateful for this opportunity. Many are not as lucky, as you are more than aware," Melina said, sadness crossing her features.

"That I am," I replied, reaching out to squeeze my grandmother's hand. "Tell me about the Persians, you said there were no survivors in Thermopylae, what happened?"

"Thermopylae fell soon after your death. After Leonidas' death," Melina supplied.

I sent a silent prayer to my fallen uncle. "What of Sparta and Athens, did they repel the invaders at the Isthmus of Corinth as they intended? Did we claim victory over the Persians?"

"No, there was no battle at the Isthmus. The Greek fleet suffered heavy losses in the Straits of Artemisium and when they heard Thermopylae had been lost, they fled to Salamis. The Persians claimed victories at Thessaly, Boeotia and Attica, burning Athens to the ground," Demi replied.

"No," I gasped.

"I am afraid it is the truth. Fortunately though, no Greek lives were lost in Athens as everyone had been evacuated. But from what we have heard, the city is a mere shell of its former self, and it may take many winters to return it to its previous glory, if ever it can be," Melina said.

"What of our soldiers, do you know if anyone survived?" I asked.

"We have not heard, but surely some would have, fleeing into the hills they know so well around Trachis," Melina replied, and I knew she was thinking of Moeris.

I nodded, allowing the silence between us to drag out before I spoke again. "I met Nikomachos at the Pass. He is a soldier now. Or at least he was, he tried to save Leonidas so I can only imagine he fell too."

"Nikomachos," Melina smiled.

"Did Xerxes return home, or does he still occupy Athens?" I asked, seeing the questions Demi held back. There would be time to tell her who Nikomachos was tomorrow.

"He has gone. His navy followed ours to Salamis, where we were victorious. He returned to Persia, leaving Mardonius to rule the conquered areas to the east, our home included. There is talk of the Greek forces engaging Mardonius in the summer but nothing has been settled as yet," Melina replied.

"How far to the west do you think the Persians will try to come?" I asked.

"Not this far, they don't intend to cross the Pindos Ranges; they don't think there's anything here worth claiming," Demi said.

"We can only hope they hold true to those beliefs," I murmured.

"Indeed," Demi nodded, pressing her lips to my knuckles. I smiled at her. My Demi. My wife. My world. We may no longer be queens of Trachis, but I didn't care. It was more than enough to be reunited with her, my boys and my grandmother. It was enough to know that we would never have to fear Ares or the line of the Keres again. I was content to live out my days being known as the wife of a fisherwoman in the small village of Gitani, western Greece.

EPILOGUE
One moon later

I walked along the shoreline of the Thyamis River, the gentle waves from Demi's incoming boat lapping at the shoreline and covering my toes. It was cool, but the evening sun remained warm as it started to set to the west.

Melina had remained at the house, preparing the evening meal, rather than joining me at the water. I didn't mind, she usually tried to help take the fish back to the house, or to the stall keeper to sell at the agora – I thought she was too old to be attempting such tasks – she didn't agree.

I sat on the riverbank, letting my toes to stir up the soft sand at the edge as I awaited the boat's arrival.

"May I join you?" a soft voice asked.

I turned, shielding my eyes. A tall woman stood beside me, her long red hair catching the rays of the setting sun. A flowing length of white and gold cloth covered her full breasts, sheer where it fell over her arms. It wasn't exactly a chiton but it did wrap around her body in a similar manner. A gold rope circled her waist and a golden necklace surrounded her throat, the colored jewels sparkling when the rippling water caught their sides.

For a moment I thought it was Aphrodite who stood beside me, but though this woman was beautiful, her body was fuller and her eyes were a deep brown, rather than the blue-green of the goddess of love.

"Please," I nodded.

The woman sat down beside me, readjusting the golden slip of material at her forehead so it kept the hair from her face. "At this time of evening, this is a lovely place to sit and wait for your loved ones," she noted.

I drew a breath, my eyes remaining on her face as I tried to place her or discover who she was without having to ask. I found myself at a loss. "It is. I haven't seen you here before. Are you from Gitani?"

The woman smiled and shook her head. "No. I am from the far north of these lands. Though it is not the first time I have travelled to Greece."

"Indeed?" I asked.

"We do not have much time to speak before your wife and children return, so allow me to speak plainly."

"How did y–" She held up her hand and I quieted.

"My name is Freyja, Norse Lady of Love and receiver of the slain at Sessrúmnir. I oversee the Valkyrie who bring the warriors to my hall, and you, my dear Ava, are the slayer of my enemy; Ares, Greek God of War."

"Your enemy? Was it not your people who helped Ares craft the amulet of his Chosen One?"

"They did, though the god of war turned against us when he broke free of the cage you sent him to. He killed nine of the Valkyrie, believing no doubt he ended all of the line in his rage."

"Why would he do that?" I asked.

"I cannot say for certain, for I was not there. Not even the great King Odin himself foresaw their fate, nor heard their demise, and he was in the great hall of Valhalla when Ares appeared there, asking to speak to the Valkyrie who had aided him.

"Many have believed there were only nine Valkyrie, but there have always been thirteen. Nine resided at the hall of Valhalla with Odin, the other four with me at Sessrúmnir, my hall within the afterlife field of Fólkvangr."

"Why have you come?" I asked, noting that Demi's boat had found a favorable wind and was bringing them to shore quickly.

"Odin and I wish to show our gratitude to you for dealing with our enemy. We would have taken great pleasure in seeking our own revenge, but when Odin saw what was fated between the two of you, he allowed it to run its course. We wish now to mark you with a symbol."

"No," I immediately replied. "I was once marked with Ares' symbol, just like my mother before me, and her mother before her were. I am not eager to be so marked again."

Freyja nodded, a smile gracing her lips. "I understand your hesitation, but I assure you, you do not need to fear my sign. It has no power, shall not speak of you having any power now or in the future. It symbolizes only my friendship and the protection you and your family would have, should it be required."

"I do not wish to offend you, lady Freyja, but I know nothing of you, your fellow gods or your kin – other than that they once aided a man I called *my* enemy. Until I have proof that you truly wish to only give your friendship to me and we've had time to get to know one another, I would ask that you do not place your mark upon my skin."

"You are cautious with matters of the gods now and I respect such wishes. Though it is not the one I would now gift you with, Ares and Eir, the Valkyrie who created the amulet, spoke of placing the Gungnir on you when they learned it was you who was to be his Chosen One. It was supposed to signify an agreement made; that when the Ragnarök came, he would allow you to aid us in the battle."

"What is the Ragnarök and the Gungnir?" I asked.

"The Ragnarök is an important battle where we Norse gods shall fight for our survival. Gungnir is Odin's magical spear, which never misses its mark. Your family is almost here. We shall speak again soon," she said, turning to watch the small boat as she stood. "Remember, Ava, friend of the Norse Gods and slayer of the Greek god of war, you shall always be welcome in the north lands. You should visit us. Allow me and my kin the opportunity to prove my words and wishes to you."

"And how would I find you if I was to go? I'm sure the mortals of the north don't know where to find your halls ... until they meet their deaths."

"I shall always be nearby. You need only speak my name and I shall come to you."

"I don't believe the far north is somewhere I will travel to, though please know I am grateful for your offer."

Kadmus jumped from Demi's boat and pulled it the rest of the way to shore. I smiled and pushed myself to my feet, giving my son a wave.

"It is not just you who may wish to visit us." Freyja said.

I rounded sharply on her, but she was already gone. "I do not wish for the gods to be so interested in my life, or that of my family. I had believed those days to be over with Ares' death." I murmured, receiving no answer.

Kadmus made his way up the beach towards me, Damon bounding along beside him. "Hello, Mother," he grinned, pushing up onto his toes to kiss my cheek. "We caught many fish today, although it could've been more if Zenon could control his stomach."

I laughed and ruffled my son's blonde curls. "He doesn't want to miss out on the adventures you and your mother have on the water. One day he'll overcome the sickness he feels and your boat will sit low in the water with the weight of your catch," I grinned.

"I hope so."

Demi lifted Zenon from the vessel, helping him with an arm around his waist as they crossed the sand.

"Hello, Mother," Zenon said with a shy smile.

"Hello, my darling," I replied, sweeping his hair from his forehead and placing a kiss on his brow. "You look a little green from your day on the waves."

"It wasn't as bad as other times, by the time the sun was high in the sky I'd only returned my morning meal to the sea four times," he admitted, dropping his eyes to the ground.

"He did well," Demi assured me, tightening her grip on Zenon for a moment before leaning across to place a kiss on my lips. "A few more trips should see him standing at the sides, helping us bring in the nets without hint of an upset stomach."

"I'm sure it will be so. Kadmus, help Zenon back to the house. I'll gather the fish and we'll meet you there. Do as Melina asks if she needs anything done."

"Yes, Mother," both boys replied.

Demi and I watched our sons make their way up the beach and into the town. "How was he really?" I asked.

"A little better. I know he wants to please me by joining Kadmus and me, but I think it's safe to say he'll never find his living as a fisherman."

I laughed and followed Demi back to the boat. "Oh well, he displays other talents. He'll find his calling when the time comes."

"I'm certain he will," Demi agreed.

"While you were gone, I had a visitor," I said, hauling one of the large baskets from the boat.

"Oh?"

"Freyja. One of the Valkyrie from the north lands."

Demi paused in her own lifting and regarded me warily. "What did she want?"

"To thank me for killing Ares actually."

Demi took her basket again and we started up the beach as I told her about the conversation I'd had with the overseer of the shield maidens.

"I've been wondering if we should travel to Sparta, to meet Leonidas' wife and son. He is some of the only kin you have left," Demi said.

"Maybe," I agreed.

"And what of Nikomachos and the other brother you spoke of? Eumelia as well, perhaps it's time to mend those old wounds too."

"I don't know of Nikomachos' fate, but assume he was killed in Thermopylae. He spoke of Pamphilos being in Athens and Eumelia remains in Iolkos."

"Then should we not visit them? We should also travel to Thrace so you can find out if any of Leandros' kin remain, to tell them of his fate and long life if nothing else."

"You sound eager to leave Gitani, yet has it not been good to you, our sons and Melina since you fled from Trachis?"

"It has, but perhaps now is the time to consolidate our family, to have everyone around us for as long as we can. Time can be so short with those we love."

"You're right but let me think about it. Maybe if we were to travel to Thrace, Melina would come too and visit Agrias' grave in Macedonia."

"I'm sure she wouldn't want to be left behind. Perhaps we will find Moeris as we travel."

"That would be nice," I nodded.

I readjusted the basket in my arms, wondering how we would be received at each home Demi had suggested we visit. Pamphilos and Eumelia might be kin but that didn't mean we'd be instantly welcomed, as much as I might want to be. I couldn't imagine what I would say to Eumelia especially after such time apart and how we'd left things. But I was willing to go and find out. Soon. After I'd spent more time here with my immediate family.

ACKNOWLEDGMENTS

So, here we are at the end. The end of our friends in Thermopylae. The end of the series. The end of Ava and Skylar and Zita's war with Ares. It's been a long journey and one that, while it hasn't always been easy (for me or for you) I could have never walked away from. Not once did I even consider it. Oh, I wondered how I was going to write what I had to or wondered how after making major changes I could bring it all back together and make it work. There was a lot of self-doubt and frustration and fear and getting the final book done took far longer than I wanted. But I knew it had to be perfect. A perfect end. A fitting end. One that did justice to everything that had come before. I hope in your eyes I have succeeded.

Once again I need to say a big thank you to DR and Ashley who willingly agreed to be my guinea pigs as I made my way through this final book and fought with it to become what it needed to be.

To Kristie – my intrepid (and super busy) editor who has been with me since this book was created and who has encouraged me and supported me through six books (and I hope many more to come). Thank you for everything you've done.

To my girls – Renee and Ava – who continue to support my writing endeavors and understand that even though I might look like I'm listening, I'm probably thinking about some plot point or story and you REALLY need to write me a note to do whatever it is you need me to so I don't forget. Saves everyone a mountain of frustration!

I have no idea what I'm going to do with myself now this final book is done … I don't know if I'm ready to leave Ancient Greece yet so there will be some 'alongside books' that come out at some stage. There are also a number of unfinished books sitting in folders around my study vying for my attention, so maybe I'll look at getting those out into the world too. But no matter which way I choose to go, you can rest assured that this is not the last you've heard from me and I hope you'll join me on my next adventure.

From the bottom of my heart, I thank you for all your support so far xo.

ABOUT THE AUTHOR

Belinda Harrison was born and raised in a country town in North East Victoria, Australia. She spent just over two years experiencing 'big city life' in Melbourne and Sydney in her twenties where she held jobs in a packaging company, various temp positions, an online gaming firm and a hair loss treatment center before the lure of the country recalled her.

She joined her family's business and spent the next eleven and a half years in the world of retail plumbing and appliance sales. She then made the brave decision to leave the familiar and join another well respected local firm in the Real Estate sector where she worked in Commercial Property Management. After five years, Belinda decided it was time for another change and moved across the road to the local newspaper where she looks after Circulation, and does a little writing for them when the need arises.

Belinda lives in 'the best part of Victoria' with her wife Renee, daughter Ava, Charlie the dog, and cats Caesar and Max.

To keep up with what's next for Belinda, join her mailing list on her website at www.belindaharrison.com

www.ingramcontent.com/pod-product-compliance
Lightning Source LLC
Chambersburg PA
CBHW031718170626
46808CB00005B/1801